A SEASON

A lady never tells…

Elena Leighton and Ellie Rosewood
might only be a lowly governess and a
lady's companion, but...
these women than meets the eye!

For their meek and respectable demeanour
hides this season's most scandalous secrets…
and all is about to be deliciously revealed!

How far will the Duke of Royston go
to lay bare the real Ellie Rosewood?

NOT JUST A WALLFLOWER
December 2013

And Lord Adam Hawthorne
makes a date with impropriety in

NOT JUST A GOVERNESS
Already available

And in eBooks
from Mills & Boon® Historical *Undone!*

NOT JUST A SEDUCTION
Already available

NOT JUST A WALLFLOWER

Carole Mortimer

First published in Great Britain 2013
by Mills & Boon, an imprint of Harlequin (UK) Limited.
Harlequin (UK) Limited, Eton House, 18-24 Paradise Road,
Richmond, Surrey TW9 1SR

© Carole Mortimer 2013

ISBN: 978 0 263 89865 1

Harlequin (UK) policy is to use papers that are natural, renewable
and recyclable products and made from wood grown in sustainable
forests. The logging and manufacturing process conform to the
legal environmental regulations of the country of origin.

Printed and bound in Spain
by Blackprint CPI, Barcelona

Carole Mortimer was born in England, the youngest of three children. She began writing in 1978, and has now written over one hundred and fifty books for Harlequin Mills & Boon®. Carole has six sons: Matthew, Joshua, Timothy, Michael, David and Peter. She says, 'I'm happily married to Peter senior; we're best friends as well as lovers, which is probably the best recipe for a successful relationship. We live in a lovely part of England.'

Previous novels by the same author:

In Mills & Boon® Historical Romance:

THE DUKE'S CINDERELLA BRIDE*
THE RAKE'S WICKED PROPOSAL*
THE ROGUE'S DISGRACED LADY*
LADY ARABELLA'S SCANDALOUS MARRIAGE*
THE LADY GAMBLES**
THE LADY FORFEITS**
THE LADY CONFESSES**
SOME LIKE IT WICKED†
SOME LIKE TO SHOCK†
NOT JUST A GOVERNESS††

The Notorious St Claires
**The Copeland Sisters*
†*Daring Duchesses*
††*A Season of Secrets*

You've read about *The Notorious St Claires* **in Regency times. Now you can read about the new generation in Mills & Boon® Modern™ Romance:**

The Scandalous St Claires:
Three arrogant aristocrats—ready to be tamed!
JORDAN ST CLAIRE: DARK AND DANGEROUS
THE RELUCTANT DUKE
TAMING THE LAST ST CLAIRE

And in Mills & Boon® Historical *Undone!* **eBooks:**

AT THE DUKE'S SERVICE
CONVENIENT WIFE, PLEASURED LADY
A WICKEDLY PLEASURABLE WAGER**
SOME LIKE IT SCANDALOUS†
NOT JUST A SEDUCTION††

And in M&B® Regency *Castonbury Park* **mini-series:**

THE WICKED LORD MONTAGUE

To Peter, the love of my life, for all of my life.

Chapter One

∽∽∽∾∾∾

June, 1817—Lady Cicely Hawthorne's London home

'You must be absolutely thrilled at the news of Hawthorne's forthcoming marriage to Miss Matthews!' Lady Jocelyn Ambrose, Dowager Countess of Chambourne, beamed across the tea table at her hostess.

Lady Cicely nodded. 'The match was not without its…complications, but I have no doubts that Adam and Magdelena will deal very well together.'

The dowager countess sobered. 'How is she now that all the unpleasantness has been settled?'

'Very well.' Lady Cicely smiled warmly.

'She is, I am happy to report, a young lady of great inner strength.'

'She had need of it when that rogue Sheffield was doing all that he could to ruin her, socially as well as financially.' Edith St Just, Dowager Duchess of Royston, and the third in the trio of friends, said, sniffing disdainfully.

Lady Jocelyn turned to her. 'How are your own plans regarding Royston's nuptials progressing, my dear?'

The three ladies, firm friends since their coming out together fifty years ago, had made a pact at the beginning of this Season, to see their three bachelor grandsons safely married, thereby ensuring that each of their family lines was secure. Lady Jocelyn was the first to achieve that success, when her grandson had announced his intention of marrying Lady Sylvianna Moreland some weeks ago, the wedding due to take place at the end of June. Lady Cicely had only recently succeeded in seeing her own grandson's future settled, his bride to be Miss Magdelena Matthews, granddaughter of George Matthews, the recently deceased Duke of Sheffield. It only remained for Edith St Just, the Dowager Duchess of Royston, to secure a future duchess for her own grand-son, Justin St Just, the Duke of Royston.

Not an easy task, when that wickedly handsome and haughtily arrogant gentle-man had avowed, more than once, that he had no intention of marrying until he was good and ready—and aged only eight and twenty, he had assured his grandmother that he did not consider himself either 'good' or 'ready' as yet!

'The Season will be over in just a few weeks...' Lady Cicely gave her friend a doubtful glance.

The dowager duchess nodded regally. 'And Royston will have made his choice be-fore the night of the Hepworth ball.'

Lady Cicely gave a gasp. 'But that is only two weeks away!'

Edith gave a satisfied smile. 'By which time St Just will, I assure you, find himself well and truly leg-shackled!'

'You are still convinced it will be to the lady whom you have named in the note held by my own butler?' Lady Jocelyn also looked less than confident about the outcome of this enterprise.

At the same time as the three ladies had laid their plans to ensure their grandsons found their brides that Season, the dowager duchess had also announced she had already made her choice of bride for her own grandson, and that Royston would find himself betrothed to that lady by the end of the Season. So confident had she been of her choice that she had accepted the other ladies' dare to write down the name of that young lady and leave it in the safe keeping of Edwards, Lady Jocelyn's butler, to be opened and verified on the day Royston announced his intention of marrying.

'I am utterly convinced,' Edith now stated confidently.

'But, to my knowledge, Royston has not expressed a preference for any of the young ladies of the current Season.' Lady Cicely, the most tender-hearted of the three, could not bear the thought of her dear friend being proved wrong.

'Nor will he,' the dowager duchess revealed mysteriously.

'But—'

'We must not press dear Edith any further.' Lady Jocelyn reached across to gently squeeze Lady Cicely's hand in reassurance. 'Have we ever known her to be wrong in the past?'

'No…'

'And I shall not be proved wrong on this occasion, either,' the dowager duchess announced haughtily, belied by the gleeful twinkle in faded blue eyes. 'Royston shall shortly find himself not only well and truly leg-shackled, but totally besotted with his future bride!'

An announcement, regarding this about the arrogantly cynical Duke of Royston which so stunned the other two ladies that neither of them felt able to speak further on the subject…

Chapter Two

Two days later—White's Club, St James's Street, London

'Is it not time you threw in your cards and called it a night, Litchfield?'

'You'd like it if I did so, wouldn't you, Royston!' The florid, sneering face of the man seated on the opposite side of the card table was slightly damp with perspiration in the dimmed candlelight of the smoky card room.

'I have no opinion one way or the other if you should decide to lose the very shirt upon your back,' Justin St Just, the Duke of Royston, drawled as he reclined back in his armchair, only the glittering intensity of his narrowed blue eyes revealing the utter contempt he felt for the other man. 'I merely wish to bring this interminable game of cards to an end!' He deeply regretted having accepted Litchfield's challenge now, and knew he would not have done so if he had not been utterly bored and seeking any diversion to relieve him from it.

Ennui. It was an emotion all too familiar to him since the fighting against Napoleon had come to an end and the little Corsican had finally been incarcerated on St Helena once and for all, at which time Justin had considered it was safe to return to London, resign his commission, and take up his duties as Duke of Royston. A scant few weeks later he had realised his terrible mistake. Oh, he still had all of his friends here, the women willing to share his bed were as abundant, and his rooms in Mayfair were still as comfortable—he had long ago decided against taking up residence at Royston House, instead leaving his grandmother to continue living there alone after the death of Justin's father, and the removal of Justin's mother to the country—but all the time feeling as if there should be something...more to life.

Quite what that was, and how he was to

find it, he had no idea. Which was the very reason he had spent the latter part of his evening engaged in a game of cards with a man he did not even like!

Lord Dryden Litchfield shot him a resentful glance. 'They say you have the devil's own luck, with both the cards and the ladies.'

'Do they?' Justin murmured mildly, well aware of the comments the *ton* made about him behind his back.

'And I am starting to wonder if it is not luck at all, but—'

'Have a care, Litchfield,' Justin warned softly, none of his inner tension in evidence at the as-yet-unspoken insult, as he reached out an elegant hand to pick up his glass and take a leisurely sip of his brandy. With his fashionably overlong golden hair, and arrogantly handsome features, he resembled a fallen angel far more than he did the devil. But regardless of how angelic he looked, most, if not all, of the gentlemen of the *ton* also knew him to be an expert with both the usual choices of weapon for the duel Litchfield was spoiling for. 'As I have said, the sooner we bring this card game to an end, the better.'

'You arrogant bastard!' Litchfield glared

across at him fiercely; he was a man perhaps
a dozen or so years older than Justin's own
eight and twenty, but his excessive weight,
thinning auburn hair liberally streaked with
silver, brown-stained teeth from an over-indulgence in cheap cigars, as well as his blus-
tering anger at his consistent bad luck with
the cards, all resulted in him looking much
older.

'I do not believe insulting me will succeed in improving your appalling skill at
the cards,' Justin stated as he replaced his
brandy glass on the table.

'You—'

'Excuse me, your Grace, but this was just
delivered for your immediate attention.'

A silver tray appeared out of the surrounding smoke-hazed gloom, bearing a note with
Justin's name scrawled across the front of
it, written in a hand that a single glance had
shown was not familiar to him. 'If you will
excuse me, Litchfield?' He did not so much
as glance in the other man's direction as he
retrieved the note from the tray to break the
seal and quickly read the contents before refolding it and placing it in the pocket of his
waistcoat, throwing his cards face down on
the table. 'The hand is yours, sir.' He nodded

in abrupt dismissal, straightening his snowy white cuffs as he stood up to leave.

'Ha, knew you was bluffing!' the other man cried out triumphantly, puffing happily on his foul-smelling cigar as he scooped up Justin's discarded cards. 'What the—?' he muttered disbelievingly at a handful of aces as the mottled flush of anger deepened on his bloated face.

Dangerously so, in Justin's opinion; he had no doubt that Litchfield's heart would give up its fight to continue beating long before the man reached his fiftieth birthday.

'The note was from a woman, then.' An even more pronounced sneer appeared on the other man's face as he looked up at Justin through the haze of his own cigar smoke. 'I never thought to see the day when the devilishly lucky Duke of Royston would throw in a winning hand of cards in order to jump to a woman's bidding.'

At this point in time 'the devilishly lucky Duke of Royston' was having extreme difficulty in resisting the urge he felt to reach across the card table, grab the other man by his rumpled shirtfront and shake him like the insufferable dog that he was! 'Perhaps it is her bedchamber into which I am jumping…?' He raised a mocking brow.

Litchfield gave an inelegant snort. 'No woman is worth conceding a winning hand of cards.'

'This woman is,' Justin assured him drily. 'I wish you joy of the rest of your evening, Litchfield.' With a last contemptuous glance, he wasted no more time as he turned to stride purposefully from the dimly lit room, nodding briefly to several acquaintances as he did so.

'Step aside, Royston!'

Justin's legendary reflexes allowed him to take that swift sideways step and turn all at the same time, eyes widening as he watched a fist making contact with the lunging and livid-faced Litchfield, succeeding in stopping the man so that he dropped with all the grace of a felled ox.

Justin's rescuer knelt down briefly beside the unconscious man before straightening, revealing himself to be Lord Bryan Anderson, Earl of Richmond, a fit and lithe gentleman of fifty years or so, the thickness of his hair prematurely white. 'Your right hook is as effective as ever, I see, Richmond,' Justin said admiringly.

'It would appear so.' The older man straightened the cuff of his shirt beneath his tailored black superfine as both men continued ignoring the inelegantly recumbent Litchfield. 'Dare I ask what you did that so annoyed the man?'

Justin shrugged. 'I allowed him to win at cards.'

'Indeed?' Richmond raised his brows. 'Considering the extent of his gambling debts, one would have thought he might have been more grateful.'

'One would have thought so, yes.' Justin watched unemotionally as the unconscious Litchfield was quietly removed from the club by two stoic-faced footmen. 'I thank you for your timely intervention, Richmond.'

'Think nothing of it, Royston.' The older man bowed. 'Truth be told, I perhaps enjoyed it more than I should have,' he added ruefully.

Justin knew, as did most of the *ton,* that the now-widowed Bryan Anderson had spent around twenty-five years tied to a woman who, following a fall from her horse during the first months of their marriage, in which she had received a severe blow to her head, had regressed to having the mind of a child and remained as such until her recent death.

Nor, despite having every reason to do so, had that gentleman ever betrayed his marriage vows. Publicly, at least. What Richmond did in private had been, and remained, his own affair, and would not have been frowned upon by the *ton* in any case; twenty-five years of marriage to a woman, who believed herself a child, must have been unendurable torture. No doubt the hours Justin knew the other man had spent sparring at Jackson's had been an attempt to alleviate some of his frustrations during that time.

As, in all likelihood, had striking Litchfield just now…

'I thank you anyway, Richmond.' Justin said, giving him a slight bow in acknowledgement. 'Now, if you will excuse me, I have another engagement.'

'Of course.' Richmond returned the gesture. 'Oh, and Royston…?' He gave him a significant look as Justin paused to raise questioning brows. 'If I were you, I would watch your back for the next few weeks where Litchfield is concerned; it would seem he is an even less gracious winner than he is a loser.'

Justin's top lip curled. 'So it would appear.'

Richmond nodded. 'I had the displeasure of serving in the army with him in India many years ago and know him to be a bully with a vicious temper. The men did not like him any more than his fellow officers did.'

'If that were the case, I am surprised one of them did not take steps to rid themselves of such a tyrant.' It was well known in army circles that the enlisted men—enlisted? Hah! They were usually men who had been forced into taking the king's shilling for one nefarious reason or another—occasionally chose to dispose of a particularly unpopular officer during the confusion of battle.

Richmond gave a rueful smile. 'That should have been the case, of course, and likely would have happened if he had lingered in the army overlong, but there was some indiscretion with another officer's wife, which caused his superior officer to see that he left India sooner rather than later.'

Justin studied the older man's bland expression for several seconds. 'And would that superior officer happen to have been yourself, sir?'

'It would,' Richmond said grimly.

'In that case I will bear your warning in mind,' Justin said. 'I wish you a good night, Richmond.' He lost no more time in making his departure as he proceeded out into the hallway to collect and don his hat and cloak in readiness for stepping outside.

'Hanover Square, if you please, Bilsbury,' he instructed his driver tersely as he climbed inside the ducal coach and relaxed back against the plush upholstery, the door closing behind him seconds before the horses moved off smartly into the dark of the night.

If any woman was worth the loss of a fabulous hand at cards, then it was surely the one he now hurried to…

Miss Eleanor—Ellie—Rosewood paced restlessly in the vast entrance hall of the house in Hanover Square as she awaited for word of the response to the note she had instructed be delivered earlier this evening. Hopefully none of her inner anxiety showed on her face as she heard the clatter of horses' hooves on the cobbles outside, followed by a brief murmur of conversation. Stanhope moved forwards and opened the door just in time to allow the handsome Duke of Royston to sweep imperiously inside, bringing the cool evening air in with him.

As always happened, at first sight of this powerful and impressive gentleman, Ellie was struck momentarily speechless, as she could only stand and stare at him.

Excessively tall, at least a couple of inches over six feet, with fashionably ruffled hair of pure gold, Justin St Just's features were harshly patrician—deep blue eyes, high cheekbones aside a long and aristocratic nose, chiselled lips and a square, determined jaw—and his wide shoulders and tapered waist were shown to advantage in the black superfine and snowy white linen, buff pantaloons and high black Hessians fitting snugly to the long length of muscled calf and thigh; he was without doubt the most handsome gentleman Ellie had ever beheld—

'Well?' he demanded even as he swept off his cloak and hat and handed them to Stanhope before striding across the vast hallway to where Ellie stood at the bottom of the wide and curving staircase.

—as well as being the most arrogant—

She drew in a breath. 'I sent a note earlier this evening requesting that you call—'

'Which is the very reason I am here now,' he cut in.

—and impatient!

And considering that Ellie had sent the note over two hours ago, she found his delayed response to that request to be less than helpful! 'I had expected you sooner…'

He stilled. 'Do I detect a measure of rebuke in your tone?'

Her cheeks felt warm at the underlying steel beneath the mildness of his tone. 'I— no…'

He relaxed his shoulders. 'I am gratified to hear it.'

Her chin rose determinedly. 'It is your grandmother whom I believe may have expected a more immediate response from you, your Grace.' Indeed, that dear lady had been asking every quarter of the hour, since she had requested Ellie, as her companion, to send a note to her grandson, as to whether or not there had been any word from him. The duke's arrival here now, so many hours after the note had been sent, was tardy to say the least.

'This is my immediate response.'

She raised red-gold brows. 'Indeed?'

Justin looked at her as if seeing her for the

first time—which he no doubt was; companions to elderly ladies were of no consequence to dukes!—his eyes glinting deeply blue between narrowed lids as that disdainful glance swept over her from the red of her hair, her slenderness in the plain brown gown, down to the slippers upon her feet, and then back up to her now flushed face. 'The two of us are related in some way, are we not?'

Not exactly. Ellie's mother had been a widow with a nine-year-old daughter—Ellie—when she had married this gentlemen's cousin some ten years ago. But as both her mother and stepfather had since been killed in a carriage accident, it rather rendered the relationship between herself and the duke so tenuous as to be practically non-existent. And if not for the kindness of his grandmother, the Dowager Duchess of Royston, in taking Ellie into her own household as her companion when she had been left alone in the world without a penny to call her own, Ellie very much doubted she would have seen any of the St Just family ever again following her mother's demise.

'We are stepcousins once removed, at best, your Grace,' she now allowed huskily.

He raised an eyebrow, the candlelight giving a gold lustre to his fashionably tousled hair, the expression in those deep-blue eyes now hidden behind those lowered lids. 'Cousin Eleanor,' he acknowledged mockingly. 'The fact of the matter is, I was not at my rooms when your note was delivered earlier this evening and it took one of my servants some time in which to…locate me.'

Justin had no idea why it was he was even bothering to explain himself to this particular young woman. She was only a distant relative by marriage. Indeed, he could not remember even having spoken to Miss Eleanor Rosewood before now. He had noticed her, of course—bored and cynical he might be, but he was also a man!

Her hair was an intriguing shade of red, despite attempts on her part to mute its fieriness and curl in the severity of its style. Her eyes were a stunning clear green and surrounded by thick dark lashes, freckles sprinkled the tops of her creamy cheeks and the pertness of her tiny nose, and her mouth—

Ah, her mouth… Full and pouting, and naturally the colour of ripe strawberries, it was far too easy for a man to imagine such a mouth being put to far better uses than talking or eating!

She was tiny in both stature and figure, and yet the fullness of her breasts, visible above the neckline of her plain and unbecoming brown gown, emphasised the slenderness of her waist and thighs, her hands also tiny and delicate, the fingers long and slender in wrist-length cream lace gloves.

Justin was well aware that his grandmother had lost no time in gathering this orphaned chick into her own household as her companion after Eleanor had been left alone in the world, following the death of her mother and stepfather, Justin's own profligate cousin Frederick; Edith St Just might like to give the outward appearance of haughtiness and disdain, but to any who knew her well, it was an outer shell which hid a soft and yielding heart.

'Your note implied the request was urgent in nature,' Justin now drawled pointedly.

'Yes.' Colour now warmed those creamy cheeks. 'I—the physician was called to attend the dowager duchess earlier this evening.'

'The physician?' he repeated sharply. 'Is my grandmother ill?'

'I do not believe she would have requested the physician be called if that were not the case, your Grace.'

Justin's eyes narrowed suspiciously as he privately questioned whether or not she was daring to mock him; the green of her gaze was clear and unwavering, with no hint of the emotion for which he searched. Which was not to say it was not there, but merely hidden behind that annoyingly cool façade. 'What is the nature of her illness?' he enquired coldly.

She shrugged. 'Your grandmother did not confide in me, sir.'

Justin barely restrained his impatience with her unhelpful reply. 'But surely you must have overheard some of her conversation with the physician?'

Her gaze lowered from his piercing one. 'I was not in the room for all of his visit—'

'Might I ask why the devil not?'

Eleanor blinked those long dark lashes as the only outward sign of her shock at the profanity. 'She asked that I collect her shawl from her private parlour. By the time I returned Dr Franklyn was preparing to leave.'

Justin's impatience deepened. 'At which

time I presume my grandmother asked that I be sent for?'

She nodded. 'She also requested that you go up to her bedchamber the moment you arrived.'

A request this lady had obviously forgotten to relay to him until now. Because his arrival had diverted her from the task, perhaps...? It was a possibility he found as intriguing as he did amusing.

He nodded. 'I will go up to her now. Perhaps you would arrange for some brandy to be brought to the library for when I return downstairs?'

'Of course.' Ellie found she was relieved to have something practical to do, her usual calm competence seeming to have deserted her the moment she found herself in Justin's overpoweringly masculine presence. 'Do you wish me to accompany you?'

The duke came to a halt on the second step of the wide staircase in order to turn and give her a pointed look. 'I believe I am well aware of where my grandmother's bedchamber is located, but you may accompany me up the stairs, to ensure I do not attempt to make away with the family silver, if that is your wish.'

'Is that "family silver" not already yours?' she asked, trying hard to keep hold of her composure against his needling.

'It is.' He smiled briefly. 'Then perhaps you fear I may become lost in my own house, Cousin?'

Ellie was well aware that this was his house. As was everything connected with the Duchy of Royston. 'I believe my time might be better served in seeking out Stanhope and requesting the decanter of brandy be brought to the library.' Even the thought of accompanying the duke up the stairs was enough to cause Ellie's cheeks to burn—something she knew from past experience to be most unbecoming against the red of her hair.

'And two glasses.'

She raised surprised brows. 'You are expecting company?' The fact that the duke had been so difficult to locate this evening would seem to imply that he had been otherwise…occupied, and perhaps less than reputably. Even so, Ellie could not imagine him inviting one of his less-than-acceptable friends here, especially if he had been spending the evening in the company of a lady.

'It is you whom I am expecting to join me there,' he explained with a sigh.

Ellie's eyes widened. 'Me?'

Justin almost laughed at the stunned expression on her face. A natural reaction, perhaps, when this was the longest conversation they had ever exchanged.

Surprisingly, he found her naivety amusing, and, Justin readily admitted, very little succeeded in amusing him.

His childhood had been spent in the country until the age of ten, when he had been sent away to boarding school, after which he had seen his parents rarely and had felt an exclusion from their deep love for each other when he did, to the extent that it had coloured his own feelings about marriage. He accepted that a duke must necessarily marry, in order to provide an heir to the duchy, but Justin's own isolated upbringing had dictated his own would be a marriage of convenience, rather than love. A marriage that would not exclude his children in the way that he had been excluded.

His three years as the Duke of Royston had ensured that he was denied nothing and certainly not any woman he expressed the least desire for—and, on several occasions, some he had not, such as other gentlemen's wives and the daughters of marriage-minded mamas!

Eleanor Rosewood, as companion to his grandmother, was not of that ilk, of course, just as their tenuous family connection ensured she could never be considered as Justin's social equal. At the same time, though, even that slight family connection meant he could not consider her as a future mistress, either. Frustrating, but true.

'Your Grace…?'

He frowned his irritation with her insistence on using his title. 'I believe we established only a few minutes ago that we are cousins of a sort and we should therefore address each other as Cousin Eleanor and Cousin Justin.'

Ellie's eyes widened in alarm at the mere thought of her using such familiarity with this rakishly handsome gentleman; Justin St Just, the twelfth Duke of Royston, was so top-lofty, so arrogantly haughty as he gave every appearance of looking down the length of his superior nose at the rest of the world, that Ellie would never be able to even think of him as a cousin, let alone address him as such.

'I believe that you may have implied

something of the sort, yes, *your Grace,*' she said stubbornly.

He arched one blond brow over suddenly teasing blue eyes. 'But you did not concur?'

'I do not believe so, no, your Grace.'

He eyed her in sudden frustration. 'Perhaps it is a subject we should discuss further when I return downstairs?'

She frowned. 'I—perhaps.'

He scowled darkly at her intransigence. 'But again, you do not agree…?'

Ellie believed such a conversation to be a complete waste of his time, as well as her own. What was the point in arguing over what to call one another? They'd probably not speak to each other again for at least another year, if this past year—which consisted of this last few minutes' conversation for the entirety of it—was any indication! 'It is very late, your Grace, and I believe the dowager duchess, if she has been made aware of your arrival, will be becoming increasingly anxious to speak with you,' she prompted softly.

'Of course.' He now looked annoyed at having allowed himself to become distracted by talking to her. 'I will expect to find you in the library, along with the decanter of brandy and two glasses, when I return,' he added peremptorily before resuming his ascent of the staircase.

Almost, Ellie recognised indignantly, as if he considered her as being of no more consequence than a dog he might instruct to heel, or a horse he halted by the rein.

Chapter Three

'I must say, you took your time getting here, Royston.'

Justin, as was the case with most men, was uncomfortable visiting a sickroom, but especially when it was that of his aged grandmother, the dowager duchess being a woman for whom he had the highest regard and affection.

Tonight, the pallor of her face emphasised each line and wrinkle, so that she looked every one of her almost seventy years as she lay propped up by white lace pillows piled high against the head of the huge four-poster bed. A state of affairs that was not in the least reassuring, despite the fact that her iron-grey hair was as perfectly styled as usual and her expression as proudly imperious.

The St Justs, as Justin knew only too well, after learning of his grandfather's long and private struggle with a wasting disease, were a breed apart when it came to bearing up under adversity; his grandmother might only be a St Just by marriage, but her strength of will was equal to, if not more than, any trueborn St Just.

He crossed the room swiftly to stand beside the four-poster bed. 'I apologise for my tardiness, Grandmama. I was not at home when Cousin Eleanor's note arrived—'

'If you lived here as you should that would not have been a problem,' she said querulously.

'We have had this conversation before, Grandmama. This is your home, not mine—'

'You are the Duke of Royston, are you not?'

Justin sighed. 'Yes, for my sins, I most certainly am.'

Edith eyed him disapprovingly. 'No doubt living here with me would put a dampener on your gambling or wenching—or both! Which diversion were you enjoying this evening to cause your delay?' She gave a disgusted sniff, but couldn't hide the twinkle in her eye.

Justin kept his expression neutral so as not to upset his grandmother; his reluctance to live at Royston House was due more to the fact that he associated this house with the frequent absences of his parents during his childhood, and his subsequent loneliness, than because he feared his grandmother would put a crimp in any supposed excesses of his in gambling and wenching, as she put it. As a consequence, he preferred to remain at the apartments he had occupied before the death of his father. 'I am sure this is not a suitable conversation for a grandson to be having with his aged grandmother—'

'Less talk of the aged, if you do not mind! And why should we not talk of such things?' She looked up at him challengingly. 'Do you think me so old that I do not know how young and single gentlemen of the *ton* choose to spend their evenings? Many of the married ones, too!'

'I believe I may only be called young in years, Grandmama,' he drawled rue-fully; these past three years as the Duke of Royston, and the onerous responsibilities of that title, had required that Justin become more circumspect in his public lifestyle, and at the same time they had left him little or no time for a private life either.

Perhaps it was time he thought seriously of acquiring a permanent mistress, a mild and biddable woman who would be only too pleased to attend to his needs, no matter what the time of day or night, but would make no demands of him other than that he keep her and provide a house in which they might meet. It was an idea that merited some further consideration.

But not here and now. 'I did not come here to discuss my own activities, when it is your own health which is currently in question.' he changed the subject deftly. 'Cousin Eleanor has informed me that Dr Franklyn was called to attend you earlier this evening. What is the problem, Grandmama?'

'Might I enquire when you decided that Ellie is to be referred to as your cousin?' Edith raised those imperious grey brows.

'Ellie?'

'Miss Eleanor Rosewood, your Cousin Frederick's stepdaughter, of course,' she supplied impatiently.

'I can hardly be so familiar as to address her as Ellie—a name I do not particularly care for, by the by—' Justin gave an irritated scowl '—when her mother, one supposes, bestowed upon her the perfectly elegant name of Eleanor. And Miss Rosewood is far too formal, in view of her connection to this family.'

'I agree.' His grandmother gave a haughty nod. 'And it is Ellie—Eleanor, whom I wish to discuss with you.'

Justin made no attempt to hide his astonishment. 'Are you telling me that you had me tracked down at my club, with all the fervour of a pack of hounds baying at the scent of fox—'

'Do not be melodramatic, Justin.' Edith eyed him with indulgent exasperation.

His brows rose. 'Do you deny having had a note delivered to my rooms late in the evening, one moreover that appeared to be of such vital urgency that my manservant instantly dispatched one of the other servants to track me down at one of my clubs?'

'I did instruct the note be written and delivered to you, yes. But it was not so late in the evening when I did so,' his grandmother added pointedly. 'Nor can I be held responsible for the actions of your manservant in dispatching a servant to seek you out so doggedly.'

Justin gave another scowl. 'But you do not deny that the reason for sending the note was so that you might bring me here simply in order to discuss your young companion?'

The dowager duchess sent him a reproachful glance. 'There is nothing simple about it, my dear. Ellie, and her future, have loomed large in my thoughts of late. Even more so this evening, when I am feeling so unwell—Justin, would you please refrain from pacing in that restless manner and instead sit down in that chair beside me? It is making my head ache having to follow your movements in this way.' She gave a pained wince.

Only one part of that statement was of any relevance to Justin at this particular moment. 'In what way are you feeling unwell?' He pounced on the statement, his expression distracted as he lowered his long length down into the chair beside the bed before reaching out to take one of his grandmother's delicately fragile hands into both of his.

Edith gave a weary sigh. 'I find I become very tired of late. An occurrence which has made me realise that—it has made me aware that I should have made much more of an effort to ensure that things were settled before now…' She gave another sigh, a little mournful this time.

Justin scowled darkly. 'Grandmama, if this is yet another way for you to introduce the unwelcome subject of my acquiring a duchess—'

'Why, you conceited young whippersnapper!' She gave him a quelling glance as she sat up straighter in the bed. 'Contrary to what you appear to believe, I do not spend the whole of my waking life thinking up ways to entice my stubborn and uninterested grandson into matrimony!' Then she seemed to collect herself and settled back once more on her pillows with another pained wince.

Justin gave a rueful shake of his head at hearing her berate him so soundly; not too many people would have dared speak to him like that and hope to get away with it! Oh, he was certain that many of the *ton* referred to him, behind his back, as being 'arrogantly haughty' or 'coldly disdainful', and even on occasion as being 'harsh and imperious' just like his grandmother was, but they would not have dared to do so to his face.

Not when they were sober, at least, Justin acknowledged derisively, as he thought of

Litchfield's insulting behaviour earlier this evening. A rash and dangerous move on Litchfield's part, when Justin was acknowledged as being one of the finest swordsmen in England, as well as one of the most accurate of shots; no gentlemen would dare to talk to him in that way when they were sober, for fear they might incite—and subsequently lose—the duel that would undoubtedly ensue.

'I am glad to hear it,' he drawled in answer to his grandmother's comment. 'Pray, then, what are these "things", which need to be "settled", Grandmama?'

'Eleanor's future, of course.' She eyed him carefully, her gnarled fingers folding and then refolding the fine bedsheet beneath them. 'She is so very young, and has no other relatives apart from ourselves, and I cannot bear to think of what might become of her when I am gone.'

Justin tensed. 'When you are gone? Is there any likelihood of that happening in the near future?' he prompted sharply as he felt the slight trembling of the hand he still held in his own.

The fact that the love his parents shared had been exclusive and all-consuming, and not one which had allowed time or particular consideration for their only child, had, as a consequence, meant that it was Justin's paternal grandparents, Edith and George St Just, who were the constant influences in his life, and with whom he had chosen to spend the majority of his school holidays, as well as Christmas and birthdays.

'Doctor Franklyn is of the opinion that I am simply wearing out—'

'Utterly ridiculous!' Justin barked, sitting forwards tensely, blue gaze fierce as he searched the unusual delicate pallor of her face. 'He is mistaken. Why, you had tea with your two dear friends only a few days ago, attended Lady Huntsley's ball with them just yesterday evening—'

'As a consequence, today I am feeling so weak that I do not even have the energy to rise from my bed.'

'You have overtaxed yourself, that is all,' he insisted.

'Justin, you are no longer a child and, sadly, neither am I.' His grandmother gave another heavy sigh. 'And I cannot say I will not be pleased to be with your grandfather again—'

'I refuse to listen to this nonsense a mo-

ment longer!' Justin released her hand to
stand up before glowering down at her. 'I
will speak to Dr Franklyn myself.'

'Do so, by all means, if you feel you must,
but bullying the doctor cannot make me any
younger than I am,' Edith reasoned gently.

Justin drew in a sharp breath at the truth
of that statement. 'Perhaps you might rally,
find new purpose, if I were to reconsider
my decision not to marry in the near future.'

'Generous of you, Royston.' She gave him
an affectionate, understanding smile, which
had the effect of shooting more fear into his
heart than anything she might say considering she'd been so hell-bent on seeing him
married off as soon as humanly possible.
'Unfortunately, the outcome would, I am
sorry to say, remain the same.'

'I simply cannot accept that!'

'You must, Justin,' his grandmother
chided gently. 'Gratified as I am to see how
the thought upsets you, it is a fact of life that
I cannot go on for ever. I should, of course,
have liked to see you settled before my time
comes, but I accept that is not to be…'

'I have already suggested I might give the
matter of matrimony further consideration,

if it would make you happy!' He scowled fiercely at the mere thought of it.

'You must, and no doubt will, do exactly as you wish. At the moment I am more concerned with my dear companion. I must know that Ellie—Eleanor's—future has been settled before I depart this world.'

'I would prefer that you not say that phrase again in my presence, Grandmama.' Justin had resumed his restless pacing, too agitated by his grandmother's news to be able to stand or to sit at her bedside any longer.

'Ignoring something will not make it go away, my dear,' Edith pointed out.

Justin was well aware of that, but even the thought of his grandmother no longer being here, gently chiding or sternly rebuking him for one misdemeanour or another, was anathema to him. She was only in her sixty-ninth year, and Justin had not so much as spared a thought for the possibility of her dying just yet; Edith St Just had been, and still was, the woman in his life on whom he had always depended, a woman of both iron will and indomitable spirit, always there, the steely matriarch of the St Just family.

'May we discuss Eleanor's future now,

Justin?' Edith continued, uncharacteristically meek.

Eleanor Rosewood, and her future, were the last things that Justin wished to discuss at this moment, but a single glance at his grandmother's face was enough to silence his protests as he noticed once again how the paleness of her face, and the shadows beneath her eyes, gave her the appearance of being every one of those eight and sixty years.

He bit back the sharpness of his reply and instead resumed his seat beside the bed. 'Very well, Grandmama, if you insist, then let us talk of Cousin Eleanor's future.'

She nodded. 'It is my dearest wish to see her comfortably married before I dep—am no longer here,' she corrected at Justin's scowl.

He raised his brows. 'It seems to me that you appear to wish this dubious state upon all those close to you. I am heartily relieved it is not just me you have set your sights on.'

'Do not be facetious, Royston!' The dowager frowned. 'As I have already stated, you must do as you wish where your own future bride is concerned, but for a young woman in Ellie's position, marriage is the only so-lution.'

'And do you also have a gentleman in mind to become her husband? More to the point, does Cousin Eleanor have such a gen-tleman in mind?' He raised mocking brows.

His grandmother sighed. 'She has been so taken up with my own affairs this past year that I very much doubt she has given the matter so much as a single thought.'

'Then—'

'Which is not to say she should not have done so.' Edith frowned him into silence. 'Or that I should not have insisted she do so, before she is of an age that is considered as being unmarriageable.'

'Exactly how old is Cousin Eleanor?' Justin eyed his grandmother incredulously, thinking of the girl's fresh, dewy complex-ion and unlined brow.

'She has recently entered her twentieth year—'

'Almost ancient then!' he teased.

'I am being serious, Justin. A young woman of Ellie's meagre circumstances, if left alone in the world, will, as I am sure you are only too well aware, have very few opportunities open to her.' She arched a pointed brow.

Yes, Justin was well aware of the fate that often befell impoverished but genteel young ladies of Eleanor Rosewood's beauty and circumstance, being neither a part of society and yet not of the working classes either. 'And exactly what do you expect me to do about it? Settle some money on her as a dowry, perhaps, in order to entice a penniless young man of the clergy or some such into offering her marriage?' he suggested sarcastically.

'The dowry would certainly be a start.' His grandmother took his suggestion seriously as she nodded slowly. 'Heaven knows the Royston fortune is large enough you would not even notice its loss! But I do not see why Eleanor should have to settle for an impoverished clergyman. Surely, somewhere amongst your acquaintances, you must know of a titled gentleman or two who would willingly overlook her social shortcomings in order to take to wife a young woman of personal fortune, who also happens to be the stepcousin of the powerful Duke of Royston?'

Justin had meant to tease with his suggestion of a providing a dowry for Eleanor, but he could see by the seriousness of his grandmother's expression that she, at least, was in deadly earnest. 'Let me see if I understand you correctly, Grandmama. You wish for me to first settle a sizeable dowry upon your companion, before then seeking out and securing a suitable, preferably titled husband, for her amongst my acquaintances?' The suggestion was not only preposterous, but seemed slightly incestuous to Justin in view of his own less than cousinly thoughts about that young lady just minutes ago!

'I do not expect you to approach the subject quite so callously, Royston.' Edith eyed him impatiently. 'I am very fond of the gel and I should not like to see her married to a man she did not like, or whom did not like her.'

His brows rose. 'So you are, in fact, expecting me to secure a love match for her, despite her "social shortcomings" as you so tactfully put it.'

'A suitable marriage does not preclude the couple from falling in love with each other,' Edith snapped. 'Your grandfather and I loved each other dearly. As did your father and mother.'

Yes, and it was the example of that deep love his parents had for each other that had made Justin so leery of entering into matrimony himself; he could not bear even the thought of ever loving a woman so deeply, so intensely, that his own offspring suffered because of it.

He suppressed a shudder. 'I believe you may be expecting too much for Eleanor to secure such a love in her own marriage.'

'We will not know until you try,' his grandmother insisted.

'And how do you propose I go about doing that?' He gave a rueful shake of his head.

'As Ellie's closest male relative—yes, I know you're about to say that technically you're not really related to her at all—you might perhaps commence by accompanying her to—to a musical soirée or two, perhaps, in order that you might introduce her to these eligible if financially bereft young gentlemen of your acquaintance?'

'I—you expect me to attend *musical soirées?*' Justin stared at his grandmother incredulously as he once again rose to his feet out of sheer incapability to know what to do next; indeed, he was starting to feel like that toy he'd had as a child which had popped out of the box when the lid was lifted! 'I believe your current indisposition has addled your brain, Grandmama!' He shook his head. 'I do not attend music soirées or balls in the normal course of events, let alone with the intention of marrying off my young step-cousin to some unsuspecting gentleman!'

'But there is nothing to say that you could not make the exception in these special circumstances, is there?' she insisted defiantly.

'No, of course there is not. But—'

'It would make me very happy if you were to do so, Justin.'

He narrowed suddenly suspicious blue eyes on the supposedly frail figure of his grandmother as she once again lay back, so small and vulnerable-looking against those snowy white pillows. 'I thought it was Cousin Eleanor's happiness which was your first and only concern?'

'It is.' Edith's eyes snapped her irritation at his perspicacity. 'And I can think of no better way to secure that happiness than you publicly acknowledging Ellie as a favoured cousin.'

'A favoured cousin of such low social standing she has been in your own employ this past year,' he reminded her drily.

'I very much doubt that any of the *ton* would make the connection between that mousy young woman and Miss Eleanor Rosewood, the elegant and beautiful cousin of the Duke of Royston.'

He very much doubted the truth of that claim, in regard to the gentlemen in society, at least; he, for one, had certainly taken note of Eleanor's understated beauty!

'And even if they did,' Edith continued firmly, 'none would dare to socially cut or slight Ellie whilst she is seen to be under your protection.'

On that subject Justin did agree. But the cost to himself, of being forced into the tedium of attending what was left of the Season, was surely too much to expect of him? His grandmother did not seem to think so...

'I am to host the Royston Ball in four days' time and you are always gracious enough to make an appearance on that occasion,' his grandmother reminded him.

'The ball may have to be cancelled if you are still feeling so fatigued,' he said slyly.

'That will not happen during my lifetime!' the dowager duchess assured him imperiously. 'The Royston Ball has taken place for the past hundred years and this year shall be no different, not even if I have to spend the evening sitting in my Bath chair overseeing events,' she continued determinedly.

'And you seriously intend to introduce Eleanor into society that evening?'

She gave a haughty inclination of her head. 'As a guest in my home she will naturally attend.'

'And you expect me to act as her escort for the evening?'

'As her guardian, perhaps, which would be perfectly acceptable as you are her closest male relative.' She nodded briskly. 'It is also the perfect opportunity for Ellie to see and be seen by the *ton*.'

Justin had the uncomfortable feeling that somewhere in the course of this conversation he had not only been manipulated, but soundly outmanoeuvred. An unusual occurrence, admittedly, but somehow his grandmother seemed to have succeeded in doing so. He—

'There is one other subject upon which I shall require your assistance, my boy.'

He eyed the redoubtable old lady extremely warily now. 'Yes?'

'I believe it might be advisable, before any marriage were to take place, to attempt to ascertain the identity of Ellie's real father...'

Justin's eyes widened in shock. 'Her *real* father? Was that not Mr Rosewood, then?'

'As that gentleman had already been dead for a full year before Ellie was born, I do not believe so, no...' Edith grimaced.

This situation, one not even of Justin's own choosing, suddenly became more and more surreal. 'And is Eleanor herself aware of that fact?'

His grandmother gave a snort. 'Of course she is not. I only discovered the truth of things myself when I had her mother investigated after that idiot Frederick ran off to Gretna Green so impetuously and married the woman.'

'So my stepcousin and ward is not only penniless, but is also a bastard—'

'Royston!'

Justin groaned out loud. 'And if I should discover that her real father is an unsavoury scoundrel fit only for the gutter?'

His grandmother raised imperious brows. 'Then you will do everything in your power to make sure that no one else is ever made privy to that information.'

'And how do you suggest I do that?'

'I have every confidence that you will find a way, Royston.' She smiled.

A confidence in his abilities which, in this particular instance, Justin did not share…

Ellie could not settle as she waited nervously for Justin to join her in the library. Even the warmth from the fire beside which she now sat, lit by Stanhope some minutes ago when he delivered the tray on which sat the two glasses and brandy decanter, did little to ease the chill of nervousness from her bones.

She had been in the dowager duchess's household for a year now and before this evening could have counted the number of words she had exchanged with the top-lofty Duke of Royston on the fingers of one hand. Nor had he ever deigned to address her by her given name until this evening.

Which was not to say Ellie had not been completely aware of him, or that his full name was Justin George Robert St Just, the twelfth Duke of Royston—and a long list of other titles which escaped Ellie's memory for the moment. Aged nine years her senior, and so obviously experienced as well as worldly, the golden-haired, blue-eyed Justin St Just had also featured largely in every one of Ellie's romantic dreams, both day and night this past year, to a degree that she believed herself half in love with him already.

Which made awaiting his appearance in the library now even more excruciatingly nerve-racking. How embarrassing if she were to reveal, by look, word or deed, even an inkling of the sensual fantasies she had woven so romantically about the powerful and handsome duke! Fantasies that made Ellie's cheeks burn just to think of them as she imagined Justin returning her feelings for him, resulting in those chiselled lips claiming her own, those long and elegant hands caressing her back, before moving higher, to cup the fullness of her eagerly straining breasts—

'Your thoughts appear to please you, Cousin Eleanor…?'

Ellie gave a guilty start as she rose hastily from the chair beside the fireplace to turn and face the man whose lips and hands she had just been imagining touching her with such intimacy.

Justin did not at all care for the look of apprehension which appeared upon Eleanor Rosewood's delicately blushing face as she rose to gaze across the library at him. Apprehension, accompanied by a certain amount of guilt, if he was not mistaken. What she had to feel guilty about he had no idea, nor did he care for that look of apprehension either. 'Perhaps not,' he drawled as he stepped further into the room and closed the door behind him before crossing to where the decanter of brandy and glasses had been placed upon the desktop.

'I trust the dowager duchess is feeling better?'

As Justin's grandmother had elicited several promises from him before allowing him to leave her bedchamber, the condition of her health being one of them, he was not now at liberty to discuss the reason for Dr Franklyn's visit, with Eleanor or anyone else. That Justin would be having words with the good doctor himself was definite, but his grandmother had insisted that neither of her two close friends, or her companion, be made aware of the reason for her fatigue.

Justin schooled his features into an expression of amusement. 'She assures me she feels well enough to continue as usual with the Royston Ball to be held here in four days' time,' he answered evasively as he turned to carry the two brandy glasses over to where she stood so delicately pale beside the glowing fire.

She made no effort to take the glass he held out to her. 'I do not care for brandy, your Grace.'

'I have a feeling that tonight shall be the exception,' he said drily.

She blinked long silky lashes. 'It will…?'

'Oh, yes,' he said distractedly. The flickering flames brought out the red-gold fire in her hair, Justin noted admiringly as he placed the glass in her hand; she really did have the most beautiful hair, in a myriad of shades, from deep auburn to red and then gold. Her eyes were a bright green, the same colour as a perfect emerald, and surrounded by the longest silky black lashes Justin had ever seen. As for those freckles upon her creamy cheeks and nose…

Justin felt a sudden urge, a strong desire, to kiss each and every one of them! He determinedly brought those wayward thoughts to an abrupt end and his mouth compressed. 'My grandmother has requested that you… assist her in the matter of the ball.'

Her little pink tongue moved moistly across those full and pouting lips, making him shift uncomfortably. 'I am not sure what assistance I could possibly be in the planning of such a grand occasion, but I shall of course endeavour to offer the dowager duchess whatever help I am able.'

Justin gave her an amused look. 'You misunderstand, Cousin Eleanor—the assistance required of you is that you attend the Royston Ball.'

She nodded. 'And I have already said that I shall be only too pleased to help the dowager duchess in any way that I can—'

'You are to attend the ball as her guest—careful!' he warned as the brandy glass looked in danger of slipping from her fingers.

Ellie's fingers immediately tightened about the bulbous glass even as stared up at him in disbelief. Justin could not seriously be suggesting that she was to attend the ball as a member of the *ton,* was he?

The implacability of his expression as he looked at her down the long length of his aristocratic nose appeared to suggest that he was.

Chapter Four

'You may find a sip of brandy to be beneficial…'

Ellie was still so stunned that she obediently sipped her drink—and immediately began to choke as the fiery liquid hit and burned the back of her throat. A dilemma Justin immediately rectified by slapping her soundly upon her back.

Perhaps a little harder than was necessary?

Ellie shook her head as she straightened, her eyes watering, her face feeling hot and flushed as she spoke huskily, 'I have no idea what her Grace can be thinking! I could not possibly attend the Royston Ball as a guest.'

'My grandmother has decreed otherwise.'

As if that announcement settled the matter, Ellie realised dazedly. 'And what is your own opinion on the subject, your Grace?' she prompted, sure that he could not approve of such a plan as this.

He gave a shrug of those wide and muscled shoulders before drawling, 'I make it a point of principle never to disagree with my grandmother.'

Ellie knew that to be an erroneous statement from the onset; if Justin listened without argument to everything his grandmother said to him, then he would have long since found himself married, with half-a-dozen heirs in the nursery! For Edith St Just made no secret of her desire to see her grandson acquire his duchess, and not long afterwards begin producing his heirs. A desire which Ellie knew he had successfully evaded fulfilling during this past year, at least.

Ellie looked up at him from beneath lowered lashes as she tried to gauge the duke's response to his grandmother's unexpected decision to invite her lowly companion to attend the prestigious Royston Ball. A fruitless task, as it happened, the blandness of Justin's expression revealing absolutely none of that arrogant gentleman's inner thoughts.

Although Ellie thought she detected a slight glint of amusement in the depths of those deep blue eyes… No doubt at her expense, she thought irritably.

Ellie was not a fool and she might well consider herself half in love with Justin, and find him exciting in a forbidden way, but that did not preclude her from knowing he was also arrogant, cynical and mocking. Or that his mockery on this occasion was directed towards her.

She drew in a ragged breath in an attempt to steady herself. 'I shall, of course, explain to her Grace, first thing in the morning, exactly why it is I cannot accept her invitation.'

'And I wish you every success with that.' There was no mistaking the amusement this time in those deceptively sleepy blue eyes.

Deceptive, because Ellie was sure that nothing escaped this astutely intelligent man's notice! 'But surely you must see that it will not do?'

'I am not the one whom you will have to convince of that, Eleanor,' the duke pointed out almost gleefully, she thought crossly. 'My grandmother, once her mind is settled upon something, is rarely, if ever, persuaded otherwise.'

That might well be so—indeed, after this past year spent in that lady's household, Ellie knew for herself that it was!—but in this case it must be attempted. Only the cream of society was ever invited into the dowager duchess's home, to attend the Royston Ball or on any other social occasion, and Ellie knew that she was far from being that. Admittedly, her mother and father had been on the fringes of that society, her father because he was the youngest son of a baron. And although her mother had been merely a country squire's daughter, she had been elevated in society by her first marriage to the son of a baron, and again at the second marriage to the son of a lord, the dowager duchess's own nephew. Even so, Ellie's own place in society was precarious at best.

'Indeed, I see no reason why you should wish to do such a thing,' the duke continued. 'If my grandmother has decided that you are to be introduced to society, then you may be assured that none in society will dare to argue the point.'

'Even you?' she couldn't help asking, then flushed at her own temerity.

Justin frowned at this second attempt on Eleanor's part to ascertain his own views on the subject. Especially when he was now unsure of those views himself…

Admittedly, he had initially dismissed the very idea of her introduction into society, but second, and perhaps third thoughts, had revealed to him that it was not such an unacceptable idea as he had first considered. His grandmother's argument, in favour of doing so, in an effort to secure Eleanor a suitable husband, although a considerable inconvenience to himself, was perfectly valid. Most especially if Justin were to provide Eleanor with a suitable dowry, as his grandmother suggested he must do.

Eleanor was both ladylike in her appearance as well as her manner. The fact that she also happened to be impoverished should not prevent her from seeking the same happiness in the marriage mart as any other young lady of nineteen years.

There was that irritating question as to whom Eleanor's real father might be, of course, but Justin had his grandmother's assurances that Eleanor knew nothing of that, believing herself to be the daughter of Mr Henry Rosewood. And if Justin's investigations into that matter, at his grandmother's

behest, should prove otherwise, then who
needed to be any the wiser about it?

The father, perhaps, if he did not already
know of his daughter's existence...

Only time, and investigation, would inform Justin as to whether or not the name of
Eleanor's real father was of any relevance to
this present situation.

His grandmother having elicited his next
promise—that he would not speak to Eleanor on that particular subject either—Justin
now turned to the reason for Edith's insistence on Eleanor's début into society. 'The
dowager duchess has decided it is time for
you to acquire a husband.'

Green eyes widened incredulously at his
announcement, even as those creamy cheeks
became flushed. With embarrassment? Or
temper? Or perhaps excitement? He wished
he knew.

Justin did not know her well enough to
gauge her present mood, but he was certainly
man enough to appreciate the added depth
of colour to the green of her eyes, and the
flushed warmth in those creamy cheeks, as
well as the swift rise and fall of the full swell
of her breasts. Indeed, if this young lady had
been anyone other than his grandmother's

protégée, then she would have been the perfect choice for the role of his mistress he had been considering earlier—

Justin called a sudden halt to his wandering thoughts. His grandmother's request had now placed him in the position of guardian to this particular young lady, and as Eleanor's guardian Justin would frown most severely upon any gentleman having such licentious thoughts, as his had just been, in regard to his own ward!

She drew in a deep breath, unwittingly further emphasising the fullness of those creamy breasts. 'I am sure I am very…gratified by her Grace's concern—'

'Are you?'

Ellie gave Justin a quick glance beneath lowered lashes as she heard the mocking amusement in his tone; grateful as she was to the dowager duchess for coming to her rescue a year ago, it had not been an easy task for Ellie to learn to hold her impetuous tongue, or keep her fiery temper in check, as was befitting in the companion of a much older lady and a dowager duchess at that, and they were faults her mother had been at pains to point out to Ellie on a regular basis when she was alive.

The duke's amusement, so obviously at her expense, which she once again saw in those intense blue eyes, was enough to make Ellie forget all of her previous caution, as she snapped waspishly, 'I am gratified to see that at least one of us finds this situation amusing and it is not me!'

'If nothing else, it has at least succeeded in diverting my grandmother's attention from my own lack of interest in the married state!' he lobbed back lazily.

Ellie eyed him in frustration. 'I am no more interested in entering into marriage, simply because it's convenient, than you are!'

Her mother's marriage, to a youngest son, had resulted in Muriel Rosewood being left a virtually impoverished and expectant widow on Henry Rosewood's death, with only a small yearly stipend from the Rosewood family coffers, and no other interest in the widow and her daughter from that family, with which to support them.

Muriel's second marriage ten years later, to a rake of a man whom she did not love, but who offered her a comfortable home for herself and her young daughter, had not been a happy one. Far from it.

As a consequence, Ellie had decided that she would never marry for any other reason than that she loved the man who was to be her husband. Far better that she remain an old maid, she had decided, paid companion to the dowager duchess, or someone very like her, than that she should end up as unhappy as her mother before her, unpaid servant and bed partner of a man who did not love her any more than she loved him.

The duke chuckled huskily. 'My grandmother is not easily gainsaid.'

'You appear to have done so most successfully all these years,' Ellie pointed out smartly.

Justin gave an acknowledging inclination of his golden head at the hit. 'And with my grandmother's determined efforts now firmly concentrated upon your own marital prospects, my dear cousin, I fully admit I am hoping to continue that enviable state for several more years to come.'

She frowned. 'I do not have any "marital prospects"!'

'But you will have, once I have settled a sizeable dowry upon you.'

'A sizeable dowry!' Ellie repeated, staring up at him incredulously. 'And why, pray, would you wish to do that?'

He lifted a brow. 'Because it would make my grandmother happy if I did?'

Ellie continued to look up at him for several long seconds, a stare the duke met with unblinking and bored implacability. Bored?

So he found the idea of marrying her off, whether she wished it or not, whether she would be happy or not, to be not only amusing but boring as well?

And to think—to imagine that she had thought only minutes ago that she was in love with Justin St Just! So much so, that she had awaited with trepidation the announcement of his betrothal and forthcoming marriage to some beautiful and highly eligible young lady. Now she could not help but feel pity for whichever of those unlucky women should eventually be chosen as duchess to this arrogant man!

Indeed, as far as Ellie was concerned, Justin St Just had become nothing more than her tormentor, out to bedevil her with threats of arranging her marriage to a man she neither knew nor loved.

It could not be allowed to happen!

Except…Ellie had no idea how she was

to go about avoiding such an unwanted outcome when the duke and the dowager duchess, both so imperious and determined, seemed so set upon the idea.

She placed her brandy glass down upon one of the side tables before commencing to pace the room, as she feverishly sought for ways in which she might avoid the state of an arranged, unhappy marriage, without upsetting the kind dowager duchess, or incurring the wrath of her devil of a grandson.

Justin replenished his brandy glass before strolling over to take a seat beside the warmth of the fire, observing Eleanor's agitated movements from between narrowed lids.

That she was displeased at the idea of an arranged marriage was completely obvious. A deep frown marred her brow as she continued to energetically pace the length of the library, which allowed Justin to appreciate the outline of her slender and yet curvaceous form in the plain brown gown and the creamy expanse of her throat above the swell of her breasts, as well as the fineness of those furiously snapping green eyes.

He couldn't help but wonder how much more beautiful she might look with that abundance of red curls loose about her shoulders and dressed in a clinging gown, or possibly a night rail, of deep green silk…

And to think he had been bored to the point of ennui earlier this evening!

Not so any longer. Now Justin felt invigorated, the future full of possibilities, as he considered the challenge ahead of him in procuring a suitable husband for the surprisingly feisty, and obviously unwilling, Miss Eleanor Rosewood.

He was not a little curious as to the reason for her obvious aversion to an arranged marriage, when, in Justin's experience, for the majority of the women of his acquaintance an advantageous marriage appeared to be their only goal in life.

Could it be—did Eleanor's tastes perhaps run in another direction entirely? No, surely not! It would be a cruelty on the part of Mother Nature if a woman of such understated beauty, and surprisingly fiery a temperament as Eleanor, was not destined to occupy the arms, the bed, of some lucky gentleman. In other circumstances, she would almost certainly have made the perfect mistress—

No, he really must not think of her in such

terms. He must in future consider himself as purely a guardian where she was concerned.

Even if his extremely private inner thoughts strayed constantly in the opposite direction!

'Have you drawn any conclusions yet as to how you might thwart my grandmother's plans for your immediate future?' Justin teased after several long minutes of her pacing. 'If so, I wish you would share them with me, if only for my own future reference?'

Ellie came to an abrupt halt to glare across the library at the lazily reclining form of the relaxed duke, the glow from the flames of the fire turning his fashionably styled hair a rich and burnished gold, those patrician features thrown into stark and cruel relief, and causing Ellie's pulse to quicken in spite of herself.

The rapidity of her pulse, and sudden shortness of breath, told her that, although she now doubted herself in love with him any more, she was still not completely averse to his physical attributes, at least.

His arrogance and mockery, when directly aimed at her, as they now were, were something else entirely, the former frustrating her and the latter infuriating her.

She drew in a deep and steady breath before answering him. 'I do not see why I cannot, politely but firmly, inform her Grace of my feelings of aversion to an arranged marriage—you find something amusing in that approach?' she prompted sharply as he laughed out loud.

'Truth be told, I find it ridiculous in the extreme.' Justin flashed his even white teeth in an unsympathetic grin. 'My grandmother, as I am sure you are aware, has all the subtlety of a battering ram. That being so, I doubt your own feelings on the matter will even be considered. Nor will anything you have to say on the subject shake her unwavering certainty that she feels she knows what is best for you,' he added firmly as Ellie would have protested.

'Perhaps if you were to—no, I see that you are so entertained by the whole idea, you would not even consider coming to my aid!' Ellie eyed him in utter disgust as he continued to grin at her in that unsympathetic manner.

He eyed her mockingly. 'Perhaps if you were to tell me of the reasons for your reluctance in this matter, I'd feel more inclined to help you out?'

Ellie gave an impatient shake of her head. 'No doubt they are the same as your own. I could never marry anyone whom I did not love with the whole of my heart and who did not love me in the same way.'

All amusement fled as he stood up abruptly, his eyes now a cold and glittering sapphire blue. 'There you are wrong, Eleanor,' he rasped. 'My own feelings on that particular subject are in total opposition to your own,' he elaborated harshly as she raised questioning brows, 'in that I would never consider marrying anyone who declared a love for me, or vice versa.'

Ellie's eyes widened at his words and the coldness of the tone in which he said them. She had believed that the duke's aversion to marriage was because he had not yet met the woman whom he loved enough to make his duchess. His statement now showed it was the opposite.

Ellie could not help but wonder why…

She was aware, of course, that many marriages in the *ton* were made for financial or social gain, as her mother's had been to Frederick St Just. But often the couples in those marriages learnt a respect and affection for each other, and in some cases love itself. Again, that had not happened in her mother's case, her marriage to Frederick, an inveterate gambler and womaniser, tolerable at best, painful at worst, certainly colouring Ellie's own views on the subject.

But for any gentleman to deliberately state his intention of never feeling love for his wife, or to have her feel love for him, seemed harsh in the extreme.

And surely it was asking too much of any woman, if married to Justin St Just, not to fall in love with him?

Or perhaps the answer to his stated aversion to loving his future wife had something to do with why he could not initially be found earlier on this evening...?

Ellie knew that many gentlemen of the *ton* had mistresses, women society dictated they could never marry, but for whom they often held more affection than they did their wives. Perhaps he had such a woman in his life? A low-born woman, or possibly a married woman of the *ton,* whom he could never make his duchess, but for whom he had a deep and abiding love?

Yes, perhaps that was the explanation for his stated desire for a loveless marriage.

'Would such a situation not be unfair to your future wife?' she ventured softly.

He looked down the length of his nose at her. 'Not if she were made aware of the situation from the onset.'

She gasped. 'Surely no woman would accept a marriage proposal under such cold and unemotional conditions?'

He gave her a pitying smile. 'It has been my experience that most, if not all women, would maim or kill in order to marry a duke and love be damned.'

'But—'

'The hour grows late, Eleanor, and I believe we have talked on this subject long enough for one evening.' Justin abruptly placed his empty brandy glass down upon the mantelpiece before turning away, no longer in the least amused by this conversation. 'If I might ask that you send word to me tomorrow regarding my grandmother's health?'

'I—of course, your Grace.' Eleanor seemed momentarily disconcerted by the abrupt change of subject. 'Hopefully I might also be able to inform you of her change of mind in regard to my attending the Royston Ball.'

Justin grimaced. 'You are an optimist as well as a romantic, I see.'

A faint flush darkened her cheeks even as she raised her chin proudly. 'I would hope I am a realist, your Grace.'

He gave a slow shake of his head. 'A realist would know to accept when she is defeated.'

'A realist would accept, even with your generous offer of providing me with a dowry, that I am not meant to be a part of society. Indeed,' she continued firmly as he would have spoken, 'I have no ambitions to ever be so.'

Justin raised his brows. 'You consider us a frivolous lot, then, with nothing to recommend us?'

He found himself the focus of dark-green eyes as Eleanor studied him unblinkingly for several seconds before giving a brief, dismissive smile. 'There is no answer I could give to that question which would not result in my either insulting you or denigrating myself. As such, I choose to make no reply at all.'

It was, Justin realised admiringly, both a clever and witty answer, and delivered in so ambiguous a tone as to render it as being at least one of the things she claimed it was not meant to be!

Again he found himself entertained by this surprisingly outspoken young woman, to appreciate why his grandmother was so fond of her; Edith St Just did not suffer twittering fools any more gladly than he did himself.

He gave her a courtly bow. 'I greatly look forward to being your escort to the Royston Ball.' And it was true, Justin realised with no little surprise; it was diverting, to say the least, to anticipate what this young woman might choose to do or say next!

Her eyes widened in alarm. 'My escort?'

He shot her a disarming grin. 'Another request from my grandmother.'

'But why should I be in need of an escort, when I already reside here?'

Justin smiled. 'Because a single lady, appearing in society for the first time, must be accompanied by her nearest male relative and guardian, and it appears I have that honour.'

Panic replaced the alarm in those deep-green eyes. 'Everyone would stop and stare, and the ladies would gossip speculatively behind their fans if I were to enter the ball-room on the arm of the Duke of Royston!'

'I believe that to be the whole point of the exercise, Cousin.'

'No.' Eleanor gave a decisive shake of her head, several red curls fluttering loosely about her temples as she did so. 'If I am to be forced to attend, as you believe I will be, then I absolutely refuse to make such a spectacle of myself.'

He raised haughty brows. 'Even though *you* will have the honour of being the first young woman whom the Duke of Royston has ever escorted anywhere?'

She looked startled for a moment, but recovered quickly. 'That only makes me all the more determined it shall not happen.'

Justin's smile widened at her stubborn optimism. 'I do not believe there is any way in which you might prevent it—other than your possibly falling down the stairs and breaking a leg before then!' He laughed in earnest as he saw by Eleanor's furrowed brow that she was actually giving the suggestion serious consideration. 'Would it really be such a bad thing to be seen entering the ballroom on my arm, Eleanor?' he chided softly as he crossed the room to stand in front of her. 'If so, then you are not in the least flattering to a man's ego.'

'I do not believe your own ego to be in need of flattery,' Ellie murmured huskily, totally disconcerted by Justin's sudden and close proximity. Indeed, she could feel the warmth of his breath ruffling those errant curls at her temple.

'No?' Long lean fingers reached up to smooth back those curls, the touch of his fingers light and cool against the heat of her brow.

Ellie swallowed before attempting an answer, at the same time inwardly willing her voice to sound as it normally did. 'How can it, when you are the elusive but much-coveted prize of the marriage mart?'

She sounded only a little breathless, she realised thankfully, at the same time as she knew her disobedient knees were in danger of turning to water and no longer supporting her.

'Am I?' A smile tilted those sculptured lips as those lean fingers now trailed lightly down the warmth of her cheek.

Her throat moved as she swallowed before answering. 'Elusive or much coveted?'

'Either.'

Ellie found she was having trouble breathing as his fingers now lingered teasingly close to, but did not quite touch, the fullness of her lips. Suddenly she possessed both dry lips and a throat she necessarily had to moisten before attempting to speak again. 'This is a ridiculous conversation, your Grace.'

'Ah, once again you seek to put me firmly in my place with the use of formality,' he murmured admiringly.

'I do no such thing!' Ellie attempted to rally her indignation—not an easy task when the soft pad of the duke's thumb was now passing lightly across her bottom lip, and sending rivulets of excitement to the tips of her breasts and an unaccustomed warmth to gather between her thighs. 'Your Grace—'

'Justin,' he correct softly. 'Or Cousin Justin, if you prefer.'

'I do not,' she stated firmly, knowing that if she did not stop his teasing soon she would end up as a boneless puddle at his highly polished, booted feet. 'It is late, and I— Perhaps there is some—someone anxiously awaiting your returning to her tonight?'

He stilled as those narrowed blue eyes moved searchingly over her flushed face. 'You implied something similar when I arrived earlier tonight...'

'Your Grace?'

'It becomes more and more obvious to me that you, like my grandmother, believe my delay in arriving here this evening to be because I was in the arms of my current mistress,' he said speculatively.

Ellie felt her cheeks flush even warmer, no doubt once again clashing horribly with the red of her hair, as well as emphasising the freckles across her cheeks and nose that had long been the bane of her life. 'I am not in the least interested as to the reason for the delay in your arrival—'

'Oh, but I think you are, Eleanor,' he contradicted softly. 'Very interested.'

She gave a pained frown as she looked up into those intent blue eyes and decided she had suffered quite enough of this gentleman's teasing for one evening. 'Is your conceit so great that you believe every woman you meet must instantly fall under the spell of your charm?'

'Not in the least.' Those blue eyes now twinkled down at her merrily. 'But it is gratifying to know that you at least find me charming, Eleanor—'

'What I *believe,* your Grace, is that you are a conceited ass—' She fell abruptly silent as Justin lowered his head and bit lightly, reprovingly, on her bottom lip.

Ellie stiffened as if frozen in place and her heart seemed to cease beating altogether as she acknowledged that the coldly arrogant Duke of Royston, the mockingly handsome Justin St Just, had just run the moistness of his sensuous tongue over her parted lips…

Chapter Five

Justin knew, almost the instant he began to gently nibble on the enticing fullness of Eleanor's bottom lip, tasting her heady sweetness against the sweep of his tongue, that he had made a mistake. A mistake of monumental proportions.

Admittedly he had been intrigued by that plump curve for some time now and had wondered at the depth of sensuality it implied, but to have acted upon that interest, given that his grandmother had so newly appointed him Eleanor's unofficial guardian, was unacceptable. To himself as well as it must be to Eleanor. Indeed, she appeared to be so horror-struck by his advances that she stood in front of him as still, and as cold, as the statue she now resembled.

Justin pulled back abruptly, his hands grasping the tops of her arms as he placed her firmly away from him, at the same time unable to stop himself from noticing that her lip was a little swollen from where his teeth had seconds ago nibbled upon it. 'Perhaps, in future, it would be as well if you desisted from challenging me by insulting me?' he added harshly in a desperate attempt to divert her attention away from his despicable behaviour.

'You—I—' Ellie gasped her indignation, eyes wide and accusing at the unfairness of being blamed for his shockingly familiar behaviour. She now wrenched completely out of his grasp to glare up at him. 'You are worse than conceited, sir! You are nothing more than—'

'Yes, yes,' he dismissed in a bored voice, knowing he had to carry on now as he had started. 'I have no doubt I am a rake and a cad, and many other unpleasant things, in your innocent eyes.' He eyed her mockingly as he straightened the lace cuffs of his shirt beneath his jacket. 'You will need to be a little more subtle, my dear, if you are to learn to rebuff the advances of the gentlemen of the *ton* without also insulting them.'

'And why should I care whether they feel insulted, if they have dared to take the same liberties you just did?' Ellie asked scornfully.

'Because it is part of the game, Eleanor,' he explained, hoping she would believe him.

She stilled, eyes narrowed. 'Game…?'

He gave a slight inclination of his head. 'How else is a man to know whether or not he likes a woman enough to marry her, let alone bed her, if he does not first flirt with her and take a liberty or two?'

She breathed shallowly. 'You are saying that you—that your reason for—for making love to me just now was your way of preparing me for the advances of other gentlemen?'

He raised a golden brow at her comment. 'A mere taste of your lips cannot exactly be called lovemaking, Eleanor.'

Her cheeks flushed. 'You will answer the question!'

He shrugged wide, indifferent shoulders. 'Are you now prepared?'

Was Ellie 'prepared' for the assault upon her senses that had resulted when he had nibbled upon, and tasted, her lips? Could anything have 'prepared' her for having her heart stop beating as it leapt into her throat? For the aching heat that had suffused her body? For the way her legs had turned to jelly, threatening to no longer support her? For the thrill of the excitement that had run so hotly through her veins!

And all the time she had been feeling those things he had merely been 'preparing' her for the advances of the other gentlemen of society...

She straightened, her shoulders back, chin held proudly high. 'I am "prepared" enough to know I shall administer my knee to a vulnerable part of any gentleman's anatomy should he ever attempt to take such liberties with me!'

The duke gave a pained wince. 'Then my time with you this evening has not been wasted.'

Had there ever existed a gentleman as arrogant, as insufferable, as this particular one had just proved to be? Somehow Ellie doubted it. Nor did she intend to suffer his company this evening for one minute longer!

She stepped back, her gaze cool. 'I believe it time that I went upstairs and checked upon the dowager.'

Blond brows rose in disbelief. 'Are you *dismissing* me, Eleanor?'

Her mouth set stubbornly as she refused

to be cowed by his haughty arrogance. 'Did it sound as if I were?'

'Yes.'

She gave a small smile of her own. 'Then that is what I must have been doing.'

Justin gave a surprised bark of laughter at the same time as he cursed the fact that he had realised only this evening that he found this particular young woman so damned entertaining. It was, to say the least, inconvenient, if not downright dangerous, to his peace of mind, if nothing else. As he had realised when he had kissed her just now. A mistake on his part, which Justin had felt it necessary to explain by dismissing it as a lesson for Eleanor's future reference—even if the lesson *he* had learnt had been not to kiss her again. 'I am a duke, Eleanor, you are an impoverished stepcousin; as such it is not permissible for you to dismiss me.'

She raised auburn brows. 'Another lesson in social etiquette, your Grace?'

Gods, this woman had enough pride and audacity to tempt any man— Justin brought those thoughts to an abrupt halt, a scowl darkening his brow as he looked down at her between narrowed lids. 'One of many ahead of me, I fear,' he taunted. 'Your social skills appear to have been sadly neglected, my dear.' And he, Justin acknowledged bleakly, would have to take great care in future not to 'enjoy' those lessons too much!

Colour blazed in Eleanor's cheeks at his deliberate insult. 'I assure you that I am perfectly well aware of how to behave in the company of both ladies and gentleman without your help, sir.'

'Your implication being that you do not consider me as being one of the latter?'

There was no missing the dangerous edge to his tone now, and Ellie—in keeping with her changed circumstances in life a year ago—wisely decided to heed that warning. This time. 'There was no implication intended, your Grace. Now, if you will excuse me…' She gave a brief curtsy before crossing to the library door.

'And if I do not excuse you?'

Ellie came to an abrupt halt, her heart pounding loudly in her chest, the hand she had raised to open the door trembling slightly as she turned to face Justin. 'Do you have something more you wished to say to me tonight, your Grace?'

What Justin 'wished' to do at this moment was place this determined but politely rebellious young lady across his knee and administer several hard slaps to her backside; indeed, he could not remember another woman infuriating him as much as this one did—or who tempted him to kiss her as much as this one did either, and all without too much effort on her part, it seemed. 'You will remember to send word to me concerning my grandmother's health,' he commanded instead.

'I have said I will, your Grace.' She gave another cool inclination of her head. 'Will that be all?'

Justin's hands clenched at his sides as he resisted the impulse he felt to reach out and clasp her by the shoulders before soundly shaking her. After which he would probably be tempted into pulling her into his arms and kissing her once again. And heaven— or more likely hell—only knew where that might lead! 'For now,' he bit out between clenched teeth.

She turned and made good her escape, closing the library door softly behind her.

Leaving Justin with the unpleasant knowledge that he might have given his grandmother's companion little thought until this evening—apart from noticing those kissable lips and the tempting swell of her breasts like any other red-blooded male would!—but he was now far too aware of the physical attributes, and the amusement to be derived from the sharp tongue, of one Miss Eleanor Rosewood.

'Would you care to explain to me exactly why it is I am out riding with you in the park this afternoon, your Grace, chaperoned by her Grace's own maid...' Ellie glanced back to where poor Mary was currently being bounced and jostled about in the dowager duchess's least best carriage '...when I am sure my time might be better occupied in helping her Grace with the last-minute preparations for the Royston Ball later this evening?' She shot the duke a questioning glance as she rode beside him perched atop the docile chestnut mare he had requested be saddled for her use.

His chiselled lips were curved into a humourless smile, blue eyes narrowed beneath his beaver hat, his muscled thighs, in buff-coloured pantaloons, easily keeping his own feisty mount in check, so that he might keep apace with her much slower progress as the horses walked the bridal-path side by side.

'I believe you are riding with me in the park because it is my grandmother's wish to incite the *ton*'s curiosity by allowing you to see and be seen with me before this evening.'

Ellie shot him a curious glance. 'And what of your own wishes? I am sure that you can have no real interest in escorting me for a ride in the park?'

Justin bit back his irritated reply, aware as he was that Eleanor was not the cause of his present bad temper. He had spent much of his time these past three days hunting down Dr Franklyn, determined as he was to learn the full nature of his grandmother's ill health and what might be done about it.

To his deep irritation, the physician, once found, had been adamant about maintaining his doctor/patient confidentiality. A determination that neither the threats of a duke, nor the appeal of an affectionate grandson, had succeeded in moving. Nor had he been in the least comforted by Dr Franklyn's answer, 'We all die a little each day, your Grace', when Justin had questioned him as to whether or not the dowager duchess was indeed knocking at death's door.

The physician's professionalism was commendable, of course—with the exception of when, as now, it was in direct opposition to Justin's own wishes. As a consequence, he had left the physician's rooms highly frustrated and none the wiser for having visited, and spoken with, the good Dr Franklyn.

His evenings had been no more enjoyable, spent at one gaming hell or another, usually with the result that he had arrived back at his rooms in the late hours or early morning, nursing a full purse, but also a raging headache from inhaling too much of other gentlemen's cigar smoke and drinking far too much of the club's brandy. Last night had been no exception, resulting in Justin having risen only hours ago from his bed. He had then had to rush through his toilet in order that he might be ready to go riding in the park with Eleanor at the fashionable time of five o'clock.

An occurrence which had made him regret ever having agreed to his grandmother's request today. 'My own wishes are unimportant at this time,' he dismissed flatly.

Eleanor eyed him with a slight frown. 'I had thought her Grace seems slightly improved these past few days?'

Justin gave her a rueful glance, having no intention of discussing his grandmother's health with this young woman, or anyone else. 'You believe my grandmother's possible ill health to be the only reason I would have consented to ride in the park with you?'

Eleanor shrugged slender shoulders, her appearance thoroughly enchanting today in a fashionable green-velvet riding habit and matching bonnet, the red of her curls peaking enticingly from beneath the brim of that bonnet. 'You obviously have a deep regard for your grandmother's happiness, your Grace.'

'But I have no regard for your own happiness, is that what you are saying?'

Ellie avoided that piercing blue gaze. 'I do not believe anyone actually enquired as to whether or not I wished to go riding in the park with you, no…'

'Then I shall enquire now,' the duke drawled as some of the tension seemed to ease from those impossibly wide shoulders shown to advantage in the cobalt-blue riding jacket. 'Would you care to go riding in the park with me this afternoon, Miss Rosewood?'

Ellie had tried in vain these past three days to persuade the dowager duchess into changing her mind about Ellie attending the

Royston Ball, or accepting Justin St Just as her escort for that evening.

Having failed miserably in that endeavour, Ellie had then been forced to spend much of those same three days being pushed and prodded and pinned into not only the velvet riding habit she wore today, but also several new gowns, one of which she was to wear to attend the Royston Ball this evening. Tediously long hours when the poor seamstress had been requested to return again and again by the dowager duchess, in order that the fit of Ellie's new gowns should meet the older lady's exacting standards.

As a consequence, Ellie would much rather have spent the day of the ball composing herself for this evening, than putting herself through the equally unpleasant ordeal of first riding in the park with the arrogantly indifferent, and highly noticeable Duke of Royston. Especially when his taciturn mood and scowling countenance showed he was obviously as reluctant to be here as she was!

'No, I would not,' she now answered him firmly.

Once again Justin found it impossible not to laugh out loud at her honesty. 'Even though, as I have previously stated, it is well known amongst the *ton* that I never escort young ladies, in the park or anywhere else?'

'Even then,' she stated firmly. 'Indeed, I do not know how you manage to stand all the gawking and gossiping which has taken place since we arrived here together.'

Justin raised surprised brows as he turned to look about them. Having been lost in his own sleep-deprived drink-induced misery until now, he had taken little note of any interest being shown in them.

An interest that became far less overt when openly challenged by his icy-blue gaze. 'Ignore it, as I do,' he advised dismissively as he turned back to the young woman riding beside him.

Green eyes widened in the pallor of Eleanor's face. 'I find that somewhat impossible to do.'

'Perhaps a compliment or two might help divert you?' he mused. 'I should have told you earlier what a capable horsewoman you so obviously are.' Far too accomplished for the docile mount he had allocated to her. A horse, Justin now realised, whose chestnut coat was very similar in colouring to the red of her hair.

'Are you so surprised?' she taunted before

giving him a rueful smile. 'My stepfather, your own cousin Frederick, may have been offhand in his attentions, but he possessed an exceptionally fine stable, which he regularly allowed me to use.'

Justin's gaze narrowed. '"Offhand in his attentions"…?' he repeated slowly. 'Was Frederick an unkind stepfather to you?'

'Not at all.' Eleanor gave a reassuring shake of her head. 'He was merely uninterested in either my mother's or my own happiness once his interest in bedding my mother had waned.'

'Eleanor!'

She shrugged. 'It is not unusual amongst the gentlemen in society to marry for lust, I believe.'

'No,' Justin acknowledged abruptly. 'And you are saying that Frederick married your mother for just that reason?'

Eleanor nodded. 'So she explained to me when I had attained an age to understand such things, yes. Frederick married my mother because he desired her, my mother married him in order to secure the future for both herself and her daughter. Once Frederick's desire for her faded, as it surely must have without the accompaniment of love—'

she grimaced '—it was not a particularly happy marriage.'

Justin began to understand now Eleanor's own aversion to a marriage without love. How ironic, when his parents' exclusive love for each other had determined his own aversion to a marriage *with* love.

Ellie was unsure as to the fleeting emotions that had settled briefly on the duke's harshly etched features, before as quickly being dismissed in favour of him looking down the length of his nose at her with his usual haughty arrogance. 'Will your own mother be attending the ball this evening?' she prompted curiously, not having met Rachel St Just as yet.

Her son scowled darkly. 'My mother never leaves her country estate.'

'Never?'

'Never.'

He answered so coldly, so uncompromisingly, it was impossible for Ellie not to comprehend that his mother was a subject he preferred not to discuss. Not that she was going to let that stand in her way! 'Was your own parents' marriage an unhappy one?'

'Far from it,' he rasped. 'They loved each

other to the exclusion of all else,' he added harshly.

To the exclusion of their only child? she pondered, slightly shocked. And, if so, did that also explain his own views on the married state? It was—

'Good Gad, Royston, what a shock to see your illustrious self out and about in the park!'

Ellie forgot her musings as she turned to look at the man who so obviously greeted the duke with false joviality. A gentleman who might once have been handsome, but whose florid face and heavy jowls now rendered him as being far from attractive, and his obesity was obviously a great trial to the brown horse upon which he sat.

'No more so than you, Litchfield,' Justin answered the other man languidly, causing Ellie to look at him searchingly before turning her attention back to the man he had addressed simply as Litchfield.

As if sensing Ellie's curiosity, the older man turned to return her gaze before his pale hazel eyes moved from her bonneted head to her booted feet, and then back again, with slow and familiar deliberation. 'Perhaps it is your charming companion we have to thank for your presence here today?' he suggested admiringly.

Justin's tightened. 'Perhaps.'

The other man raised pepper-and-salt brows. 'Not going to introduce us, Royston?'

'No.' The duke's steely gaze was uncompromising.

The other man's pale eyes, neither blue nor green nor brown, but a colour somehow indiscriminately between them all, returned to sweep over Ellie with critical assessment. 'You seem somewhat familiar, my dear. Have we met before?'

'I am sure I should have remembered if we had,' Ellie replied ambiguously.

Litchfield turned to grin at Justin. 'She's a beauty, I grant you that,' he drawled appreciatively.

Ellie might be slightly naïve herself when it came to the subtleties of society, but even so she was perfectly well aware that this Litchfield was, in fact, challenging the duke and he was using her as the means with which to do it. 'You are too kind, sir.' She gave Litchfield a bright and meaningless smile. 'If you will excuse us now? We were about to leave.'

'Indeed?' Litchfield gave her a leering

smile, revealing uneven and brown-stained teeth in his unpleasantly mottled face, wisps of auburn hair, liberally streaked with grey, peeping out from beneath his hat and brushing the soiled collar of his shirt.

'Indeed,' Ellie confirmed coolly.

'If you would care to…ride, another afternoon, then I should be only too pleased to offer my services as…your escort. You have only to send word to my home in Russell Square. Lord Dryden Litchfield is the name.'

The man's familiar manner and address, considering the two of them had not so much as been formally introduced—deliberately so, on Justin's part?—were such that even Eleanor recognised it as being far from acceptable in fashionable circles. As she also recognised that Lord Litchfield was far from being a gentleman. Which begged the question as to how Justin came to be acquainted with such an unpleasant man.

'I will join you shortly, Eleanor,' Justin bit out harshly.

'Your Grace?' she said in surprise as, having turned her horse back in the direction they had just come, she now realised he had made no effort to accompany her, the two men currently seeming to be engaged in an ocular battle of wills.

A battle of wills she had no doubt the duke would ultimately win, but it was one which Ellie would prefer not take place at all; not only would it be unpleasant to herself, but she very much doubted the dowager duchess would be at all pleased to learn that Ellie had been present during an altercation in the park between her grandson and another gentleman.

Justin's hands tightly gripped the reins of his restive black horse as he continued to meet Dryden Litchfield's insolently challenging gaze. 'You will wait for me by the carriage, Eleanor,' he commanded firmly.

'But—'

'Now, please, Eleanor.' He did not raise his voice, but she must have realised by the coldness of his tone that it would be prudent not to argue with him any further on the matter, and he thankfully heard her softly encourage her horse to walk away from the two men. 'Do you have something you wish to say to me, Litchfield?' he prompted evenly.

The other man feigned an expression of innocence. 'Not that I recall, no.'

Justin's mouth thinned. 'I advise that you

stay well clear of both me and mine, Litchfield.'

Those pale eyes glanced across to where
Eleanor now sat on her horse, talking to the
maid inside the waiting carriage. 'Is she
yours, Royston?'

'Very much so,' Justin confirmed instantly.

'If you say so…' the other man taunted.

His jaw clenched. 'I do.'

'For now, perhaps.'

'For always as far as you are concerned,
Litchfield.' Justin scowled darkly.

'And if the lady should have other ideas?'

Justin drew in a sharp breath at his insolent persistence. 'Do not say you have not
been warned, Litchfield!'

'You seem mightily possessive, Royston.'
The older man gave him a speculatively look.
'Can this be the same young lady whose missive caused you to end our card game so that
you could run eagerly to her side?'

Eleanor's note was indeed responsible for
that occurrence, but certainly not in the way
in which Litchfield implied it had.

'Ah, I see that it is indeed the case.'
Litchfield nodded in satisfaction at Justin's
silence. 'As I said, she is certainly a rare
beauty—'

'And as I have said, she is not for the likes of you,' Justin bit out tautly.

'Well, well.' The older man eyed him curiously. 'Can it be that the top-lofty Duke of Royston has finally met his match? Are we to expect an announcement soon?'

'You are to *expect* that I shall not be pleased if I hear you have made so much as a single personal remark or innuendo about the young lady who is my ward,' Justin snarled, wanting nothing more than to take this insolent cur by the throat and squeeze until the breath left his body. Either that, or take a whip to him. And Justin would cheerfully have done either of those things, if he had not known it would draw unwanted attention to Eleanor.

Litchfield's eyes widened. 'Your ward…?'

Justin gave a haughty nod. 'Indeed.'

The other man continued to look at him searchingly for several seconds before giving a shout of derisive laughter and then turning to look at Eleanor speculatively once again. 'How very interesting…' He raised a mocking gloved hand to his temple before turning his horse and deliberately riding in the direction of the Royston carriage, raising his hat to Eleanor as he passed and so forcing her to give an acknowledging nod in return.

Justin scowled as he recalled Anderson's previous warning for him to beware of Litchfield in future, with the added comment that the other man was at the very least a nasty bully, and at worst, a dangerous adversary. Indeed, if not for the fact that it would have been damaging to Eleanor's reputation, then Litchfield would have been made to pay for his insulting behaviour just now, possibly to the extent that the other man found himself standing down the sights of Justin's duelling pistol. As it was, Justin had dared not involve Eleanor in the scandal of a duel before she had even appeared in society!

Tomorrow, or possibly the next day, was another matter, however...

'What an unpleasant man.' Ellie could not resist a quiver of revulsion when Justin finally rejoined her and the two of them turned to walk their horses back to Royston House.

'Very,' he agreed.

'Will he be attending the ball this evening...?'

The duke gave a scathing snort. 'My grandmother would never allow one such as he to step over her threshold.'

She eyed him curiously. 'And yet he is obviously a man of your own acquaintance, is he not?'

'We have shared a card game or two, which he has invariably lost.' Justin shrugged dismissively. 'His reputation is such that much of society shuns him. And while we are on the subject,' he added harshly, 'I forbid you to so much as acknowledge him should you ever chance to meet him again.'

'You *forbid* it?' Ellie gasped incredulously.

The duke looked implacably at her. 'I do, yes. Unless, of course, I am mistaken and you would welcome Litchfield's attentions?'

She gave another shudder just recalling that unpleasant man. 'Of course I would not.'

'Then—'

'Whilst I accept that we are distantly related by marriage, *Cousin*—' Ellie's bland tone revealed none of her inner anger at his high-handedness '—and that you are the grandson of my employer—'

'—and your newly appointed guardian—'

'Perhaps that is so—'

'There is no perhaps about it!' the duke swiftly interjected.

'Even so, I cannot—I simply cannot allow you to forbid, or allow, any of my future actions,' Ellie informed him firmly, with far too many memories of how his cousin Frederick had held such sway over her poor mother for the last years of her life.

Justin reached out and grasped the reins of her horse as she would have urged her horse into a canter. 'In this instance I must insist you obey me, Eleanor.'

Tears of anger now blurred her vision. 'You may insist all you please, your Grace, but I refuse to allow myself to be bullied by any man.'

Justin scowled his frustration as Eleanor wrenched her reins from his grasp, leaving him to sit and watch as she urged her horse forwards and away from him.

Damn Litchfield.

Damn his troublemaking hide!

Chapter Six

'I believe, Royston, that if you do not cease scowling, you are in danger of taking your duties as Ellie's guardian to such a degree that you will succeed in scaring away all but the most determined of eligible young gentlemen!'

Justin turned to raise one arrogant brow as he looked down to where his grandmother had moved to stand beside him at the edge of the crowded dance floor in her candlelit ballroom. Still slightly pale, and uncharacteristically fragile in her demeanour, the dowager duchess had, as she had said she would, rallied from her sickbed in order to take her place as hostess of the Royston Ball.

Justin's mood had not improved since he

and Eleanor had parted so frostily upon returning to the stables behind Royston House. For the most part because Justin knew he had handled the situation badly, that issuing orders to a woman as stubborn as Eleanor was proving to be was sure to result in her doing the exact opposite of what was being asked of her—an accusation, which if repeated to Eleanor, would no doubt earn him the comment of 'the pot calling the kettle black'! Not that Justin thought for a moment that she would ever encourage Litchfield's advances, but he had no doubt she would find some other way in which to bedevil him for what she had considered his high-handedness this afternoon.

He had known, the moment Eleanor walked down the grand staircase at Royston House earlier, and he had seen the light of rebellion in those emerald-green eyes and the defiant tilt to her chin, that she intended for that punishment to begin this very evening…

At first glance Justin had wondered at his grandmother's choice of attire for her young protégée. But the longer he gazed upon Eleanor's appearance, the more he realised how astutely clever the old lady had been; brightly coloured silks were now the preferred fashion for the ladies of the *ton,* as were the garishly matching feathers and silks worn in their hair.

In contrast, Eleanor's gown was the palest shade of green silk Justin had ever seen, as were the delicate above-elbow-length lace gloves that covered her hands and arms. Her hair, those glorious red curls, had been swept back and up and secured at her crown, before being allowed to cascade gently down to brush lightly against the slenderness of her nape. Her bare nape. For, unlike the other women of society, of any age, who often chose to wear their wealth, quite literally, upon their sleeves and about their throats, Eleanor was not wearing a single piece of jewellery. Her wrists, her hair, the lobes of her ears, the creamy expanse of her throat and breasts, were all completely unadorned.

As a consequence, Justin realised that Eleanor Rosewood's understated elegance gave her the appearance of a dove amongst garishly adorned peacocks. A pure, unblemished, perfectly cut diamond set amongst roughly hewn and gaudy-coloured sapphires, emeralds and rubies.

As predicted, the crowded ballroom had fallen deathly silent the moment Stanhope had announced their entrance. But Justin was fully aware the speculative attention was not directed solely towards him this evening, but included the young lady standing so coolly self-contained at his side—admittedly, it was a façade of calm only, as hinted at by the slight trembling of her gloved hand as it rested lightly upon his arm, but to all outward appearances Eleanor was a picture of composure and elegance. She was also, as his grandmother had intended, instantly recognised as the same young woman who had been seen riding in the park with him this afternoon.

The ladies, as Eleanor had previously suggested might be the case, had gazed openly and critically at her from behind fluttering fans—with not a single sign of recognition, Justin noted ruefully, that the elegant Miss Eleanor Rosewood was also Ellie, the previously nondescript companion of the dowager duchess. The gentlemen, Justin had noted with more annoyance, had been much more open in their admiration.

An admiration confirmed by the fact that at least a dozen of those same gentlemen had crowded around begging to be introduced the moment Justin had finished presenting Eleanor to his grandmother and her two close friends, the Dowager Countess of Chambourne and Lady Cicely Hawthorne, all of them expressing a wish to claim a dance with her before the evening should come to an end.

As her guardian and protector, it had been Justin's duty to claim Eleanor for the first dance, of course, and he had politely done so—much to the increasing interest of his grandmother's other guests; the Duke of Royston never stood up to dance on these occasions. Indeed, Justin had always made a point of not doing so, making his attentions to Eleanor all the more noticeable. It would, as his grandmother had always intended it should, secure her place in society.

The two of them had not exchanged so much as a word as they danced that first set together, Eleanor's expression one of cool detachment as Justin studied her beneath hooded lids, finding himself pleasantly surprised by her grace and elegance on the dance floor; proving that she had indeed been shown how to 'behave in the company of ladies and gentlemen'.

Justin had not been quite so pleased by those same gentlemen who had rushed to fill Eleanor's dance card the moment he escorted her back to his grandmother's side. Or the fact that Eleanor appeared to blossom under their avid attentions.

His mouth thinned anew as he continued to gaze across to where Eleanor was now laughing merrily at something amusing her current dance partner had said to her. 'Lord Braxton can hardly be considered young or entirely eligible,' he remarked curtly to his grandmother.

'Nonsense!' Edith dismissed as she continued to smile benevolently at her young protégée. 'Jeremy Caulfield is a widower as well as being an earl.'

Justin grimaced. 'He is also twice Eleanor's age and in need of a stepmother for all of those children he keeps hidden away in the nursery at Caulfield Park!'

His grandmother raised iron-grey brows. 'There are but three children, Justin, the heir, the spare and a girl. And anyone with eyes in their head can see that Braxton is smitten with Ellie herself, rather than having any thoughts of providing his children with another mother.'

Justin was only too well aware that Jeremy Caulfield's admiration of Eleanor was personal; that was made more than obvious by the warm way the other man gazed upon her so intently, and the way in which Caulfield's hand had lingered upon hers as they'd danced together. That Eleanor returned his liking was obvious in the relaxed and natural way in which she returned the earl's smiles and conversation. Nor could Justin deny, inwardly at least, that it would be a very good match for Eleanor if Caulfield were to become seriously enamoured of her, enough so that he made her an offer of marriage.

It would, Justin also acknowledged, bring a quick end to his reluctant role as Eleanor's guardian.

An occurrence which, surprisingly, he found far less pleasing than he had thought he might.

'—am afraid that I have already promised to eat supper with the dowager duchess, Lady Hawthorne and the Countess of Ambridge, my lord,' Ellie shyly refused the invitation of the handsome and attentive Lord Jeremy Caulfield, Earl of Braxton, placing her hand upon his arm as they left the dance floor together.

After the disastrous end to her ride in the

park with Justin earlier, Ellie had been in a turmoil of trepidation about attending the Royston Ball with him this evening, only to find, once the tension of dancing the first set with Justin had been dealt with, that she was actually enjoying herself. Mainly due, she admitted, to the genuinely warm regard of such gentlemen as the attentive earl.

Her smile faded somewhat as she looked up and saw the imposing Duke of Royston standing so disapprovingly beside his smiling grandmother; he had certainly made no effort to put Ellie at her ease this evening. How could he, when he had barely spoken two words to her since his arrival some hours ago, causing her to give a sigh of relief when their dancing together finally came to an end?

Surely it only confirmed how deeply Justin disapproved of his grandmother's determined interest in settling Ellie's future, and his own reluctant involvement in it? He had made it more than obvious he would never have contemplated agreeing to it if not for his deep regard for Edith and that lady's recent bout of ill health.

Thankfully, the dowager duchess really had seemed to improve a little over the last few days, and although she was still pale, she gave every appearance of enjoying the evening; Ellie knew that dear lady well enough by now to know that Edith St Just would never admit to it if she were not!

The Earl of Braxton looked genuinely disappointed by Ellie's refusal to sit with him at supper. 'Perhaps if I were to ask the dowager duchess's permission—'

'As Miss Rosewood is my own ward, it is my permission you would need to receive, Braxton,' the cold voice of Justin St Just cut in.

The older man turned, a pleasant smile curving his lips. 'Then perhaps you might consent to allowing me to escort Miss Rosewood into supper, Royston?'

'I am afraid that would not do at all, Braxton.' The duke looked down the length of his nose at the other man.

'Oh, but—'

'It will not do, Eleanor,' Justin repeated firmly as she started to protest. 'Forgive my ward, Braxton.' He turned back to the earl. 'I am afraid Eleanor is new to society. As such she is unaware of the attention she has already drawn to herself by her naivety and flirtatiousness.'

Ellie's eyes widened at the unfairness of the accusation. Admittedly she had not sat down for a single dance since that first one with Justin, but she believed that her popularity was only because she was considered something of a curiosity, an oddity, if you will. Certainly she had not sought out any of the attentions that had been shown to her, nor did she consider she had been in the least flirtatious!

'If you will excuse us, Braxton?' Justin did not wait for the earl's response as he took a firm grasp of Ellie's arm before turning away.

'Justin—'

'We will await you in the supper room, Grandmother,' he said to the old lady who had come up behind them, his expression grimly unapproachable as he strode rapidly towards the room in which supper was now being served, practically dragging Ellie along beside him.

'Now who is the one responsible for drawing attention? To us both?' Ellie's cheeks burned with humiliation as she stumbled to keep up with the duke's much longer strides, at the same time as she kept a smile fixed upon her lips for those watching them.

Justin's jaw clenched and he ground his back teeth together as he glared at the members of the *ton* who dared to so much as glance in their direction. Glances which were hastily averted under the fierceness of his chilling blue gaze.

'Your Grace—'

'Do not "your Grace" me in what can only be described as a feeble attempt to mimic my grandmother's disapproving tones!' Justin rounded on Eleanor sharply, only for his breath to catch in his throat as he saw how pale her cheeks had now become, those freckles more evident on her nose and cheeks, and that there were tears glistening in those deep-green eyes as she looked up at him reproachfully.

Damn it to hell!

He forced himself to slow his angry strides and loosen his tight grip upon her arm before speaking again. 'It may not appear so, Eleanor,' he explained, also attempting to soften the harshness of his tone, 'but I assure you I am only acting in your best interests. For you to have singled Braxton out so soon, by eating supper alone with him, would have been as good as a declaration on your part.'

A puzzled frown marred her creamy brow

as she blinked back the tears. 'A declaration? Of what, exactly?'

'Of your willingness to accept a marriage proposal from him should one be forthcoming.'

'That is utterly ridiculous…' she recoiled with a horrified gasp '…when I have only just been introduced to him!' If anything her face had grown even paler.

Justin nodded grimly. 'And being new to society, you are as yet unaware of the subtle nuances of courtship.'

She shook her head, red curls bouncing against the slenderness of her creamy nape. 'But I am sure the earl meant no such familiarity by his supper invitation. He merely wished to continue our discussion, to learn my views, on the merits or otherwise, of engaging a companion or governess for his five-year-old daughter.'

Justin's breath caught in his throat. 'He discussed the future care of his young daughter with you?'

'Well, yes…' Ellie could see by the grim expression in his hard blue eyes that she had obviously done something else unacceptable. 'It was a harmless enough conversation, surely?'

He gave her a pitying glance. 'It is the sort of conversation that a gentleman has with the lady who might perhaps become the new mother of that child.'

Ellie eyes widened. 'Surely you cannot be serious? I hardly know the man!'

Justin gave a derisive snort. 'Can it be that you are really as naïve as you appear to be, Eleanor? Because if that is so, then I believe my grandmother should have waited a while longer before introducing you into society.'

'I do not—'

'This afternoon you were all but propositioned by one of the biggest blaggards in London,' Justin continued remorselessly. 'And this evening you have committed the *faux pas* of discussing a man's nursery with him!'

Ellie's cheeks now burned with humiliated colour, but she was determined not to give in without a fight. 'Must I remind you that I would not have so much as spoken to that "blaggard" this afternoon, if not for your own acquaintance with the man? And I truly believe the earl was merely making polite conversation just now—'

The duke cut her off with an incredulous look. 'By consulting with you on what is best for the future education of his young, motherless daughter?'

Ellie gave a pained frown. 'Well…yes.'

Had she been naïve in taking Lord Caulfield's conversation at face value? She had not thought so at the time, but Justin knew the ways of society far better than she, after all. Yet it had seemed such a harmless conversation, Jeremy Caulfield so terribly bewildered and at a loss as to how best to bring up a little girl on his own—

Oh, good lord…!

'I believe my evening has now been quite ruined!' Ellie almost felt as if she might quite happily sit down and cry rather than attempt to eat any of the delicious supper laid out so temptingly before her.

Justin gave her a humourless smile. 'Do not take on so, Eleanor, a single inappropriate conversation with a gentleman does not commit you to spending a lifetime with him. Indeed, I should not give my permission for such a marriage even if such an offer were forthcoming. And I have no doubt my grandmother is even now excusing your behaviour by reiterating to Braxton your inexperience in such matters.'

'And that makes me feel so much better!'

Ellie snapped, her earlier feelings of well-being having completely dissipated during the course of this conversation.

She had believed herself to be doing so well, to be behaving with all the dignity and decorum as befitted the supposed ward of the Duke of Royston, and instead it now seemed she had been encouraging the Earl of Braxton into believing she was in favour of him furthering his attentions towards her.

She gave a forlorn sigh. 'How on earth have you managed to avoid the pitfalls of the marriage mart for so long and so expertly, your Grace?'

And just like that, Justin's scowling and dark mood of the past twelve hours became a thing of the past, and he began to chuckle even as he moved forwards to pull back a chair for her. 'I believe I may attribute my own success in that regard to both stealth and cunning!'

Eleanor pursed her lips as she sat down. 'Then perhaps you might consider tutoring me into how I might do the same, for I fear I am completely at a loss as to how to deal with it myself.'

Justin eyed her curiously as he lowered his long length into the chair beside her, waiting until one of the footmen had placed plates of sweetmeats on the table for their enjoyment before answering her. 'You would not consider yourself fortunate in becoming Braxton's countess?'

She shook her head. 'He is a pleasant enough gentleman, I am sure, but I—I have no ambition to become the wife of any man who does not love me with all of his heart, as I intend to love him.'

Justin studied her closely. 'Because of the unhappy circumstances of your mother's marriage to Frederick?'

Eleanor nodded. 'I can imagine nothing worse than suffering such a fate myself.'

Justin could not help but admire the strength of her conviction, even if his own feelings on the matter were in total contradiction to her own. He thought it was far better to marry a woman for her lineage and ability to produce healthy children. On which subject… 'And what of children, Eleanor?' he enquired. 'Do you have no desire to have a son or daughter of your own one day?'

Green eyes twinkled mischievously as she looked about them pointedly, the supper room now filling with other members of the *ton* seeking refreshment. 'Is our present conversation not as socially unacceptable as discussing the education of Lord Caulfield's young daughter with him?' she murmured softly before leaning forwards to pierce a piece of juicy pineapple with a fork and lifting it up to her lips.

'Perhaps,' Justin allowed ruefully. Then he found himself unable to look away from the fullness of her lips as they closed about the juicy fruit.

Her expression was thoughtful as she chewed and swallowed the fruit before innocently licking the excess juice from the plumpness of her lips. 'Then of course I would dearly love to have children of my own one day, both a son and a daughter at least. But only—'

'If you were to have those children with "a man who loved you with all of his heart",' he finished drily.

Ellie smiled. 'Why are you so cynical about falling in love, your Grace…? Your Grace?' she prompted quizzically as he started laughing again.

He raised an eyebrow. 'You do not find it slightly ludicrous to ask me such a personal question at the same time as continuing to address me with such formality, Eleanor?'

'Perhaps,' she allowed huskily, colour warming her cheeks.

'Perhaps, Justin,' he insisted.

She blinked, aware that an underlying, inexplicable something seemed to have crept into their conversation, although she had no idea what it was or why it was there. 'Would calling you Royston as your grandmother does not be more appropriate?'

'Far too stuffy,' he dismissed gruffly.

Ellie lowered her lashes. 'I am not sure the dowager duchess would approve—'

'Not sure I would approve of what?' Edith prompted briskly as she joined them, Lady Cicely and Lady Jocelyn accompanying her.

Her grandson rose politely to his feet and saw to the seating of those three ladies in the chairs across the table from them, before resuming his own seat beside Ellie. 'I was endeavouring to persuade Eleanor into calling me Justin when we are alone together or in the company of family or close friends,' he explained with an acknowledging bow of his head towards Lady Cicely and Lady Jocelyn.

Lady Cicely looked flustered as she

glanced nervously towards the dowager duchess. 'I am not sure…'

'Is that quite the thing, Edith…?' Lady Jocelyn frowned her own uncertainty as she too deferred to the dowager duchess for her opinion on the matter.

Edith gave her grandson a searching glance before answering the query. 'I do not see why not. They are cousins by marriage, after all.'

'Yes, but—'

'I am still unsure as to whether—'

'You were rather abrupt with Braxton just now, Royston,' the dowager duchess cut off her friends' continued concerns as she turned to look at her grandson.

'Was I?' the duke returned unconcernedly.

'You know very well that you were.' His grandmother frowned.

'I am sure he will recover all too soon,' he murmured distractedly as he reached out to pierce another piece of fruit before holding it temptingly in front of Ellie.

Something Ellie—even in her 'naivety and inexperience'—knew to be entirely inappropriate. Nor did she care for the piercing intensity of Justin's glittering gaze at it rested on her parted lips.

At the same time she realised that *this* was what had changed so suddenly between them just minutes ago; one moment Justin had been berating her for her 'flirtatiousness' in what he believed to be her encouragement of Lord Caulfield and the next he had been shamelessly flirting with her himself. Just what was he up to?

Was this perhaps another lesson, to see if she had learnt anything from their conversation just now?

Whatever the reason for his behaviour, it had resulted in his drawing unwarranted attention to the two of them. As Ellie glanced nervously about them, she could see several of the older matrons in the near vicinity looking positively shocked at the intimacy of his gesture in offering to feed her the sliver of pineapple. Indeed, Lady Cicely and Lady Jocelyn both seemed to be holding their breath as they waited to see what Ellie would do next. Edith's expression was, unfortunately, as enigmatic and unreadable as her grandson's.

Ellie gave a cool smile as she sat back in her chair, not quite touching the chair back itself, as she had been taught to do by her mother long ago. 'I find I am no longer hungry for pineapple, your Grace,' she informed him repressively. 'Perhaps you should eat the fruit yourself? I can vouch for it being truly delicious.' She held her breath tensely as she waited to see what Justin would do or say next.

Chapter Seven

Madness.

Absolute bloody madness!

For there could be no other reason why Justin gave every appearance of behaving like a besotted fool, enticing his ladylove with succulent titbits of fruit.

Justin considered himself to be neither besotted nor a fool, Eleanor Rosewood was most certainly not his ladylove—nor would she ever be—and the only enticing that had ever interested him, where any woman was concerned, took place between silken sheets—and it was fruit of the forbidden kind!

He looked into those emerald-green eyes just inches from his own and knew from the uncertainty, the slight panic he detected in their depths, that Eleanor's casual dismissal just now was purely an act she had assumed for their audience. That the widening of her pupils, the bloom of colour in her cheeks, her slightly parted lips, and the barest movement of her breasts as she breathed shallowly, were indicative of what she was really feeling.

And Justin had no trouble at all recognising that.

Arousal.

For all that she might express her resentment of him in the role he now held in her life as her guardian and protector, and despite her rebelling against any and all restrictions he might choose to place upon her actions, she could not hide the fact she also found him physically attractive, despite her stated aversion to 'lust' being the reason for her mother's marriage to Frederick.

A knowledge that caused Justin's lips to curl into a satisfied smile as he straightened. 'Much better, Eleanor,' he drawled as he discarded both the fork and pineapple on to his plate before turning to the three older ladies seated across from them. 'I am endeavouring, at her request, to tutor Eleanor in how best to deter over-zealous gentlemen of the *ton,* without also offending them,' he explained wryly as Lady Cicely and Lady Jocelyn, at least, continued to look upon him in obvious shock.

His grandmother's expression was no less disapproving. 'And in that you appear to have been successful. Unfortunately,' she continued irritably, 'your chosen method of doing so has now also succeeded in rousing the speculation of the *ton* regarding the Duke of Royston's intentions towards his young ward!'

Justin gave a scornful laugh. 'An occurrence which will likely render Eleanor popular with the gentlemen and unpopular with the ladies!'

'It is not in the least amusing, Royston.'

'Of course it is, Grandmama.' He relaxed against the back of his chair. 'How can it be anything else when we all know I have no romantic intentions whatsoever where Eleanor is concerned.'

'I really must thank you for your most recent lesson, your Grace.' Ellie had heard quite enough of 'the Duke of Royston's' opinions for one evening. Arrogant, mocking, insufferable gentleman that he was!

Unfortunately, she also found him verbally challenging, dangerously handsome and physically exciting, to the extent that she suspected she might still be in love with him, despite previous private denials to the contrary.

Just to look at this man, to be in his company, to exchange verbal swords with him, still, in spite of her inner remonstrations with herself, caused her heart to beat faster, her breathing to falter and every nerve ending in her body to become thrillingly aware of everything about him. And Ellie knew she had almost succumbed to his dangerous allure as he had held that sliver of pineapple up in front of her so temptingly.

It had been so intimate an act, the noise and chatter about them seeming to disappear as the world narrowed down to just the two of them, and Ellie had found herself totally unable to look away from those piercing sapphire-blue eyes.

Much, she realised now, like a butterfly stuck on the end of a pin by its curious captor!

Certainly his next comment had shown that he had felt none of the physical awareness of her that she now had of him. Indeed, he had merely confirmed what she had suspected all along: that the arrogant Duke of Royston was merely being his usual insufferable self by teaching her another 'lesson'.

'If you will all excuse me, I believe I will go and tidy my appearance before the dancing recommences?' She placed her napkin down upon the table before standing up.

Justin also rose politely to his feet. 'I will accompany you.'

Ellie raised one mocking brow, in perfect imitation of the duke's own haughty arrogance. 'To the ladies' retiring room, your Grace?'

Those chiselled lips twisted. 'I will obviously wait outside in the hallway for you.'

Ellie frowned her irritation. 'I am sure that is unnecessary—'

'I beg to differ.' His mouth tightened. 'Unless you have a previous arrangement to meet with Braxton in one of the private rooms?'

She gasped. 'Of course I have not!'

He straightened his shoulders. 'Then I think it best that I accompany you to ensure he does not waylay you. Ladies.' He gave a polite bow to the three older women seated opposite them before pointedly raising his arm for Ellie to take, leaving her no choice but to place her gloved hand upon that arm and walk along stiffly at his side as he coolly nodded acknowledgement of acquaintances as they made slow progress across the crowded, noisy room.

But that did not mean Ellie did not bristle inside with indignation, at his highhandedness, for the whole of that time!

She removed her hand from his arm the moment they were outside in the less crowded Great Hall. 'How dare you! Who are you to embarrass me in front of other people, by questioning whether or not I might have behaved so scandalously as to have arranged to meet Lord Caulfield privately?'

Justin eyed her calmly, knowing himself to be once again in control—thankfully—of this situation. And himself. For he had not been as immune to Eleanor's physical awareness of him just now, when he'd attempted to feed her the pineapple, as he had given the impression of being...

No, indeed, he had risen to the occasion in spite of himself and had been forced to remain seated at the table for several minutes longer than necessary in order to wait until the bulge in his breeches became less obvious.

Much to his increasing annoyance.

Eleanor Rosewood's role as a protégée of his grandmother's, and his own ward, now rendered her as being completely unsuited to ever becoming his mistress. Nor did she meet the stringent requirements of a prospective duchess. As such there was no place for her in his well-ordered life, other than the annoyance of being forced by circumstance into acting as her guardian. All was not lost, of course; any number of women here this evening could, and in the past had, assuaged his physical needs.

'Who am I?' Justin repeated in a suddenly steely voice. 'I believe, for the moment at least, I am placed in the role of acting as your guardian and protector. Whether you feel you are in need of one or otherwise,' he added as she parted her lips with the obvious intention of protesting. 'As such, I have no intention of allowing you to embarrass me, or my grandmother, by behaving in an unsuitable manner through ignorance.'

Ellie eyed him hotly. 'You truly are the most insufferable man I have ever met!'

'So you have remarked before, I believe.'

'Then I must believe it to be true!'

The duke gave a deliberately weary smile. 'And I am fortunate in that I find your opinion of me to be of little interest.'

Just as Ellie knew she herself was of little interest to him either, other than as an appeasement to his grandmother's plans for her, the dowager the only woman whom he so obviously did care about; Ellie had heard a definite coldness in his tone when she had mentioned his mother to him.

Unfortunately, she now had no choice but to curl her fingers painfully into the palms of her gloved hands, in order to prevent herself from giving in to the temptation she felt to slap that supercilious and arrogant smile from his perfect lips!

She drew in a deep and controlling breath. 'Is it any wonder, then, that I have come to prefer the company of such polite gentlemen as the Earl of Braxton?'

Those blue eyes narrowed. 'I should warn you that it would be unwise to challenge me, Eleanor.'

Ellie's throat moved as she swallowed nervously, once again aware of the sudden tension that had sprung up between them, of how the very air that surrounded them now seemed charged with—with she knew not what.

The only thing she was sure of was the fluttering of excitement beneath her breasts, of the dampness to her palms inside her lace gloves, of the burn of colour blooming in her cheeks as his eyes continued to glitter down at her.

She swallowed again before speaking. 'I do not believe that is what I was doing.'

'No?'

'No,' she said defiantly.

A nerve pulsed in his tightly clenched jaw. 'I disagree.'

'That is your prerogative, of course—what are you doing?' she squeaked as the duke took a firm grasp of her arm before pulling her down the shadowed hallway, away from the crowded public salons, to where the private family rooms were situated. 'Justin?' she prompted sharply as he threw open the library door and pushed her unceremoniously inside the darkened room.

He followed her inside before closing the door firmly behind him. 'Of all the times I have asked you to do so, you must choose now to decide to call me Justin?' He towered over her in the darkness. 'I do believe you are challenging me, after all, Eleanor,' he murmured huskily.

It took Ellie several moments to adjust her eyes to the gloom of the library, at which time she realised it was not as dark as she had at first imagined, that the moonlight shone in brightly through the windows, giving his overlong-blond hair a silvery rather than golden sheen, his eyes glittering a much paler blue, the light and shadows giving his hard, chiselled face a darker, more dangerous sharpness, than it usually had.

Not that any of that was important, when placed alongside the scandal that would ensue if anyone were to discover them alone together in the darkness of the library! 'We should not be in here, your Grace.'

'Yes, you are most certainly challenging me, Eleanor,' he remarked in reproof. 'Did no one ever warn you that it is dangerous to wake the sleeping tiger?'

'You are likening yourself to a tiger?' she asked incredulously.

'Now I believe you are mocking me.'

He took a deliberate step forwards, causing Ellie to take a step backwards, only to find she could go no further as she came up against the closed door. Her eyes widened in alarm as she watched him place a hand flat against the door either side of her face, at once holding her captive between that door at her back and the hardness of his body just inches in front of her own.

Too few inches. Indeed, Justin stood so close to her now that she could feel the heat of his body through the thin silk of her gown, felt surrounded by the clean male smell of him as much as his impressive height and breadth. Her senses began to swim as she scented the sharp tang of his cologne, her breasts suddenly feeling fuller, firmer, the tips tingling with an almost painful ache, an inexplicable dampness between her thighs, the whole experience making her legs feel weak.

As clear evidence that she did indeed love this man…

The warmth of his breath brushed softly, sweetly, against her temple as he bent his head closer to her own before murmuring, 'Little girls who deliberately wake the tiger deserve to be…punished, just a little, do you not think?'

Ellie quivered in awareness, felt as if his close proximity had sucked all the air from the room, her head beginning to whirl as she tried to breathe, and failed. 'Please…!' she gasped at the same time as she lifted her hands to his chest with the intention of pushing him away, of allowing her to draw in a breath. Only to find she had no strength left to do so, that instead of pushing him away her hands lingered, as if with a will of their own, her fingers splaying almost caressingly against the heat of his broad chest.

'Please what, Eleanor?'

'I—' She moistened lips that had become suddenly dry. 'I should go…'

'You should, yes.' He nodded slowly as he moved even closer, so that the silk of her gown and his own clothing were all that now separated them. 'The question is, are you going to do so?'

She looked up at him searchingly, the shadows cast by the moonlight making it impossible for her to read the expression on the male face only inches above her own. Even so, she could see enough to know the duke's expression was one of hard determination and not the tender softness of a lover. 'I believe you are playing another game with me, your Grace,' she accused.

'Am I?'

'Yes!'

'Does this feel like a game to you, Eleanor?' He shifted slightly, allowing the length of his body to press against her much softer one, allowing her to feel the swollen hardness bulging in his breeches, which now pulsed insistently against the soft swell of her abdomen.

She raised startled lids; she might be young, and both naïve and as inexperienced as this man had called her earlier, but she was not so ignorant that she did not know what that throbbing hardness pressed against her meant.

As she had told him earlier today, her stepfather had kept a fine stable at the country house where Ellie had spent much of the ten years of Frederick's marriage to her mother, and she knew exactly what took place when the stallion was brought to the mare for breeding. And that impressive hardness, which had risen up between Justin's thighs, was the same as had been between the stallion's back legs when he had caught the scent of the mare in season.

Had he smelled her arousal and in turn had become aroused by her? she wondered.

* * *

If Justin had thought his behaviour earlier was madness, then this had to be insanity.

Complete insanity!

Not only should he not be here alone in a darkened room with Eleanor, but he should certainly have kept his distance from her, and definitely not given in to the temptation to feel her slender curves so soft and sensuous against his much harder ones.

He could not even put his rashness down to an overindulgence in brandy this evening, either, having been watching Eleanor so intently, as she danced with what seemed like a legion of other gentlemen, that there had not been the time to allow a single drop of the restorative liquid to pass his lips.

No, it was Eleanor herself who had intoxicated him this evening. Whose every word challenged him. Who had aroused him earlier, causing him to swell and throb inside his breeches, just by watching her lick the juice of the pineapple from the swell of her lips, until Justin had desired, hungered, for the sweet taste of those lips for himself. As he still hungered.

'Well, does it feel like a game?' he repeated as she didn't answer.

Her little pink tongue moved moistly across her lips before she finally responded in a breathy voice. 'Not any game I have ever played before, no.'

'Good.' Justin gave a hard, satisfied smile. 'And would you like to know what happens next in this particular…game?'

'Your Grace—'

'Justin, damn it!' He glared down at her, watching her face as he pressed his thighs against her, only to give a low and aching groan in his throat as pleasure immediately shot hotly down the length of his arousal.

Her eyes widened in alarm. 'Justin, are you all right?'

'Do not look so concerned.' He gave a strained smile. 'It may not appear so, but I assure you it is pleasure I am feeling, not pain.'

Ellie eyed him uncertainly now. 'Pleasure?'

Strange, because when she had secretly observed the stallion and the mare together in the stable yard, it had seemed to her as if the stallion were in pain, head tossing in agitation, eyes wide and wild, as he snorted and stomped on the cobbles beneath his hooves as he strained to get close to his quarry.

The terrified mare had seemed to fair no

better, pinned restlessly in place as she was beneath those thrashing hooves, her silky neck bitten several times as the stallion mounted her, squealing and trying to move out from beneath him as that thick rod between his back legs disappeared inside her body, before being thrust in again, time and time without end it had seemed to Ellie, before she could stand to watch the wild coupling no longer and she had run crying from the stables in search of her mother.

Muriel had wiped away her tears, of course, soothing her fears as she explained that the mare had not been in pain as she had thought, that it was merely how baby horses were made, and that the mare would be happy enough when her foal was born in the spring.

It was in the course of that conversation that Ellie had added a codicil to her earlier conviction that she would never marry any man she did not love and who did not love her. Observing the stallion and mare together, Ellie had known that she could never be intimate in that way with a man she did not love and who did not love her, either. It was too personal, too carnal, too—too wild, for her to ever contemplate such personal intimacy taking place with a man whom she merely *liked*.

Justin's expression softened slightly as he obviously now saw, or perhaps sensed, her uncertainty. 'You do not believe me?'

'I—I do not know what to think, or say…' A slow shake of her head accompanied the hesitancy of that denial.

He grinned. 'Well, that is certainly a novelty in itself!'

'You are laughing at me again.'

Justin sobered, glittering gaze fixed intensely on the pale oval of her face. 'What would you like me to do with you?'

She caught her bottom lip between small pearly white teeth, nibbling that tender flesh for several seconds before her chin rose in challenge. 'I believe I should like for you not to treat me as a child.'

He smiled. 'Oh, I assure you, Eleanor, at this moment you are far from appearing as a child to me.'

She nodded. 'Then you will please tell me what happens next in this game?'

Justin drew in a sharp breath. 'Usually the gentleman now nuzzles his lips against the lady's throat. Like this.' He suited his actions to his words, enjoying her perfumed and silky skin against his lips.

She gave a soft sigh even as she arched her throat to allow him easier access. 'And next?'

Justin continued to taste and kiss that tender column. 'Next he perhaps dares to venture a little lower…'

'Lower…?' Her breath caught and held, causing the fullness of her breasts to push against the low neckline of her gown.

'Here.' Justin trailed a path of kisses down to that magnificent swell, feeling himself grow even longer, thicker inside the confines of his breeches, as he tasted her breasts with his lips and tongue and breathed in her intoxicating, heady perfume.

Ellie heard another low and aching groan, only to realise that it was she this time who was making that sound, that the feel of Justin's lips and tongue against her swollen and heated flesh, the slow thrust of his throbbing hardness against the juncture between her thighs, did indeed give her pleasure. A hot and burning pleasure that coursed through the whole of her body, causing the rosy tips of her breasts to swell, and increasing the dampness between her thighs. 'I—oh…!' she gasped low in her throat, her back arching instinctively, as that slowly thrusting hardness against her thighs rubbed against a part of her there that also felt swollen and oh, so sensitive.

'Do you like that, pet?' he asked gruffly as he continued to kiss her breasts even as he slowly moved his thighs against hers a second time.

Ellie drew in a sharp breath. 'I—do—not—know.' The thrill of the sensations currently coursing through her body were so completely new to her, felt so strange, but not unpleasant, a mixture of both a shivery and hungry ache, and heated pleasure.

'Hmm, then perhaps we should continue until you do know.' Justin nibbled deliciously on the swollen flesh above her gown, his hips arched into hers as he continued that slow and leisurely thrusting.

And each time he did so Ellie felt that same pleasure, that swelling and moistness between her thighs becoming more intense as she now moved restlessly against him, seeking, wanting, oh God, aching for she knew not what…!

Her hands reached up to grasp tightly on

to those impossibly wide shoulders, steadying her, anchoring her, even as she arched her thighs up to meet his thrusts, her breath now coming in short, strangled gasps. 'Please! Oh, Justin, please do not torture me any longer!'

Justin drew back slightly as he heard the anguish in her voice, knowing by the glazed look in her eyes, the flush to her cheeks, that she was close, so very close to orgasm. An orgasm, that in her innocence, she was completely unprepared for.

An innocence which he had been seriously in danger of shattering!

It took every effort of will he possessed to place his hands on her shoulders and pull away from her, feeling like the bastard he undoubtedly was as he saw the bewilderment in her expression. 'And it is for this reason, my dear Eleanor,' he drawled with deliberate lightness, 'why you would do well never to arrange private trysts with gentleman such as the Earl of Braxton!'

Chapter Eight

Ellie blinked dazedly, wrapping her arms about herself as she felt suddenly cold, bereft, now that the heat of Justin's body had been withdrawn from her, that chill entering her veins, and then her heart, as she saw the expression on his arrogantly disdainful face, and realised that the past few minutes had been all about teaching her yet another of those 'lessons' in how to *not* behave in society.

Physically roused he might have been, but it had been a controlled and deliberate arousal on his part, and obviously nothing like the unbelievable pleasure Ellie had experienced when he had kissed and caressed her. No doubt even the proof of his arousal had been deliberate on his part, as a way of showing her just how little she really knew about men, and the weakness of her own body in responding to them, while he seemed to have put the whole incident behind him as if totally unmoved by it.

Her arms dropped back to her sides as she drew herself up stiffly, determined that this arrogant duke should not see the humiliation she now suffered for having allowed herself to become so aroused by his deliberately intimate caresses. 'It seems I have reason to thank you once again, your Grace—' she gave him a cool smile '—in that I shall now know in future exactly how to deal with any gentleman who might attempt to take such liberties with me.'

His eyes narrowed. 'You will?'

'Oh, yes.' Ellie shot him another saccharine-sweet smile even as her hand rose in an swift arch before making sharp and painful contact with one of his arrogant cheeks. 'Tell me,' she continued calmly once he had straightened from the recoil of that hard slap, 'is that suitable punishment for such familiarity, do you think?'

Justin eyed her appreciatively as he slowly ran his fingers against his now-burning cheek. 'I am sure that it is,' he finally answered her drily.

'Good.' She stepped away from the door to straighten her gown. 'I believe it is now past time that I rejoined the dowager duchess in the ballroom.' She raised her brows as she gave a pointed glance towards the closed door.

Justin could not help but admire her coolness, in both her actions—painful as that forceful slap upon his cheek might have been!—and her demeanour. She looked, he decided, as he stepped forwards to open the door to allow her to sweep past him and out into the hallway, every bit as regally disdainful at this moment as his grandmother when she was least pleased with him.

Eleanor paused to turn in the hallway. 'I trust I may safely assume that you have no more "lessons" for me this evening, your Grace?'

'You may,' he confirmed, having already decided that he had attended his grandmother's ball for quite long enough. Far too long, in fact, when he considered how close he had been, just minutes ago, to making passionate love to Eleanor Rosewood in his grandmother's library!

Nor was that passion completely dampened even now, this distant, haughty Eleanor equally, if not even more challenging, than the defiant one of a few minutes ago. But it was a challenge Justin could not, dared not, allow himself to take up. Even if the uncomfortable throbbing of his unappeased shaft might demand otherwise.

As he already knew, there was an easy solution to that last problem. Instead of seeking one of the women here tonight, he would go to one of the houses of the *demi-monde,* settle on one of the pretty and willing woman to be found there and satisfy those demands in that way. Without expectation on either side. More importantly, without complication.

For it was quickly becoming obvious to Justin that his desire for Eleanor could become—indeed, if it was not already—a serious complication in his life.

'Royston?'

Justin, having already instructed Stanhope to bring his cloak and hat, with the intention of leaving Royston House following that less-than-satisfactory incident with Eleanor, now closed his eyes briefly before slowly turning to face the gentleman who had halted his departure. 'Richmond,' he recognised pleasantly. 'Forgive me, I had not realised you were here this evening.'

'Your grandmother was kind enough to invite me.' The older man nodded as he strode across the hallway to join Justin near the doorway. 'I rarely attend these things, but no one refuses an invitation from the Dowager Duchess of Royston,' he added ruefully.

'No.' Justin's reply was harder than was warranted as he thought of the inconvenient, and deeply irritating, request his grandmother had made of him some days ago, regarding Eleanor Rosewood.

'You were just leaving,' Richmond stated the obvious.

Justin affected an expression of boredom as he smiled. 'There is only so much of the simpering misses and the over-eager young gentlemen that I can tolerate in one evening, even to please my grandmother.'

Bryan Anderson did not return his smile. 'I particularly noticed one of those young ladies as you danced with her earlier.'

'Indeed?' It was Justin's standard non-committal reply when he was unsure as to what it was the other person wanted from him. For, much as he liked Bryan Anderson, the only young lady Justin had danced with this evening had been Eleanor, and he was completely out of patience if Richmond was yet another middle-aged widower wishing to court her. 'I believe you are referring to my ward, Miss Eleanor Rosewood?'

'Just so.' Richmond ran an agitated hand through his prematurely white hair. 'I— would it be impertinent of me to enquire as to her exact age?'

'It would, yes.' Surely Eleanor was too young for him?

The earl's eyes widened as he realised what his question had sounded like to Justin. 'No, no, Royston, it is nothing like that. Miss Rosewood is far too young for my interest,' he assured hastily. 'I just—if not her age, would it be possible for you to tell me who her mother is?'

'Was,' Justin corrected guardedly, having absolutely no idea, now that Richmond had assured him so positively he had no marital intentions towards Eleanor, what this conversation was about. But he felt sure, from the intensity of the earl's mood, that it was something which would further add to the complication Eleanor had already become in his life. 'Eleanor's mother was married to my cousin Frederick and, if you recall, he and his wife were both killed in a carriage accident just over a year ago.'

The earl gave a thoughtful frown. 'Frederick's wife was previously Muriel Rosewood…?'

'I believe I have just said so.'

'I had no idea… Of course, I have not been much in society for many years, and but even so I had not realised—' He broke off with a shake of his prematurely white head. 'Look, Richmond—'

'Would you mind very much if I were to accompany you to wherever it is you are going?' The earl now looked at him appealingly. 'I would very much like to talk with you more on this subject, and here and now really is not the time or the place.' He looked pointedly at the attentive Stanhope, only to wince as several overly raucous young bucks also emerged from the supper room, glasses of champagne in their hands.

They all fell silent, however, the moment they were treated to a single infamously reproving lift of one of the Duke of Royston's eyebrows. 'Perhaps you are right, Richmond, and we should discuss this some other time?' Justin turned back to the earl. 'I am, however, presently on my way to a…private engagement, so perhaps we can make an appointment for some time tomorrow? In the afternoon would be best for me,' he added, thinking about spending a night of unbridled passion in some willing woman's bed, before making his leisurely way back to his own apartments in the late hours of the morning, and spending several hours sleeping off those excesses in his own bed.

The other man drew in a sharp breath. 'I suppose it could wait until tomorrow…'

'Best to do so, then.' Justin said. 'Perhaps we might have a late lunch together at White's?'

'As I said, I would rather we spoke on this matter in private,' Richmond insisted. 'Three o'clock suit? At your rooms?'

Justin looked taken aback. 'Now see here, Richmond, I do not—'

'Tell me, have you seen or heard any more of Litchfield?'

Justin's patience, never his strongest quality at the best of times—and this evening could certainly not be called that!—was almost non-existent as Richmond's conversation became even more obscure. 'As it happens we met him quite by accident whilst we were out riding in the park earlier today.'

'We? Miss Rosewood was with you?' the earl asked anxiously.

'What on earth does it matter whether Eleanor was with me or not?' Justin snapped.

'Everything! Or perhaps nothing,' the earl said vaguely. 'Did—is Litchfield now acquainted with Miss Rosewood?'

'I did not feel inclined to introduce the two of them, if that is what you are asking!'

Richmond sighed his relief. 'That is something, at least.'

'What does Eleanor riding with me earlier today have to do with the unpleasantness which exists between myself and Litchfield?'

'I shall not know the answer to that until we have spoken together tomorrow.'

Justin's previous interest in spending a passion-filled night with a willing woman was now fading as quickly as his patience. 'You are being very mysterious, Richmond.'

'I do not mean to be.' The earl sighed heavily, his face unnaturally pale. 'It is just, having now seen Miss Rosewood, and realising that she is your ward, I feel I must—' He stopped and ran an agitated hand through his hair. 'Do not underestimate Litchfield,

Royston.' His eyes glittered with intensity. 'I know him to be both a dangerous and vicious man and—we really must talk very soon!'

'Very well.' Justin acquiesced slowly. 'My rooms in Curzon Street at three o'clock tomorrow.'

'Thank you.' Richmond looked relieved.

Justin raised that infamous brow once again. 'And do I have your word that you will not attempt to approach my ward about this matter—whatever it might be—before the two of us have had chance to talk together tomorrow?'

'Good God, of course you have it!' The earl looked shocked at the suggestion. 'I would never discuss this with her—God, no.'

'I believed you the first time, Richmond,' Justin smiled wryly as he turned to finally allow Stanhope to place his evening cloak about his shoulders before donning his hat. 'Until tomorrow, then.'

'Tomorrow.'

Justin's mood was darker than ever as he walked rapidly down the steps to his carriage. What on earth could the other man want to discuss with him, about Eleanor of all people, that was so urgent and mysterious that Richmond had got himself into such a froth of emotion about it? And what did it have to do with Litchfield? Whatever it was Justin now felt almost as unsettled as Richmond so obviously was.

Perhaps he should not have delayed the conversation until tomorrow, after all? It had been sheer bloody-mindedness on his part that he had done so in the first place; being guardian to Eleanor had already caused enough chaos in his life for one week—good God, had it really only been four days since his grandmother had made that ridiculous request of him?—and, as such, Justin had been unwilling to allow her to disrupt the rest of his plans for this evening.

'Where to, your Grace?' his groom prompted as he stepped forwards to open the door of the ducal carriage.

Justin ducked his head as he stepped up and inside. 'Curzon Street,' he said wearily as he sank back into the plush upholstered seat. 'You may take me home to Curzon Street, Bilsbury.'

Justin could see little point now in going on somewhere, or even in attempting to rouse his enthusiasm for any other woman, when his conversation with Richmond just now had succeeded in deflating any last vestiges of interest his libido might have had in partaking in such an exercise.

Damn his grandmother and her infernal interference.

Damn Richmond.

But, most of all, damn the irritating thorn Eleanor Rosewood had become in his side.

'It is such a beautiful day, ideal for a drive in the park!' Ellie smiled her pleasure at the outing as she sat in the open carriage beside Edith St Just during the fashionable hour of five and six. 'So kind, too, that so many of your guests from the ball yesterday evening have stopped to pay their respects and comment on their appreciation of the evening.'

'I would have been surprised if they had not.' The dowager nodded gracious acknowledgement of yet another group of ladies as they travelled past in their own carriage. 'Lord Endicott seems to have especially enjoyed the evening, if his enthusiasm today is an indication,' she added with a knowing smile.

Ellie felt the warmth enter her cheeks, only to chuckle as she saw the mischievous twinkle in the dowager's eyes. 'He was very appreciative of your hospitality, yes.' Charles Endicott, having stopped to speak with them just a few minutes ago, had also been most complimentary to her.

'He is very appreciative of your own charms, child!' Edith insisted. 'As were many other gentlemen, if the florist's shop of flowers that has been delivered to you today is any indication.'

The blush deepened in Ellie's cheeks beneath her bonnet of pale lemon, a ribbon of deeper yellow secured beneath her chin, wearing a high-waisted gown of the same pale lemon, with another deeper yellow ribbon beneath her breasts. 'I have never seen so many flowers all together, have you, your Grace?'

Edith's eyes now warmed with humour. 'I do believe I may have seen almost as many at least once or twice in my own youth.'

Ellie smiled as she realised she was being teased. 'I am sure that you did. It is only— I have never received so much as a single bunch of freshly picked spring flowers from a gentleman before, let alone so many beautiful displays.' The dowager duchess's private parlour was awash with the vases of flowers that had been delivered throughout the day, following the Royston Ball the evening before. Half a dozen of them were for the dowager duchess herself, of course, sent by other society matrons, as acknowledgement of the success of the ball, but the other dozen or so were for Ellie alone.

Notably, she had not received so much as a single blossom from the Duke of Royston. Oh, no, that top-lofty gentleman would never deign to send a woman flowers, not even to his ward as a mark of the success of her introduction into society.

'I was only teasing, child.' Edith smiled across at her encouragingly. 'I could not be more pleased at your obvious success.'

Ellie forced the smile back to her lips. 'And you are not too tired from the ball and your late night?' Doctor Franklyn had been called to attend the dowager duchess this morning, but once again Ellie had been excluded from the bedchamber. Although she had not seemed to be too fatigued when she had joined Ellie for lunch in the small, family dining room earlier—it had been Edith's suggestion that the two of them go out for a carriage ride this afternoon.

Nevertheless, keeping true to her promise to Justin, Ellie had sent a short, formal note round to his rooms earlier today informing him of Dr Franklyn's visit this morning.

'Not too much, no,' Edith claimed.

'And will your grandson be calling upon you today, do you think?' Ellie posed the question as casually as she was able, in view of the unpleasant circumstances in which she and the duke had parted the evening before.

Not that she regretted slapping his arrogant face, for he had surely deserved it. The confusion of her own feelings for him aside, Justin St Just was, without doubt, the most infuriating gentleman she had ever known. Nothing at all like those charming young bucks who had clamoured to talk to her once it became known that her watchful guardian had departed the ball.

Ellie's own reaction to that abrupt departure was less straightforward. To the point that she could not completely explain her feelings, even to herself...

A part of her had been so relieved not to have him scowling at her so darkly every time she so much as glanced across at him. But another part of her had known that the thrill of excitement had gone out of the evening for her and that she had merely played the role expected of her for the remainder of the evening, the charming and smiling Miss Eleanor Rosewood, ward of the Duke of Royston and protégée of the Dowager Duchess of Royston.

It…concerned Ellie, that she should feel this conflict of emotions. She had been so angry with Justin for the things he had said to her after he had kissed her. Furious at his mockery. And yet… To know that the duke was no longer even in the house, let alone the ballroom, had seemed to turn the evening flat, without purpose. Although what purpose a ball was supposed to have, other than dancing and flirtation, in which Ellie had engaged fully after Justin's departure, she had no idea!

She had fared no better, once the last guest had departed from Royston House and she was at last able to escape up the stairs to her bedchamber, her pillow seeming too lumpy for her to find any comfort, the covers either too hot or too cold. Unable to sleep, Ellie had not been able to prevent her thoughts from drifting to the time she had spent in the library with Justin.

Privately she could admit that it had been the most thrilling, the most physically sensuous, experience of her life. Of course, that might be because the only sensuous experiences of her life had been with Justin, rather than a confirmation of any softer emotions she might feel towards him.

There was some comfort to be found in that, she supposed. She had nothing, no other gentleman, with whom to compare her responses to Justin St Just. Perhaps any man turned a lady's legs to water when he kissed her and made her heart beat faster, caused her breasts to tingle and between her thighs to dampen? Ellie could only hope that might be the case.

'I doubt Royston will stir himself,' the dowager duchess answered Ellie's query dismissively. 'No doubt he will have gone on somewhere after he left us last night and will not have seen his bed until the early hours of this morning!'

Considering that Justin had not wished to attend the Royston Ball at all, he would most certainly have gone in search of more scintillating entertainment for his jaded senses after departing it. Indeed, Ellie had overheard the gossips fervently speculating as much the previous evening once he had left...

'Knowing my grandson—'

'Good afternoon, ladies.'

Ellie knew, just from looking at Edith's sudden and stiffly offended demeanour, that the gentleman who had now approached them on horseback was not someone the dowager considered as being an acceptable part of society, let alone of her social equal. One glance at that gentleman was enough for Ellie to know the reason for that.

Lord Dryden Litchfield appeared immune to both the dowager duchess's disapproval, and Ellie's unsmiling face, as he raised his hat to them both politely. 'Your Grace. And Miss Rosewood, too,' he added silkily. 'How gratified I am to have the pleasure of seeing you again so soon.'

Ellie had no idea what to do or to say in the face of such boldness as this. She had not liked this man when she met him yesterday and she knew from the duke that neither he or the dowager duchess approved of Lord Litchfield, either, but to cut the man direct, and a lord at that, was surely beyond Ellie's own low social standing?

'I was not aware that you were acquainted with my grandson's ward, Lord Litchfield?' Edith St Just was the one to answer coldly as she eyed him with chilling frost.

Dryden Litchfield bared those brown-stained teeth in a smile. 'Royston introduced us yesterday.'

Ellie gasped softly at the blatant lie; the duke had not even attempted to introduce the two of them—indeed, Ellie believed Justin had gone out of his way not to do so. For just such a reason as this, no doubt; without the benefit of a formal introduction, Lord Litchfield should not have approached or spoken to her at all.

'Indeed?' The dowager gave Ellie a long and considering glance before that gaze became icier still as she turned back to Dryden Litchfield. 'You must excuse us, Lord Litchfield, I am afraid Miss Rosewood and I have another engagement which we must attend.' She nodded to him dismissively.

'But of course,' he drawled with feigned graciousness. 'Perhaps I might be allowed to call upon Miss Rosewood at Royston House…?'

Ellie gave another soft gasp, this time clearly of dismay, and Edith's mouth thinned disapprovingly at the man's bad manners. 'I do not think—'

'Miss Rosewood's time is fully engaged for the next week, at least.' A steely cold voice, easily recognisable to them all as Justin's, cut firmly across his grandmother's reply.

Ellie looked at him, only to shrink back against the carriage seat as those icily contemptuous blue eyes glanced briefly in her direction before returning to Litchfield.

'Then perhaps the week following that?' the other man persisted challengingly.

'Not then, either,' the duke refused coldly. 'Now, if you will excuse us? I believe it is past time the two ladies and I returned to Royston House.'

'But of course. Ladies.' Lord Litchfield raised his hat once again in a mockery of politeness, before wheeling his horse about and urging it into an unhurried walk in the opposite direction.

'What a disgustingly dreadful man,' Edith muttered with distaste.

'Indeed,' her grandson agreed.

'Thank heavens you came along when you did, Royston.'

'I have no doubts you would have succeeded in routing him quite thoroughly yourself, Grandmama,' he said with a twinkle, 'once you had recovered from the shock of his incivility in daring to speak to you at all.'

'No doubt. I am nevertheless grateful for your intervention, Royston,' the dowager duchess said.

'Perhaps we should be thanking Stanhope. I called at Royston House earlier,' he explained, 'and it was he who told me that the two of you were out driving in the park.'

'I cannot imagine what Litchfield imagined he was doing by approaching my carriage in the first place.' Edith gave one of her disdainful sniffs.

'Perhaps that is because it was Miss Rosewood whom he wished to see again…?'

The dowager looked at her grandson sharply. 'What do you mean, Royston? Surely you are not meaning to imply that Ellie would ever encourage the interest of such an obnoxious gentleman as that?'

Ellie was wondering the same thing. Surely he did not seriously imagine for one moment that she had encouraged Lord Litchfield in any way?

A single glance beneath lowered lashes at the duke's cold blue eyes, thinned lips and tightly clenched jaw, showed her that he was, to all intents and purposes, furious.

Was he furious with her? And if so, why?

The drive back to Royston House was

completed in silence, but Ellie was only too aware of the duke's continued anger as he rode beside the carriage on his magnificent black hunter, the expression on his face daring any in society to approach or speak to them. Wisely, none did.

Why Ellie should continue to feel quite so much as if that anger was directed personally at her was beyond understanding; despite what the duke might think, she had done nothing to encourage Lord Litchfield.

And yet still she felt as if all of the seething emotions she sensed behind Justin's stony façade were directed at her: anger, irritation and, for some inexplicable reason, resentment.

Quite why he should resent her was a mystery. If anyone should be feeling *that* particular emotion, then it should be Ellie herself, for she was the one who had once again been made a fool of the evening before, with her undeniable responses to this impossible man. Yes, indeed, all of the resentment should be on her side, not his!

Justin handed his hat and gloves to Stanhope as he entered Royston House, knowing that if the two ladies had not been present in the park, he would have been unable to stop himself from committing a public scandal, by punching Dryden Litchfield on his drink-bloated nose!

But, of course, if they had not been present, Eleanor in particular, then Justin doubted that such a confrontation would ever have taken place.

But it was only a matter of time before it did so, for Justin was certain that he and Litchfield would come to blows one day. And, after the things Richmond had related to him at their meeting earlier today, it was a day Justin anticipated with the greatest of pleasure.

But not yet. For the moment he intended to keep his own counsel and protect Eleanor without her knowledge. 'Perhaps we might partake of tea in your private parlour, Grandmama?'

'Tea, Royston?' His grandmother looked suitably surprised by this concession to civility by her wayward grandson. 'I had not thought you a great advocate of tea, my dear?'

'Brandy, then,' he conceded wryly.

'See to it, would you, Stanhope,' Edith

instructed even as she walked up the grand staircase.

'At once, your Grace.' The butler departed for the back of the house, leaving Eleanor and Justin alone in the grand entrance hall.

He was very aware that it was the first time he had been alone with her since their strained parting of the evening before. And yet it seemed as if days had passed since that time instead of hours, so much had transpired.

Usually Justin had no trouble sleeping, but he had found it impossible to fall into slumber the night before, physically frustrated of course, which was never a good thing, but also angry with himself for having kissed Eleanor yet again, and more than a little troubled as to what Richmond wished to discuss with him.

But he would never have guessed, could never have envisaged the full horror of the things Richmond had related to him earlier this afternoon.

Justin could not help but frown now as he looked down at Eleanor's bent head, her innocent head, and wonder how, if Richmond's suspicions should turn out to be correct, he would ever be able to tell her the truth, without utterly destroying the spirit in her that he so admired, as much as the fragile hold she now had in society.

No doubt Eleanor, never having needed that society before, would dismiss the importance of it in her life now, but Justin found he could not bear the thought of her independence of spirit also being trampled underfoot, snuffing out that light of either challenge or mischief he so often detected in her unwavering green gaze during their lively exchanges.

No, he would not tell Eleanor anything of that conversation as yet, preferring to make his own private and discreet enquiries, at least going some way towards proving—or disproving—Richmond's fears, before so much as attempting to broach the subject to her. Fears, which, in view of his grandmother's own doubts on the subject, Justin had no choice but to take seriously.

For what decent young woman, especially a young and beautiful woman newly entered into society, would want to be burdened with the stigma of learning that her father, her real father, might be none other than Lord Dryden Litchfield, an inveterate rake and gambler, whom all of decent society shunned?

Chapter Nine

Ellie was painfully aware of Justin's sinfully handsome appearance as he stood beside her in a perfectly tailored superfine of sapphire blue, setting off buff-coloured pantaloons and brown-topped Hessians. There was an awkward silence between them, forcing her into making some sort of conversation.

She lifted her chin even as she tilted her head back in order to look up at him, feeling the physical discomfort at her nape in having to do so. 'Goodness, you are prodigiously tall!'

Blue eyes, the exact same shade as his superfine, widened briefly, before those chiselled lips twisted into a rueful smile. 'And you, brat, are incredibly rude, that you can never address a gentleman in the normal fashion of a well-bred young lady!'

'Perhaps I have been keeping company with you for too long?' she came back pertly.

'Perhaps you have,' he allowed. 'Shall we?' He held out his arm to her. 'Unless you wish to put my grandmother to the trouble of coming in search of us, which I am sure she will do if we do not soon join her in her parlour,' he prompted as Ellie hesitated.

No, she had no wish to involve the dowager duchess in this battle of wills that ensued between herself and that lady's grandson each and every time they met.

Her hesitation in taking his arm was for another reason entirely. Already aware of everything about him, she had no wish to place herself in the position of touching him, of once again feeling his warmth beneath her gloved fingertips, the leashed strength of his tautly held muscles. To be so close to him that she could not help but be aware of that intensely seductive smell that was unique to him—clean healthy male and a fresh yet sensual cologne, which seemed to wind itself in and about her, until she longed for nothing more than to have him kiss her again, touch her again, make love to her again…

She straightened her spine in defence of that onslaught to her emotions as she deliberately placed her hand lightly upon the duke's arm. 'I should not at all wish to put the dowager duchess to such trouble as that.'

'And, in your opinion, how is she today?' her grandson enquired as they ascended the staircase together.

Ellie gave him a startled glance. 'You want my opinion…?'

He nodded. 'I received your note earlier, informing me of Dr Franklyn's visit this morning, and as that gentleman prefers to keep his opinion of my grandmother's health to himself,' he added with clear disapproval, 'it leaves me with no choice but to try to elicit the opinion on the subject from the one person who is with her the most.'

In truth, with all the excitement of the flowers arriving constantly throughout the day, the ride in the park, the encounter with the disagreeable Lord Litchfield, and then Justin's unexpected arrival a short time ago, Ellie had all but forgotten the note she had sent him following Dr Franklyn's visit.

Although Ellie could not help but admit to a certain grudging admiration for Dr Franklyn, in that he was insistent upon protecting his patient's confidentiality…much to the duke's obvious annoyance. She gave an inward smile.

'I believe her to be quite well, considering she was hostess to a ball yesterday evening, and the late hour at which we finally retired for the night,' Ellie said. 'Perhaps the doctor's visit was simply a precautionary one rather than a necessity?'

Justin pursed his lips. 'Perhaps.'

But, in Ellie's opinion, he did not sound at all certain. 'The dowager duchess did breakfast in her rooms, which is not her usual custom. But she did join me not long after that and we ate luncheon together. And it was her suggestion that we should ride in the park this afternoon.'

Justin's expression turned grim as he recalled who had been there with them when he had finally found Eleanor and his grandmother in the park earlier. 'I believe I warned you as to the unsuitability of Lord Litchfield's company?'

'You did, yes.'

'And?'

Two wings of angry colour brightened Eleanor's cheeks as she came to a halt in the hallway outside Edith's private parlour. 'And, as your grandmother has already informed you, Lord Litchfield chose to inflict his company upon us without the least encouragement. From either of us.'

Justin's nostrils flared. 'I cannot emphasise how strongly I wish for you to avoid that man's company!'

'And I cannot emphasise how strongly I resent this second implication from you that I would ever wish to encourage the attentions of such an unpleasant man!' Green eyes sparkled with that same anger as Eleanor glared up at him.

Justin held back the sharpness of his own reply and instead drew in a deep breath in an effort to calm his own turbulent emotions, knowing the worst of them, his anger, was caused by fear—for her safety, for her emotional well-being.

Litchfield was proving to be something of a nemesis in their lives at the moment, somehow seeming to be there, whenever Justin turned around. And, after Richmond's revelations about the man, Justin did not wish for Dryden Litchfield to be anywhere near Eleanor. Or for Eleanor to be anywhere near him.

He forced the tension from his shoulders

as he straightened. 'I believe you are determined to misunderstand me—'

'Is that you at last, Royston, Eleanor?' his grandmother, obviously having heard the sound of their voices outside in the hallway, now called out impatiently.

Justin bit back his own impatience at this interruption as he lowered his voice so that only Eleanor might hear him. 'We will talk of this again later.'

'No, your Grace, I do not believe we will,' she snapped back, and obviously tired of waiting for him to open the parlour door for her, opened it for herself and preceded him into the room.

'Do not believe you will what, my dear?' the dowager enquired.

Justin followed Eleanor into the room. 'Will not—Good God, it is like a florist's shop in here!' He almost recoiled from the overabundance of perfume given off by the multitude of flowers in the room, vases and vases of them, it seemed, on every available surface. 'How on earth can you possibly breathe in here, Grandmama?' He strode across the room to throw open a window before turning to glare across at Eleanor. 'I suppose we have your success last night to thank for this gratuitous display?'

'Royston!' his grandmother rebuked sharply.

Justin' continued to glare at Eleanor. 'I am only stating the obvious, Grandmama!'

'That is no excuse for upsetting Ellie.' The dowager duchess rose to her feet to cross to Eleanor's side and place an arm about her shoulders. 'I am sure Royston did not mean to be so sharp with you, my dear,' she soothed as the younger woman looked in danger of succumbing to tears.

He *had* meant to be sharp with her, Justin realised in self-disgust. In fact, that was exactly what he had meant to do!

Because he felt somehow…unsettled by this garish tribute to her obvious success the evening before, he acknowledged.

And also, he realised uncomfortably, because it had not so much as occurred to him to send Eleanor flowers himself.

Why should it have done? Even the women whose bodies he availed himself of for however long before he grew tired of them had never received flowers from him. A pretty and expensive piece of jewellery as a parting gift, perhaps, but never flowers. Justin considered flowers as being somehow more personal, a gift chosen for the woman herself, rather than with an eye to how much money they might cost.

And here Eleanor had received dozens of such tokens of admiration, probably from all those young bucks who had flocked about her at the ball!

Again Justin asked why that should bother him? If those young idiots wished to make fools of themselves over a new and beautiful face, then who was he to care one way or the other?

He stood stiffly across the room, arms behind his back. 'I was merely taken by surprise at—'

'—such a gratuitous display,' Eleanor completed challengingly as she straightened out of the dowager's embrace, her chin held proudly high, sparks of anger in her eyes now rather than tears as she glared across at him. 'If you will both excuse me, I believe I will go to my room and tidy my appearance before dinner.' She sketched a brief curtsy before leaving the parlour with a swish of her skirts.

'Royston, what on earth was that all about?'

Justin closed his eyes momentarily before opening them again to look across at his grandmother, sighing deeply as he saw the reproach in her steely blue gaze. 'You no doubt wish for me to go to Eleanor and apologise for my churlishness?'

The dowager gave him a searching glance before replying. 'Only if that is what you wish to do yourself.'

Did he? Dare he follow Eleanor to her bedchamber? Allow himself to be in a position, a place, where he might be tempted into kissing her, making love to her once again?

'Obviously not,' his grandmother said acidly at his lengthy silence. 'Ah, Stanhope.' She turned to greet the butler warmly as he arrived with the brandy and tea. 'Wait a moment, if you please, and take this cup of tea to Miss Rosewood in her bedchamber.' She bent to pour the brew into the two delicate china teacups.

Justin was still fighting an inner battle with himself, aware that he had been overly sharp with Eleanor just now, and that he did owe her an apology for his behaviour, if not an explanation. For he had no intention of admitting to anyone, not even himself—least of all himself!—the real emotion that had washed over him when he had first looked upon all those flowers and realised they were tangible proof of the admiration Eleanor had received from so many other gentlemen the evening before.

Jealousy…

Insufferable, impossible, cruel, heartless man! Arrogant, hateful, *hateful* man!

And Ellie did hate at that moment. Hated his cynicism. His sarcasm. His mockery. His overbearing arrogance. His—

'I have brought you a cup of tea…'

Ellie turned sharply, from where she lay on the bed, to look across at Justin as he stood in the doorway to her bedchamber, aware of her reddened cheeks and the soreness of her eyes from the tears that she had allowed to fall the moment she entered the room and which had been flowing unchecked ever since.

Tears of frustration and hurt, at the unfairness of his accusations.

Tears of pain and humiliation, at his unkindness about the flowers that had been sent to her today, and which she had so enjoyed receiving.

They were also tears which Eleanor had never intended for Justin to bear witness to!

She sat up and began dabbing at the evidence of those tears with the lace handkerchief she had retrieved from the pocket of her gown. 'Are you sure you should be in here?'

His answer to that was to step further into the room and close the door behind him. 'I have brought you a cup of tea,' he repeated. 'And I will bring it across to you if you promise not to throw it over me the moment I place it in your hand!' he teased gently.

Ellie replaced the handkerchief in her pocket. 'You are an exceedingly cruel man.'

'Yes.'

'An insufferable man.'

'Yes.'

She frowned. 'Hateful, even.'

'Yes.'

Ellie blinked at his unexpected acquiescence to her accusations. 'Why do you not defend yourself?'

He sighed deeply. 'Possibly because, on this occasion, I know you are correct. I am all of the things you have accused me of being.'

Ellie eyed him guardedly, looking for signs of that sarcasm or cynicism she had also accused him of to herself just minutes ago. He met her gaze unblinkingly, the expression in those blue eyes neither cynical nor sarcastic, but merely accepting. 'I do not understand…'

'I am merely agreeing with you, Eleanor.' He crossed the room until he stood before her, the delicacy of the saucer and teacup he held out to her looking slightly incongruous in his lean hand.

She reached up slowly and took the cup and saucer from him. 'That is what I do not understand.'

He looked down at her beneath hooded lids as he gave a shrug of those broad shoulders. 'I have no defence, when everything you accuse me of, I undoubtedly am.'

'And that is your apology for such insufferable behaviour?' Ellie asked.

A humourless smile curved his lips. 'No.'

'Because you offer no apology,' she realised. 'Only tea.'

'Is it not the panacea to all ills?' he drawled as Eleanor took several sips of the steaming brew.

'I believe I should have appreciated an apology more!'

'Would you?' he asked enigmatically.

Where had all her anger towards this man

disappeared to? Ellie wondered crossly as she continued to sip her tea. Because, she realised, she was no longer angry. Or tearful. In fact, a part of her felt decidedly like smiling. Or perhaps even laughing at the incongruousness of seeing such a guilty-little-boy expression on the face of one as impossibly arrogant as he was. It was also totally illogical, in view of the way his sarcasm had hurt her just a few short minutes ago.

Except…

That ridiculous expression aside, she very much doubted that Justin had ever bothered himself to take tea to a woman in the whole of his privileged life before today. The fact that he had done so now, and to her, was in itself an apology of sorts. Not the grovelling appeasement that some would have made in the circumstances, but from this arrogant duke, Ellie recognised it was as good as another gentleman having got down upon his knees and begged her forgiveness.

She placed the empty teacup and its saucer on the bedside table. 'Thank you. I do feel slightly better now.'

'Good.' He moved to sit on the side of the bed beside her and took one of her hands in both of his much larger ones. 'And I do sincerely apologise for my bad temper to you just now, Eleanor.'

Ellie, already disconcerted at the touch of his hands on hers, now looked at him in surprise. 'You do?'

He nodded. 'I was boorish, to say the least. I was a little…unsettled after seeing Litchfield, of all people, beside my grandmother's carriage in the park. But I accept I should not have taken that bad temper out on you.'

Ellie's heart had begun to beat faster at his sudden proximity, her cheeks feeling warm, her breathing shallow, and he surely must be able to feel the way her hand trembled slightly inside his? 'I really do not think it quite proper for you to be in my bedchamber. The dowager duchess—'

'Made it plain to me just now that she, at least, considers me to be nothing more than an uncle to you and, as such, feels it is perfectly permissible for me to visit you here,' he revealed drily.

The utterly disgusted expression on his face that accompanied this revelation only made Ellie feel like laughing again. How strange, when just minutes ago she had felt as if she might never laugh again…

Justin was completely unprepared for the way in which Eleanor's lips now twitched with obvious humour, before it turned into an open smile, to be followed by husky laughter. 'I fail to see what it is you find so amusing?'

'That is probably because—' She broke off, still smiling as she shook her head. 'The thought of you being considered in an avuncular role by any young woman is utterly ridiculous!'

Justin scowled. 'I could not agree more.'

Those green eyes danced. 'Your reputation in society as a rake would be ruined for ever if that were to become the general consensus!'

He stilled. 'My reputation in society is that of a rake?'

'Oh, yes.' She nodded.

'And is that what you think of me, too?' He frowned darkly. 'That I choose to spend all of my days and nights bedding young women at every available opportunity?'

'Well…perhaps not all of your days,' Eleanor allowed mischievously. 'You do, after all, have to find the time in which to attend to your ducal responsibilities! And there was gossip, yesterday evening at the ball, that not

all of those ladies have been quite so young
or available…'

'I am accused of bedding married women,
too?'

She raised auburn brows at his harshness.
'You sound surprised that your affairs are
quite so widely known.'

'What I am surprised at is that you were
subjected to overhearing such errant nonsense!' He released her hand and stood up
to restlessly cross the room before standing
stiffly in front of the window. 'Who made
these scurrilous remarks?'

She looked puzzled. 'I am not sure that I
remember who exactly…'

A nerve pulsed in his tightly clenched jaw.
'Try!'

She gave a slow shake of her head. 'The
remarks were not made to me directly, I
merely overheard several people speculating as to who your current mistress might
be, and which husband was being made the
cuckold last night.'

'I assure you—' Justin broke off, realising he was angry once again, but this time
at remarks made in Eleanor's hearing as to
what society thought of him—a reputation
which had not bothered him in the slightest

until he had heard it from her lips… 'I wish you to know that I have the deepest respect for the married state, and as such have never shown the slightest inclination to bed a married woman. Nor,' he continued grimly, 'do I have a "current mistress".'

Ellie could tell by his expression that by repeating such gossip she had somehow succeeded in seriously insulting him. 'I did not mean to give offence, your Grace.'

'I am not in the least offended,' he denied.

'I beg to differ…'

His expression softened slightly. 'I am not offended by anything you have personally said to or about me, my displeasure is for those people who obviously have nothing better to do with their time than make up scandalous and inaccurate gossip!' His voice had hardened again over the last statement.

Ellie realised that his displeasure at hearing of society's opinion of him was completely genuine.

Gossip, which Ellie, in view of their own recent intimacies, had found extremely hurtful to overhear. So much so that just imagining Justin having a mistress, and that he had gone to be with her once he had left the ball, had only added to her inability to sleep the night before.

But Justin now appeared to be denying it most vehemently.

Too vehemently to be believed?

Somehow she did not think so. Justin was all of those things she had accused him of being earlier—he could be cruel on occasion, insufferable and hateful—but at the same time she knew him to be a truthful man; indeed, it was that very honesty, his bluntness, which was usually to blame for all of those other, infuriating traits!

As such, if he now said he did not have a current mistress, married or otherwise, then she believed him...

It was an acceptance which made her feel as if a weight had been lifted from her chest. A weight she had not even realised had been there until it was removed...and which once again caused her to question her feelings towards this unattainable duke. A question she knew, even as she asked it, that she shied away from answering!

She rose to her feet. 'I am sure the dowager duchess has been most forbearing, but perhaps it is time for you to rejoin her in her parlour?' She linked her gloved hands tightly together in front of her. 'I really do have to change before dinner.'

'You have not said yet whether or not you believe my denials.'

She shrugged. 'Does it matter whether or not I believe you?'

Justin narrowed his lids as he noted the challenging tilt of her chin and the directness of her unreadable gaze.

He also realised that his own mood just now had been a defensive one. A feeling which was surely totally misplaced; it should not matter to him what his young ward thought of him, or his reputation. 'Not in the least,' he finally drawled.

Her gaze dropped from his. 'As I thought.'

Justin gave her a terse bow before striding across to the doorway. 'I will see you at dinner.'

'What?'

He paused to turn, his hand already on the door handle. 'I said we will meet again at dinner.'

She blinked. 'I had not realised her Grace had invited you to dine here this evening.'

Justin smiled. 'Of course…you were not present just now during the last part of my conversation with my grandmother.' He stood with his arms folded across his chest. 'If you had been, then you would know that it is my intention to dine here every evening for the foreseeable future. Breakfast, too, on the mornings I rise early enough to partake of it. I may be absent for the occasional luncheon—as you say, I do have other ducal responsibilities in need of my attention.'

Ellie gasped. 'I do not understand...'

His smile widened. 'It is quite simple, Eleanor. After years of my grandmother's interminable nagg—er, helpful suggestions, I have decided it is time that I moved back into the ducal home. As such I, and my belongings and personal staff, will be taking up permanent residence at Royston House as from tomorrow morning.'

Chapter Ten

'Why are you so surprised by my decision, Eleanor?' Justin asked as Ellie could only stare wide-eyed and open-mouthed across the bedchamber at him in the wake of his announcement. 'After all, you are responsible for alerting me to the fact that Dr Franklyn made yet another visit to my grandmother this morning.'

That might be so, but she certainly had not thought it would result in his decision to move into Royston House!

No doubt the dowager duchess was beside herself with pleasure at this unexpected turn of events, but it was equally as unthinkable to Ellie that she would have to suffer this disturbing man's presence every hour of every day 'for the foreseeable future'!

She moistened suddenly dry lips. 'Well, yes, I did do that, of course. But I did not mean it to—I had not expected—'

'You did not envisage it would result in your now having to suffer my living here?' Royston guessed drily.

No, she most certainly had not! Nor did there seem any point in her denying that was her response, when she had moments ago gawked at the duke like a dumbstruck schoolgirl, no doubt with a look of horror upon her face. 'Will the dowager duchess not think it…strange that you have capitulated now, when you have always resisted her pleadings in the past?'

The duke's mouth quirked. 'My grandmother does not plead, Eleanor, she suggests or instructs. And, no, I do not see why she should find my decision in the least strange.'

Ellie nibbled her lower lip. 'Surely she will realise, eventually, that someone—notably myself—must have informed you of Dr Franklyn's visit earlier today?'

'Not unless you or I were to tell her of it.' He arched golden brows. 'Do you intend telling her?'

'No, of course I do not.' She frowned her agitation in the face of his infuriating calm. 'I just—your grandmother will be too pleased by your decision at the moment to question it, but once she does—what reason will you give her for this change of heart?'

He looked down the length of his arrogant nose. 'Why should I give her any reason? This is, after all, the official London home of the Duke of Royston. That I have not chosen to live in it for some years does not mean I was not at liberty to do so at any time I chose.'

Ellie was aware of that. But she was also aware that the dowager duchess was a woman of astuteness as well as intelligence, and once that dear lady had opportunity to think, to fully consider Royston's sudden unexpected change of heart, she would most assuredly question as to why it should have occurred now, of all times.

Ellie had dashed off that note to Royston this morning for the simple reason he had asked her to do so should such a thing occur, but she had not, as he so easily guessed and obviously found so amusing, expected to now have him thrust into her own life on a daily basis. Indeed, the very idea of it, given the circumstances of their own fraught relationship, was a total nightmare for her!

It was not too difficult for Justin to read the emotions flickering across her expressive face.

It was the last emotion—horror at the prospect of living with him—which irritated Justin the most. Especially when his real reason for moving into Royston House had everything to do with her, with the conversation that had taken place with Richmond this afternoon, and its possible repercussions upon Eleanor, rather than his grandmother's health, or any real desire on Justin's part to reside here.

It really was too insulting, given those circumstances, for him to have to suffer Eleanor's obvious dismay at the very thought of being under the same roof as him, of sharing even so large a residence as Royston House with him. But it was an insult he had no choice but to endure, unless he wished to tell her of the contents of his conversation with Richmond this afternoon, which, for the moment, he had no intention of doing.

Far better if Justin were to proceed with his previous decision to privately and quietly check into those details for himself, before facing the possibility of having to burden her with any of them.

She did not need to know, for instance, of the scandal that had ensued in India twenty years ago, in which Dryden Litchfield had been accused of attacking and raping the recently widowed wife of a fellow officer. A rape that Richmond, after seeing Eleanor the previous evening, and noting her likeness to Muriel Rosewood, and the richness of her auburn hair so like Litchfield's had once been, now believed might have resulted in Eleanor's very existence; Muriel Rosewood had not been with child when her husband had died, nor had there been any sign of it when she'd left India. The timing of the incident certainly suggested that Eleanor could well be Litchfield's daughter...

No, Justin wouldn't trouble Eleanor with any of that until he was sure, beyond any doubt, that Litchfield was, in fact, her biological father. And possibly not even then, either...

He straightened his shoulders. 'The decision has been made and tomorrow morning will be acted upon,' Justin said firmly. 'As such, I will see you at dinner this evening.'

'I—yes. Of course, your Grace—'

'I have repeatedly requested that you not call me that,' he growled.

Silky dark lashes lowered demurely over those expressive green eyes. 'Then perhaps I should consider calling you "Uncle" Justin?'

'Why, you little—!' He did not even bother to finish the sentence as he strode furiously across the room towards her.

Too late, Ellie realised her mistake in goading him, looking up just in time to see him powering towards her, fury blazing in those sapphire-blue eyes, causing her to step back even as she held her hands up defensively. 'Your Gr—er—Sir—Justin—'

'It's too late for that, Eleanor!' His arms moved about her waist as he pulled her in tightly against him, her hands trapped between the softness of her breasts and the muscled hardness of his chest. 'You are fully aware,' he grated, 'my feelings towards you are far from avuncular!'

How could she help but be aware of it when she could feel the evidence of his desire pressing into her abdomen!

Heat suffused her cheeks, her legs starting to tremble, as she looked at his face and saw evidence of that same desire blazing in the depths of the glittering blue eyes glaring down at her, high cheekbones thrown into sharp relief by the tight clenching of his jaw.

'You are crushing me, Your—Justin.' She turned her hands and began to push against the hardness of his chest in an unsuccessful attempt to free herself.

He bared his teeth in a humourless smile. 'And so now you learn, too late, my dear, the lesson that baiting the tiger is much worse than simply awakening him!'

She blinked. 'I was only—I merely—'

'I know exactly what you were doing, Eleanor—and *this* is my answer!' His head swooped downwards as he captured her lips with his own even as he took a step forwards, taking Ellie with him.

She gasped as her legs hit the mattress of the bed and she lost her balance, toppling backwards. Justin swiftly took full advantage of her parted lips in order to deepen the kiss, one of his hands moving to curve possessively about her chin as he followed her down, his heavier weight landing on top of her and crushing her into the mattress.

Ellie was so stunned to find herself lying on her back on the bed, Justin's body pressing intimately against hers, that she no longer fought the onslaught as his lips continued to devour hers. Instead, she felt compelled to return that fever of passion, her arms moving up and over his shoulders to allow her to entangle her fingers in the silky softness of the hair at his nape as she kissed him back.

Quite when his punishing onslaught changed—when Justin's lips became less demanding and instead sipped and tasted her own as he adjusted his position, the hardness of his arousal now pressing against her hip as one of his legs lay between hers, allowing the warmth of his hand to curve about the full softness of her breast—she had no idea.

Nor did she care, as the thrill of arousal coursed through her, causing her breast to swell into the heat of his palm as the soft pad of his thumb sought, and unerringly found, and began to caress, the swollen and sensitive berry pressing against the soft material of her gown.

Ellie felt hot, feverish, her throat arching as he continued to kiss and caress her, moving restlessly against him as she dampened between her thighs, groaning low in her throat, as his knee moved up to press gently against that sensitive nubbin she had recently discovered nestled there, even as his thumb and fingers plucked rhythmically at her now hardened and oh-so-sensitive nipple.

He dragged his lips from hers to trail

kisses hotly across her cheek and down her throat, his breath warm, arousing, against the heat of her flesh, that tingling in her breasts rising to fever pitch as his lips and tongue now tasted the swell visible above her gown and causing another rush of dampness between her thighs.

'Justin!' she cried out achingly as his hand left her breast.

'Yes—Justin,' he growled intensely, his hand sliding up her back. 'Say it, Eleanor. Say it, damn it!'

'Justin,' she breathed obediently. 'Oh God, Justin, Justin, Justin…!' That last trailed off to a groan as she felt his tongue laving the throbbing, engorged tip of her bared breast, having no idea how that had come about, only knowing that it gave her pleasure beyond imagining as he now took that hardened tip fully into the moist heat of his mouth.

Her fingers became entangled in the silkiness of his hair even as she arched up into that demanding mouth, sensations such as she had never known existed coursing through her as she felt his hand now cup her other bared breast, thumb and finger capturing the ripe tip, and causing exquisite pleasure as he continued to caress and then squeeze that tingling, aching fullness.

Justin raised his head slightly, his movement releasing Eleanor's nipple from his mouth with a softly audible pop as he looked down in satisfaction at the swollen berry. The nipple and aureole were coloured a deep rose, the nipple engorged from the ministrations of his mouth and tongue, and continuing to flower as he blew on it gently, his gaze heating as his hand now lifted her breast until that nipple brushed against his lips.

He looked up into Eleanor's face as he slowly ran his tongue skilfully against that responsive berry, groaning low in his throat as he saw she was looking back at him with fevered eyes, several tendrils of her hair having escaped their confines and falling enticingly about the warmth of her cheeks. She looked gloriously, wantonly, beautiful!

And he should stop this now. Should put an end to this before it was too late—

'Justin…?' she moaned even as her fingers tightened in his hair and she arched her back, pushing her nipple between his parted lips and back into the moist heat of his mouth.

All thoughts of stopping fled, his lashes lowering as he obediently suckled deeply, drawing that nipple up to the roof of his mouth, tongue flicking, teeth gently biting, at the same time as his hand caressed a path down to her thighs to her knees, pushing the material of her gown aside so that he might touch the bare, silken flesh beneath.

The backs of her knees held the warmth of velvet, her thighs as smooth as silk, satin drawers posing no difficulty as Justin sought, and found, the slit in that material between her thighs, allowing his fingers to slip inside to gently stroke her swollen, wet folds.

He dipped his fingers into that moisture even as he heard Eleanor's gasp, half in shocked protest, half in pleasure, stroking her again and again, bathing his fingers in that moisture between each stroke, drawing her nipple deeply into his mouth in the same rhythm, until she no longer protested but groaned her pleasure as she writhed beneath him.

Justin was aware of the moment her hands fell down on to the bed beside her in surrender, of her head moving restlessly from side to side on the pillows, and he at last parted the silky folds and bared her sensitive and swollen nubbin to his caressing fingers and began to stroke in earnest. Softly and then harder, each time increasing the pressure, measuring his strokes to the rhythmic lifting of her hips, as she met each and every one of them, until he knew she was poised on the brink of a shattering release.

'Oh, it is too much…!' she gasped in protest, yet at the same time unable to stop herself from arching up into those caresses, her fingers once again entangled tightly in his hair as she held his mouth against her breast. 'Justin, do something…!'

Justin knew he was damned if he did. Damned if he did not. Because, he knew, whether he gave her the release she so obviously craved, or stopped this before that should happen, no doubt leaving her aching and wanting for hours afterwards, that she was never going to forgive him for arousing her to such a pitch that she lost control so completely she begged him for satisfaction.

Ellie had never known such pleasure as this existed. Had never dreamt—never so much as guessed it was there for the taking.

It really was too much, overwhelming even, as Justin turned his attention to her other breast, at the same time as he stroked between her thighs, fingers dipping into her sheath, but never quite entering, those moist fingers then moving higher to stroke the hardened nubbin above.

Such a tiny nubbin of flesh, and one that she had barely been aware of until Justin touched her, and yet it was such pleasure to have him touch her there, stroking her, his fingertip now tapping lightly against it, driving her higher, and then higher still, taking her up to a plateau of exquisite pleasure, before just seconds later she felt herself falling over the edge and down into a sea of never-ending sensations.

Again and again mindless pleasure washed over her, becoming the centre of her existence, all of her senses concentrated on those sensations: the feeling of her sheath as it pulsed and contracted, the fullness of that nubbin as it swelled and throbbed, the pleasure-pain of Justin's lips and teeth capturing each of her nipples in turn, his breath so hot and arousing against her cooler flesh.

Ellie had no idea how long it lasted, how many minutes, hours, had passed as she lost herself to that release as Justin demanded and took every last measure of that pleasure.

But finally, immeasurable minutes later, he gentled those stroking fingers between her thighs, softened his tongue against her now throbbing and aching breasts, placing one last lingering kiss against each swollen tip before he rolled to one side and moved up on his elbow to look down at her. 'I did not hurt you, did I?'

The gruffness of his voice was a thrill in itself as it wound itself sinuously along Ellie's already sensitive nerve-endings. Yet at the same time it broke the sensuous spell she had been under, allowing her to become aware of exactly what she had allowed to happen.

The Duke of Royston had just made love to her, touched her, more pleasurably, more intimately than any man had ever dared to attempt before now. More intimately than Ellie should have allowed any man to touch her before her wedding night!

Something that would never happen for her with the cynically arrogant Justin St Just, who wasn't interested in loving his bride or having those feelings returned. And she had probably just added to that cynicism and arrogance, with her easy capitulation to his seduction!

She scrambled up into a sitting position, blushing as she drew her legs up beneath her defensively, to clutch her gaping gown against her to cover her now painfully aching breasts. It allowed her to see that he was still fully and impeccably dressed, necktie still in place, waistcoat still buttoned, his hair only slightly tousled, from where her fingers had entwined and clutched at that silkiness in the throes of her pleasure, whereas he had obviously remained unmoved throughout!

She drew in a shaky breath. 'I asked you to leave some time ago.'

'Eleanor—'

'Get out!' she instructed firmly as she averted her gaze from his, not wishing to see the disgust that must surely be in his eyes. Or perhaps it would be pity or triumph there and she knew she could not bear to suffer any of those emotions being directed towards her just now.

Dear lord, she was in love with this man. A love she could never, must never, allow him to find out about. It would destroy her utterly.

'Whatever you are thinking, Eleanor, I wish you to stop it this minute!'

Her eyes glittered with unshed tears as she turned back to him. 'Do not tell me what I should or should not think!' she flared, falling back upon anger to hide her real emotions.

His eyes narrowed. 'I could have stopped, should have stopped—indeed, I had thought of doing so—but you would not have thanked me for it if I had—'

'I am not thanking you now!'

'No,' he accepted heavily before standing up and looking down at her bleakly. 'Eleanor—'

'You "could have stopped"? You "thought of doing so"?' Ellie's voice rose indignantly as she realised what he had just said, knowing that she'd had no will to call a halt, no strength to resist his caresses. But he had. Oh, yes, the arrogant Duke of Royston had remained completely in control of his own senses, whilst her feelings for him meant that she had melted at his first touch. How humiliating. 'I told you to leave,' she repeated woodenly.

'Eleanor, listen to me, damn it!' He frowned down at her in frustration. 'If I had stopped you would now be berating me for leaving you in a state of dissatisfaction that would have clawed at you for hours, instead of which—'

'Instead of which I can now claim to have been the latest recipient of the irresistible

Duke of Royston's expert lovemaking!' she threw back.

He drew in a sharp breath. 'I refuse to take offence at your insults. I realise that you are...upset.' He ran agitated hands through his hair, those golden waves instantly falling back into their artfully dishevelled style. As if he had made the gesture a hundred times before and knew its effect. After making love to a hundred different women, no doubt!

It infuriated Ellie all over again to know that she was nothing more to this man than another notch on his bedpost. 'Oh, by all means take offence,' she invited scathingly. 'For, I assure you, I am not so upset that I do not know exactly what I am saying when I warn you never to touch me ever again!'

'We will talk of this when you are calmer—'

'No, we will not,' she insisted firmly.

Too late, Justin realised the seriousness of the error he had made. Damn it, he was a man known for his icy control. A man who maintained his calm no matter what the provocation. A legendary control that had come about because of those lonely childhood years when he had felt the pain of his parents' exclusion and which he had eventually only been able to live with by learning and adopting that coolness of temperament for which he was now so well known. But Justin knew, had always known, that deep inside himself lay something else entirely, a heat, a quickness of emotions which he had no control over whatsoever. And it seemed Eleanor brought out that heat in him when no one else had managed it.

Tonight, with her, his control had been totally stripped away, his emotions so totally engaged in their lovemaking that his claim of thinking of stopping was an empty one. The unpalatable truth was, he could not have stopped kissing, caressing and making love to Eleanor if the devil himself had been at his back. That he had wanted, *ached,* to give her pleasure, as much as he had wanted to feel and see her in the throes of it, just because he had given it to her.

He sighed. 'It is a little naïve of you to expect us never to refer to this incident again—' He broke off as she gave a bitter laugh.

'Thanks to you I am no longer in the least naïve!'

'Oh, yes, Eleanor, in all the ways that matter you are still very much an innocent,' Justin argued, hands clenching into fists at his sides. 'Nor have we done anything this evening that in the least damages that innocence, or your reputation in society.'

She looked at him wordlessly for several long seconds before giving a slow shake of her head. 'I have little or no regard for my reputation in society, sir, but my innocence is certainly now questionable.'

'No—'

'Yes,' she hissed. 'You, of all people, must know that I had no idea—no knowledge of—' She stopped and gathered herself. 'My maidenhead may indeed still be intact, but my innocence is not.' Her cheeks were flushed. 'Now, would you please, please leave me.' Her voice finally wavered emotionally, the over-bright glitter in her eyes confirming that she was on the edge of tears.

Tears, which Justin knew with a certainty, she would not wish him to see fall. 'I trust you understand how impossible it is for me to even attempt to explain to my grandmother why I have changed my mind about moving into Royston House?'

Eleanor's shoulders straightened proudly. 'I understand. Just as I am sure that the two of us are adult enough, and both have enough affection for the dowager duchess, if not for each other, to do everything in our power to be polite to one another whenever we are in her company or that of others.'

Telling Justin, more surely than anything else could have done, that Eleanor had no intention of being in the least polite to him when they were alone…

He breathed out his frustration. 'Perhaps if you had listened to me when I advised you not to bait the tiger—'

'Are you saying,' Ellie interrupted with deceptive softness, 'that you consider this as being just "another lesson" you felt the need to demonstrate?'

He was taken aback. 'No, I am merely— Eleanor, put down that cup!' he instructed sharply as she turned to grab it up from its saucer. 'Eleanor!'

She did not so much as hesitate, drawing back her arm and launching the china cup across the bedchamber towards his arrogant head. Only to be thoroughly frustrated in that endeavour when he ducked at the last moment, allowing the cup to hit and smash against the door behind him.

He straightened, his face thunderous. 'My grandmother is very fond of those cups—'

Determined not to be thwarted, Ellie immediately took up the saucer and threw that at him too, succeeding in giving him a glancing blow on the side of his arrogant head, at the same time as it dishevelled the fashionably styled hair that had so annoyed her just minutes ago. 'How pleasant it is to know that my years of playing cricket with the local village children were not in vain!' She smiled her satisfaction with her accuracy.

'You are nothing but a damned hellion!' Justin winced as he raised a hand to gently probe the spot where the saucer had hit him. 'By all that's holy, you deserve to have your backside soundly smacked!'

'Lay so much as a finger more on me this evening, your Grace, and I assure you, I will scream until all the household comes running!' Ellie warned him with icy pride; she might have allowed herself to be seduced by her feelings for this man, but that did not mean he would ever know of them.

He straightened, eyes glittering. 'This is far from over, Eleanor.'

'Oh, but it is,' she insisted. 'There will be no more "lessons" for me from you tonight. Or, indeed, any other night! Now please leave my bedchamber.' She turned her face away to indicate an end to the conversation, her heart pounding in her chest as she waited to see if Justin would do as she asked. Having no idea what she would do if he did not!

There was deathly silence for several minutes, then Ellie heard the opening of the door, before it was gently closed again seconds later.

At which time she allowed the tears to fall as she began to cry as if her heart were breaking.

Which it was.

Chapter Eleven

'Is this a bad time, Royston...?'

Justin arched a brow as he looked up at the man standing in front of him, stirring himself to sit up from his slouched position in his chair beside one of the unlit fireplaces at White's, as he recognised Lord Adam Hawthorne, the grandson of one of his grandmother's dearest friends.

And there had not been so much as a single 'good time' for anyone to approach and speak to Justin over the past three days, not since the evening he had made love with Eleanor and she had then so soundly routed him from her bedchamber.

Three days when he and Eleanor had, as agreed, maintained a perfectly civil, if stilted, front whenever they were in the company of his grandmother. Away from the old lady's curious, shrewd gaze it was a different matter entirely; Eleanor avoided his company whenever she could, spending hours in another part of the house from him when she was at home, and other times out visiting, accompanied by her maid or the dowager. And, without Eleanor being aware of it, one of the footmen from Royston House, as extra protection from the threat Justin now considered Litchfield to be.

Not that Justin could blame Eleanor for that avoidance. No, despite that bump on his head from the blow of the saucer, and the headache that had followed, she was not the one to blame for the strain which now existed between them. The blame for that clearly lay entirely on Justin's own shoulders. He had fully deserved her anger, her physical retribution, had seriously overstepped a line with her. One Justin, even with his nine more years of maturity and experience, had absolutely no idea how to cross back over. Eleanor's frosty demeanour towards him certainly gave him the clear impression she had no wish for him to even try healing the breach between them!

Justin had spent the same three days trying to ascertain more about the events of twenty years ago, where Muriel Rosewood had gone to live once she returned to England, and what had become of her. Something which, without the help of Muriel herself, was not proving as easy as Justin had hoped it might. Many of the soldiers who had been in India at the same time as Litchfield, but later also returned to England, had died during the battles against Napoleon, and their widows, or the soldiers who had survived, were scattered all over England.

The Rosewood family had proved most unhelpful, too, the note of query Justin had delivered to their London home having only returned the information that they knew absolutely nothing about Henry's widow, none of the family having so much as set eyes on her again after Henry's death. And the widow's allowance, paid to her by the family lawyer on behalf of the estate, had ceased the day she had married Frederick, severing all ties with that family.

Except for Eleanor…whom the Rosewoods seemed to have no knowledge of whatsoever. As further proof that she was definitely not Henry's child?

The only other way of finding an answer as to where Muriel had settled on her return to England from India, would have been to question Eleanor about her childhood before her mother had married his cousin Frederick.

There were two very good reasons why Justin had not done so; for one, Eleanor was barely speaking to him any more, and secondly, he was trying to avoid telling her about any of this for as long as possible. There was, after all, still the possibility that Richmond could be completely wrong about this whole situation.

And yet, he mused, the coincidence of the earl's concerns, coming so quickly on the heels of his grandmother's request for Justin to try to discover who Eleanor's real father was, as well as the Rosewood family's lack of knowledge of Eleanor's very existence, made that highly unlikely.

'It would appear that it is,' Hawthorne commented ruefully at Justin's lack of reply to his query. 'Sorry to have disturbed your reverie, Royston.' He turned to leave.

'No! No, really, Thorne,' Justin repeated wearily as the other man turned to arch one dark, questioning brow. 'Please, do excuse my rudeness and join me, by all means.' He indicated the chair on the opposite side of the fireplace.

The same age as Justin, Adam Hawthorne had never been a particular friend of his until recently, despite their grandmothers' lifelong friendship. But the two men had been involved together in a matter personal to Hawthorne just weeks ago. One, which, thankfully, had been resolved in a manner most satisfactory to Hawthorne and the woman to whom he was now betrothed.

Justin waited until the other man was seated before speaking again. 'Was there something in particular you wished to discuss with me?'

'As it happens, yes.' Hawthorne, known in the past for his taciturn and prickly nature, hence the reasoning for that shortened version of his surname, now gave a boyish grin. 'You are aware, no doubt, of my upcoming nuptials…?'

'Oh, yes.' Justin rolled his eyes. It was the announcement of Hawthorne's betrothal, and forthcoming marriage, which had caused Edith to renew even more strongly her urgings that it was past time he chose a bride for himself.

Hawthorne gave a sympathetic smile. 'The dowager still proving difficult?'

'Well, your betrothal has certainly not helped my own desire not to marry as yet!' Justin admitted.

'I would imagine not.' Hawthorne laughed. 'I hear that you have once again taken up residence at Royston House.'

'Yes.' No need for Justin to ask from whom the other man had heard that snippet of information; the dowager duchess and Lady Cicely, along with Lady Jocelyn Ambrose, were, and always had been, as thick as thieves!

'My grandmother mentioned how happy it has made the dowager duchess,' Hawthorne confirmed Justin's surmise.

Happy did not even begin to describe Edith's jubilation in having Justin living with her at Royston House. Indeed, the dowager was so contented with the arrangement that her health seemed to have improved exponentially, to a degree that there had been no need for any further calls to Dr Franklyn.

A fact which relieved Justin tremendously. Although he couldn't help being a touch suspicious of this rapid improvement in her health...

Cynical of him, perhaps even egotistical, but Justin found he could not help but wonder if the dowager's recent ill health had been yet another ruse on her part, one that had succeeded in his agreement to reside at Royston House, at least, and as such put him another step closer to the idea of matrimony?

It would please him, of course, to know that his grandmother's health was not as precarious as she had given him the impression it was, but it would irritate him immensely if he were to learn that he had fallen victim to her wily machinations.

Except Justin knew he wasn't living with her solely out of concern for her health, that it was also concern for Eleanor—which she would likely not appreciate if she knew of it—that had been the main factor in his decision. He was only too well aware now of Litchfield's viciousness of nature, which in turn made Eleanor, and Justin's grandmother, both prime targets if the earl should decide to act upon that viciousness.

'Royston…?'

Justin gave himself a mental shake as he returned his attention to Hawthorne. 'You mentioned your upcoming nuptials…?'

The other man nodded. 'You have made

quite an impression on my darling Magdelena, you know.'

'Indeed?' He eyed the other man warily; Miss Matthews was a beautiful and charming young woman, and he had been pleased to assist Hawthorne in freeing her of the devil who had been so determined to ruin her life, but other than that he had no personal interest in her, and if Hawthorne thought otherwise—

'So much so,' Hawthorne continued, 'that she will hear of nothing less than that you stand as one of the witnesses at our wedding.'

'Me?' Justin could not have been more shocked if Hawthorne had invited him to dance naked at Almack's!

Hawthorne's eyes gleamed with devilish laughter. 'I realise how unpleasant that task must be to one as opposed to matrimony as you are, but Magdelena is set upon the idea.' And he was obviously a man so much in love with his future bride that he would allow nothing and no one to deny her smallest desire.

Ordinarily Justin would have found it repugnant to witness such a change in character as he had seen in Hawthorne since he had fallen in love with Miss Matthews. But, for some inexplicable reason, Justin now found his main emotion to be curiosity.

An unhappy first marriage had soured Hawthorne to repeating the experience. Until he had met and fallen in love with Magdelena Matthews, an occurrence which Hawthorne did not at all seem to regret. Indeed, the very opposite was true; Justin had never seen the other man look happier than he had these past few weeks.

Where were Hawthorne's feelings of resentment at the thought of conceding his freedom? Of being led about by his nose and his manhood for the next forty years? Of the possibility, unless he took a mistress, of sharing his bed with the same woman for decades? Also, Hawthorne had a young daughter from his first marriage—had he thought of her welfare in all of this—?

'Magdelena and your ward, Miss Rosewood, have become such fast friends these past few days.'

Justin straightened abruptly as he realised he had once again allowed himself to become so distracted by his own thoughts, he had not been paying attention to Hawthorne's conversation. 'Did you say Miss Matthews and Eleanor are now friends?'

The other man nodded. 'They have become inseparable since the night of the Royston Ball.'

Which explained why Eleanor had been accompanying the dowager on her visits to Lady Cicely's home recently, as Miss Matthews was residing with Lady Cicely until after the wedding.

'Indeed,' Hawthorne continued, 'the two of them are out together now, in the company of our mutual grandmothers, deciding upon material for Magdelena's wedding gown.'

Damn it, it appeared that Hawthorne knew more about Eleanor's movements than he did! Which, given the circumstances of her complete aversion to his own company, was not so surprising…but was incredibly galling.

'My young daughter, Amanda, who is to be a bridesmaid, is also with them,' Hawthorne relaxed back in his chair. 'A great concession on her part, believe me, as she would much rather be in the stable with her pony than shopping for dresses. I believe it was her deep affection for Magdelena and Magdelena's for her—and, of course, the

bribe of calling at Gunter's for ice-cream,
once the unpleasant task has been completed—which went a long way towards convincing Amanda otherwise!'

So it seemed that Hawthorne's daughter
from his first marriage had not been in the
least excluded from her father's happiness
in his forthcoming marriage. Or, quite obviously, the time and affections of her future
stepmother.

Hawthorne quirked a questioning brow.
'Why are you looking at me so strangely?'

Justin's jaw tightened; he had not realised
he was being so obvious. 'You appear—' He
stopped, gave a wave of his hand and then
tried again. 'You actually seem to be happily anticipating remarrying, Hawthorne.'

The other man grinned. 'Incredible, is it
not, considering our conversation on the subject just weeks prior to the announcement of
my betrothal?'

A conversation in which both men had
voiced their aversion to entering into the
married state—Hawthorne ever again, Justin until some distant time when he could no
longer avoid his duty of providing the heir—
both men bemoaning their grandmothers'

machinations in trying to bring that unhappy event about for them.

'Perhaps we are all to receive news of another betrothal quite soon…?' Hawthorne suggested.

Justin stiffened warily. 'What on earth do you mean?' Close as Eleanor's friendship with Miss Matthews was purported to be, he could not imagine Eleanor confiding their lovemaking to the other woman. And even if she had, Eleanor's aversion to his company did not in the least give him the impression that she hoped there would be more of the same, or that it would eventually lead to a proposal of marriage. The opposite, in fact! It was—

'I am referring to Endicott and Miss Rosewood, of course.' Hawthorne eyed him curiously.

Lord Charles Endicott and Eleanor?

That young pup Charles Endicott and *Eleanor!*

What the devil was going on? He almost couldn't think straight as lights seemed to explode behind his eyes.

'It would be considered a good match for your young ward,' Hawthorne continued conversationally, seemingly unaware of

Justin's sudden turmoil of emotions. 'Endicott is both wealthy and second in line to a dukedom.'

Admittedly, Endicott was indeed as Hawthorne described, and at two and twenty, he was also considered charming and handsome by those society mamas looking for a suitable and wealthy son-in-law. But as far as Justin was aware Eleanor had only met the other man once, on the evening of the Royston Ball, when she stood up to dance a single set with him. Of course, he had noted that one of those dozens of bouquets of flowers, delivered the day after the ball, could have been sent from Endicott, but even so...

Justin gave a decisive shake of his head. 'I have no idea how you have hit upon such a misconception, Hawthorne, but I assure you that Eleanor does not have any such ambitions where Endicott is concerned.'

'Oh?' Hawthorne looked surprised. 'In that case, perhaps it might be kinder if she were to discourage his attentions, rather than appearing as if she enjoyed them.'

Justin looked confused. 'I have absolutely no idea what the devil you are talking about!'

The other man gave him a speculative

glance before replying slowly, 'No, apparently you do not...'

'What do you think, Ellie?' Miss Magdelena Matthews prompted as their party stood outside Gunter's confectioner's shop in Berkeley Square. 'Was that not the most delicious ice-cream you have ever tasted?'

Ellie returned the smile. 'Most certainly.' It was also the only ice-cream she had ever eaten; there had been no money for such extravagance as this during her childhood and she had never been to London during her years as Lord Frederick's stepdaughter, nor had there been the time, or the money, to indulge in such things since she had become companion to Edith St Just.

But Ellie had hoped—willed herself—to give every appearance of enjoying herself, as she conversed and smiled and ate her ice-cream with the others in their party, the enchanting Miss Amanda Hawthorne having most especially enjoyed the latter treat.

Yes, outwardly, Ellie felt sure she gave the impression of happiness and contentment. Inwardly, it was another matter, however...

This past three days, since the evening of her error in allowing Justin to make love to her in her bedchamber, and realising she was in totally and futilely in love with him, despite his behaviour, had been nothing short of hellish, made more so by the fact that the duke now also lived with her.

As arranged, he had duly arrived at ten o'clock the following morning, his entourage of valet and private secretary in tow, the former arranging for the excess of luggage to be placed in the ducal chambers situated at the front of the house—well away, thank goodness, from Ellie and the dowager duchess' apartments at the back of the house—whilst the latter took over the study and library for the duke's personal use.

Edith St Just, as predicted, had been beside herself with joy at this turn of events. Indeed, the dowager had been flushed with excitement ever since, thankfully showing no sign of the illness or fatigue that had previously plagued her, as she happily reorganised the household to fit around the duke's daily schedule.

Ellie had been far from joyous. In fact, she had hoped, once Justin had time to consider the matter following the incident in her bedchamber, that he would have sensitivity enough to find a way in which to delay—indefinitely!—his plans to move in.

She should have realised that would be expecting too much from a man who obviously cared for nothing and no one, other than his grandmother's comfort and, of course, his own!

Ellie was therefore left with no choice but to absent herself from Royston House as much as possible. Something that had proved only too easy to do when the invitations, to theatre parties, dances and assemblies, and alfresco dining, had flooded in following her success at the Royston Ball. And, too, she had developed a deep friendship with Magdelena Matthews, the two of them finding they had much in common as they talked together whilst the dowager was visiting with her dear friend Lady Cicely.

Indeed, if not for Justin's depressingly broody presence at Royston House, and her unrequited love for him, Ellie knew she would have enjoyed her change in circumstances immensely.

Indeed, she was determined she *would* enjoy herself, in spite of the brooding, distracting Duke of Royston!

She turned to smile at the young, handsome gentleman standing beside her. 'How fortuitous that we should meet you here today, my lord.'

Lord Charles Endicott gave a boyish grin. 'Not so much, when you consider that I overheard you and Miss Matthews discussing the outing when I chanced upon you during your walk in the park yesterday.'

'That was very naughty of you!' She laughed merrily.

His eyes warmed with admiration for her appearance in a gown of pale green with matching bonnet. 'A man has no shame when he is in pursuit of a woman!'

She raised auburn brows. 'And are you pursuing me, my lord?'

'Doing my damnedest, yes.' He nodded, a gentleman aged in his early twenties, with fashionably styled dark hair and flirtatious brown eyes set in that boyishly handsome face. 'Excuse my language, if you please,' he added awkwardly.

'I find your remark too flattering to be in the least offended,' Ellie assured with another chuckle; Lord Endicott was perhaps a little too much of a dandy in his dress for her tastes, but otherwise she found his company to be both pleasant and uncomplicated. Unlike another certain gentleman she could name!

'Will you be attending Lady Littleton's musical soirée this evening?' he enquired eagerly. 'If so, might I be permitted to—?'

'My ward plans to spend this evening at home, Endicott,' a cold voice cut repressively across their conversation.

A voice Ellie recognised only too easily.

As indeed did the others in her group as they all turned in unison to look at him, the dowager with some surprise, Lady Cecil and Miss Matthews with some considerable curiosity.

Ellie took a moment to straighten her spine—and her resolve—before she also turned to look at him, instantly aware that neither her straightened spine or her resolve were sufficient for her to withstand the icy blast of his glittering blue gaze as it swept over her before alighting on the hapless Lord Charles Endicott, as that young gentleman bowed to the older man.

Lord Endicott was a picture of dandified elegance in his superfine of pale blue and waistcoat of pastel pink, the collar of his shirt uncomfortably high, neckcloth intricately tied at his throat, and giving him all the appearance of a posturing peacock when placed next to Justin's sartorial elegance, in grey superfine, charcoal-coloured waistcoat and snowy white linen.

Although possibly only half a dozen years separated the two men, they were as different as day and night, the one so bright and colourful, the other a study of dark shadows.

Ellie bristled defensively as she saw the contemptuous curl of the duke's top lip, and the scathing amusement in his gaze, as he also took in the other man's foppish appearance. 'I believe you are mistaken in that, your Grace.' She refused to so much as blink or lower her gaze as he raised one haughty brow in question. 'I am certain her Grace will concur that we have accepted Lady Littleton's invitation for her soirée this evening.'

'Then you, at least, will have to unaccept it,' Justin informed her implacably.

Her eyes widened. 'And why should I wish to do that?'

He looked down the length of his arrogant nose at her. 'You are looking tired, no doubt from all the gadding about you have indulged in recently, and an evening at home will be far more beneficial to you than another evening out.'

Telling Ellie more succinctly, than if he had spoken the words aloud, that—despite the deliberate brightness of her gown and her efforts to give the appearance of being both contented and happy—he did not consider her to be looking her best!

As if she was not already aware of that. As if she was not also aware at whose highly polished, booted feet the blame for that lay!

Her last few days had been filled with a flurry of engagements, in an effort to keep busy and at the same time absent herself from Royston House. Her nights had been…restless and sleepless, to say the least, caught as she was in the puzzling dichotomy of deeply regretting that the intimacies she had shared with Justin had ever happened, and the quivers of pleasure, the love for him, which still coursed through her each and every time she thought of what they had done together!

Nevertheless, she did not welcome him bringing attention to her fatigue, or even in mentioning it at all! 'I have no intentions of cancelling attending Lady Littleton's soirée this evening.'

'Oh, I believe that you will,' the duke answered softly, dangerously, as their gazes remained locked, his challenging, Eleanor's defiant.

'No.'

'Yes!'

'Royston?' the dowager duchess prompted sharply at this public battle of wills.

It had not been Justin's intention to leave the carriage when he had instructed his driver to return to Royston House by way of Berkeley Square, but a single glance towards the establishment known as Gunter's had revealed Eleanor and his grandmother to be standing outside, in the company of the female members of Hawthorne's family.

And that blasted Endicott fellow!

Justin had not given himself time to think as he instructed his driver to stop, barely allowing his carriage to come to a halt before jumping out on to the cobbled road and marching towards where the happy group lingered in conversation.

Just in time, it would seem, to prevent Eleanor from making yet another assignation with Endicott, for later this evening!

Chapter Twelve

⁓⁓⁓⁓

'I trust you will forgive me for intruding on your outing, ladies.' Justin chose to ignore Eleanor's furious glare for the moment as he turned to bestow a charming smile upon the other ladies gathered outside Gunter's.

His grandmother was predictably frowning her disapproval of his behaviour, Lady Cicely and Miss Matthews gazed at him with polite curiosity and Miss Amanda Hawthorne, a beautiful little angel with golden-blonde curls, still bore evidence of her recently eaten ice-cream about her little rosebud of a happily smiling mouth.

'I happened to be passing by in my carriage,' Justin continued lightly, 'and could not help but notice you all standing here in conversation. It would have been rude of me to just drive past without stopping to pay my respects.' He made a polite bow.

A gesture of politeness that was immediately answered by his grandmother's loud and disgusted 'humph'! 'That is all very well, Royston,' she snapped. 'But what is your reason for denying Elli—Eleanor the pleasure of going to Lady Littleton's soirée this evening?'

It had been Justin's experience that such evenings were both tedious and tiresome, rather than a pleasure! 'As I have already stated, Grandmama—' he maintained a pleasant, reasoning tone '—Eleanor looks somewhat fatigued and I simply feel that an evening at home resting would be more beneficial to her health than another night out.'

'I—'

'You must forgive me, Eleanor, I had not noticed before now,' the dowager duchess spoke over Eleanor's angry protest, 'but Royston is right; you are indeed looking slightly pale and fatigued this afternoon.'

'There.' Justin turned to Eleanor, triumph glittering in his eyes. 'I do not believe the dowager and I can both be wrong?'

Ellie narrowed her eyes on her tormentor's

gaze, dearly wishing that the two of them were alone at this moment—so that she might launch another cup and saucer at his arrogant head! Or a heavy tome. Or perhaps something even deadlier than that! For she did not believe a word of what he had just said, from his 'having just been passing by' in his carriage to his obviously fake concern about her supposed 'fatigue'.

Considering the size of the city, and the numerous other pursuits the duke could have been enjoying today, it seemed far too coincidental that he should have been 'driving past' Gunter's at this precise moment. Nor did Ellie believe the duke had ever given a single thought about the state of her health, this day or any other.

No, Ellie was utterly convinced that Justin was merely determined to once again exercise his steely will upon her. As determined as she was that he would not succeed in that endeavour!

She smiled up at him now with sugary and insincere sweetness, a smile that instantly caused him to narrow his own eyes in suspicion. 'I agree the dowager is never wrong, your Grace,' she conceded lightly— at the same time implying that he, on the other hand, did not have that same distinction. 'But in this instance she is misinformed. I feel perfectly well and am greatly looking forward to attending Lady Littleton's soirée with her this evening.'

His mouth thinned. 'And I would rather you did not.'

'I have noted your objection, your Grace.' She nodded.

'But choose to ignore it?'

'Yes.' It was as if they were the only two present, so intense was their current battle of wills.

Something Justin was also aware of as his mouth tightened. 'Perhaps we should leave these dear ladies to their shopping and continue this conversation in my carriage?' he suggested through gritted teeth.

Her chin rose. 'I believe we had finished shopping, your Grace, and are now returning to have tea with Lady Cicely.'

Nostrils flared on that aquiline nose. '*We* are leaving now, Eleanor.'

'Oh, I say—'

'Did you have something you wished to add to this conversation, Endicott?' Cold blue eyes focused with deadly intent on the younger man at his interruption.

Ellie could not help but feel sorry for Charles Endicott at that moment, his face first suffusing with embarrassed colour, and then as quickly paling, as Justin continued to glower down at him, appearing every inch the powerful and haughty Duke of Royston; it was like watching a fluffy little lapdog being confronted by a ferocious wolfhound. Indeed, Ellie would not have been in the least surprised if the duke's top lip had not curled back in a snarl to bare a long and pointed incisor at the younger man!

'Perhaps it would be as well if you were to return with Royston, Eleanor.' The dowager duchess, ever sensitive to not causing a scene in public—unlike her arrogant grandson!— agreed smoothly. 'I am perfectly happy to go alone to Lady Cicely's.'

Ellie was bursting with indignation at Justin's high-handedness, longing to tell him exactly what he could do with his offer to drive her home in his carriage—which had not been an offer at all but an instruction! At the same time she knew she could not, would not, do or say anything which might upset the dowager duchess; she owed that dear lady too much to ever wish to cause her embarrassment—the very clothes she stood up in, in fact!

'Then we are all agreed.' The duke took a firm hold of Ellie's arm. 'Ladies.' He bowed to them politely. 'Endicott.' His voice had cooled noticeably, eyes once again icy blue as he scowled at the younger man.

Charles Endicott was the first to lower his gaze. 'Your Grace,' he mumbled indistinctly before his expression brightened as he turned to Ellie. 'If you are not to be at Lady Littleton's this evening, perhaps I might call upon you tomorrow—'

'My ward is otherwise engaged tomorrow, Endicott.' To Ellie's ever-increasing annoyance, it was once again Justin who answered the other man glacially. 'And the day following that one, too,' he added for good measure.

The younger man frowned. 'But surely—'

'Come along, Eleanor.' The duke did not wait for her to agree or disagree, allowing her time only to sketch a brief curtsy as her own goodbye before turning on one booted heel and walking in the direction of his waiting carriage, Ellie pulled along in his wake.

She had never felt so humiliated, so—so manhandled and managed in her life before, as she did at this moment. And by Justin St Just, of all people.

But who else would dare to treat someone—anyone!—with such overriding arrogance *but* the arrogantly insufferable Duke of Royston!

He—

'You may give vent to your feelings now, Eleanor, for we are quite alone.'

The haze of red anger shifted from in front of Ellie's eyes at this mockingly drawled comment, enabling her to realise that she had been so consumed with that fury she had allowed herself to be put into his carriage, the door having already been closed to shut them inside.

It was the first time Ellie had been completely alone with him since—well, since 'that night', as she had taken to referring to it in her mind. And to her chagrin she was instantly, achingly aware, of everything about him. The golden sweep of his hair, the glitter of deep-blue eyes set in that hard and chiselled face, the way the superb cut of his superfine emphasised the width of his shoulders and tapered waist, his legs long and powerful in pale grey pantaloons and black Hessians.

Her feelings for him also made her aware

of the tingle of sensations which now coursed through her own body, her breasts feeling achingly sensitive, that now familiar warmth between her thighs.

A reaction which only increased her growing anger towards him…

Justin did not need to look at Eleanor's face to know that she was furious with him; he could feel the heat of that anger as her eyes shot daggers across the short distance of the carriage that separated them.

Justifiably so, perhaps. He had behaved badly just now. Very badly. Towards both Eleanor and Endicott. A fact his grandmother would no doubt bring him to task over at her earliest opportunity.

And yet Justin did not regret his actions. Not for a moment. He had been incensed from the first moment he had seen that young dandy Endicott made up one of his grandmother's party. To add insult to injury, his first glimpse of Eleanor, as bright as a butterfly in her gown of pale green, had been as she was laughing at something that young popinjay had just said to her.

Justin's mouth tightened as he thought of the scowls or blank looks *he* had received from her over the past few days! 'If you have something you wish to say, then for God's sake say it now and get it over with!'

'*If* I have something to say?' she repeated incredulously. 'I—it—you, sir, have the manners of a guttersnipe!'

'It would seem that today I have, yes.' His mouth twisted into a humourless and unapologetic smile. 'And if you intend to insult me, Eleanor, then you will have to do better than that.'

'You are the most insufferable, obnoxious *bully* it has ever been my misfortune to meet!' she hissed angrily, obviously warming to the subject, her cheeks also heating, those green eyes glittering across at him like twin emeralds.

His lips thinned. 'Because I prevented you from embarrassing yourself?'

She gasped. 'I do not believe I was the one causing any embarrassment!'

'I disagree.'

'I—you—in what way was I embarrassing myself?' she finally managed to gasp through her indignation.

'By your flirtation with Endicott.'

'*What?*'

'But of course.' Justin flicked an imagi-

nary piece of lint from the cuff of his superfine. 'And, as I will never give my permission
for you to marry that young peacock, you
might just as well give it up now and cease
your encouragement of him.'

'I was *not* encouraging him—'

'I beg to differ,' he cut in harshly. 'And it is
not only I who appears to think so,' he continued as she would have made another protest. 'Indeed, the society gossips have it that
there will be an announcement made before
the end of the Season!'

Her eyes widened. 'I beg your pardon?'

Justin shrugged. 'The two of you are currently the talk of the *ton*.'

She gave another gasp. 'But I have only
spoken to Lord Endicott on three occasions,
once at the Royston Ball, again at a dinner
party the evening before last, and then again
at the park yesterday in the company of Miss
Matthews.'

'And again just now,' he reminded her.
'That would appear to be four occasions in
four days.'

'Well. Yes. But—I had no idea we would
even be seeing Lord Endicott today!'

That was something, at least; Justin had
been sure the two of them must have pre-

arranged this latest meeting. 'I doubt Endicott's presence at Gunter's was as innocent as your own.'

A blush coloured her cheeks. 'He did mention something about having overheard Magdelena and I discussing the outing yesterday. Do *you* believe that Lord Endicott has serious intentions towards me?' she asked.

'Yes.'

She looked nonplussed by the starkness of his statement. 'Oh…'

Justin's mouth compressed. 'Indeed.'

She swallowed. 'But even so—surely the *ton* cannot seriously have made such an assumption on but a few days' acquaintance?'

Justin felt a stab of remorse for the bewildered expression on Eleanor's face; her eyes were wide green pools of disbelief, her cheeks having paled, her lips slightly parted and unsmiling.

All come about, he now realised with horror, because he had taken exception to being described as a bully. Even if, in this particular case, he had most certainly behaved as one. But only for her own good, he reassured himself determinedly. If Hawthorne, a man who cared nought for the gossip of the *ton,* for society itself, had been led to believe Eleanor was seriously interested in Endicott, then the rest of society must believe it too.

Justin sat forwards on the seat to reach across and take one of Eleanor's tightly clenched hands into both of his. 'The *ton* has made such assumptions on far less, I assure you, my dear,' he murmured in a more placating tone of voice.

She looked up at him curiously. 'You sound as if you speak from personal experience.'

His mouth tightened. 'It is your own reputation that is currently in jeopardy; I accepted long ago, and you confirmed it three days ago, that my own reputation is considered beyond redemption!'

Ellie looked thoughtful. The gentlemen in society appeared to either admire or fear the Duke of Royston. The ladies, married or otherwise, to desire him. The young débutantes considered him as being the catch of the Season—any Season this past ten years or so! The mothers of those débutantes appeared to either covet or avoid coming to his attention, aware as they were that the Duke of Royston had successfully avoided the parson's mousetrap for a long time; it would be a feather in any society matron's bonnet to acquire the Duke of Royston as her son-in-law, but equally it could be the social ruin of her daughter if he were to offer that young lady a liaison rather than marriage.

As such, Ellie had no idea who would have dared to make remarks about her to him. About herself and *Lord Endicott,* of all people. Why, she considered that young man as being nothing more than an amusing and playful puppy. Oh, he was handsome in a boyish way, and pleasant enough—if one ignored his atrocious taste in clothes—but her feelings for Royston meant she did not, and never would, consider Lord Endicott as being anything more than a friend. That anyone should ever imagine she might seriously consider *marrying* the foppish boy, was utterly ludicrous!

That Justin should believe such nonsense she found hurtful beyond belief. How could she possibly be interested in any other man, when Justin himself had ruined her for all others?

And Eleanor did not mean her reputation.

No, her ruination was much more fundamental than that, in that she simply could not imagine ever wishing to share such intimacies with any other man but the one she had finally accepted she was in love with.

She had done everything she could to keep herself busy since that evening, and as such give herself little time for thought. And she had endeavoured to see as little of the duke as possible, considering they now shared the same residence. But there had been no denying the barrage of memories that plagued and tortured her once she was alone in her bed at night. No way then of ignoring how her nipples pebbled into aroused hardness and between her thighs dampened, swelled, just remembering the way Justin had kissed her and touched her there.

With those memories to haunt her, how could anyone, least of all Justin himself, ever believe she had serious intentions in regard to a dandy like Charles Endicott?

Her lashes lowered again as she looked down to where Justin's hands now held one of hers in his grasp. Those same hands had touched her so intimately, caressed and stroked her to a peak of such physical pleasure it still made her toes curl to even think of it.

A reaction she did not wish him to ever become aware of, let alone find out that she was in love with him. That would be a humiliation beyond bearing.

Ellie drew in a steadying breath as she raised her head, smiling slightly as she deftly removed her hand from his. 'It is all nonsense, of course, but how exciting to think that I might soon receive my first proposal of marriage!'

Arrogant brows arched. 'Your *first* proposal…?'

'But of course.' Her smile widened deliberately at his obvious astonishment. 'The dowager has informed me that a young lady can only really consider herself a complete success in society once she has broken at least half-a-dozen hearts and received and refused her third proposal!'

The duke's back straightened, his expression suddenly grim. 'I sincerely trust, just because of our recent interlude, you are not considering counting my own heart as among the ones which you have broken?'

Ellie forced an incredulous laugh to cover the jolt she felt at hearing Justin refer so dismissively to their lovemaking. 'I believe the only thing broken on that particular evening was a cup and saucer, your Grace. Besides,' she continued evenly, 'surely one has to be in possession of a heart for it to be broken?'

'So you do not believe I have one?'

She raised auburn brows. 'Are you not the one who once stated he has no intention of ever falling in love?'

His nostrils flared. 'I believe what I actually said was that I have no intention of being in love with my wife. But,' he continued drily as she would have spoken, 'you are actually correct. The truth is, I have no intention of falling in love with any woman.'

'Why not?' Ellie could have bitten out her tongue the moment she allowed her curiosity to get the better of her. And yet a single glance at his closed expression stopped her from instantly retracting the question.

But it *was* a curiosity that a man such as he, a man who could have any woman he wished for, had decided—no, refused, to fall in love with any of them. 'Well?' she prompted as he made no reply.

His lips quirked. 'Perhaps it is that I have observed too many of my friends succumb to the emotion, and prefer not to behave in the same ridiculous manner? It surely makes a man far too vulnerable.'

It was both a glib and insulting answer, but at the same time it somehow did not ring true to Ellie's ears. She wondered anew if his aversion did not have something to do with what he had once referred to as his own parents 'exclusive marriage'. 'Is the object of that love not showing the same vulnerability by allowing her own emotions to be hurt?'

'Then why take the risk at all?' the duke argued.

Ellie shrugged. 'Possibly because it is the natural instinct of human beings to need the love and affection of others?'

'The implication being, therefore, that my own feelings on the matter must be unnatural?' he rasped.

She looked at him for a minute, the blue of his eyes glittering—with anger or something else? 'You are avoiding answering my original question...' she finally murmured.

He gave another humourless smile. 'How very astute of you.'

'And you are still avoiding it.'

'That being the case, would it not be a prudent move on your part to move on to something else?' he suggested.

Ellie's cheeks warmed as she lowered her gaze and turned to look out of the window beside her. 'I do not believe I may claim to have been particularly "prudent" in our...relationship, to date, your Grace.'

Justin could certainly vouch for that!

Indeed, Eleanor had been anything but prudent in her dealings with him this past week, to a degree that he now knew her body almost as intimately as he did his own: the satiny smoothness of her skin, the taste of her breasts, the warm touch of her lips and the expression on her face as she climaxed against his fingers.

Just as he could not help but notice the perfection of the calm profile she now turned away from him: the creamy intelligent brow, long lashes surrounding those emerald-green eyes, her cheek a perfect curve, freckle-covered nose small and straight, her lips full above her stubbornly determined chin.

Eleanor had grown in elegance as well as self-confidence this past week, her pale-green bonnet, the same shade as her gown, fastened about the pale oval of her face, with enticing auburn curls at her temples and nape, her spine perfectly straight, shoulders back, which only succeeding in pushing the fullness of her breasts up against the low bodice of her gown, knees primly together, dainty slippers of green satin peeping out from beneath the hem of her gown.

Yes, Eleanor was certainly the picture of an elegant and beautiful young lady, and Justin realised that her air of self-confidence was due to the admiration and attentions of fawning young dandies, of which Endicott was no doubt only one.

In sharp contrast to those eager young fops, he knew himself to be both cynical and aloof, and not at all what might appeal to a young woman who was so widely admired and fêted. Indeed, her remarks about his cynicism towards the emotion of love would seem to confirm that lack of appeal. A realisation which irritated Justin immensely.

So much so that he felt a sudden urge to shatter her air of confidence and calm. 'I assure you, dear Eleanor, I have absolutely no complaints at your lack of inhibitions in the bedchamber. Nor would you hear any objections from me if you were to decide to behave that imprudently again!'

'Justin!' She gasped as she whipped round to face him, a fiery blush colouring her cheeks.

Perhaps, if in her shocked surprise Eleanor had not addressed him by his first name, Justin might have decided not to pursue this any further.

Perhaps…

Chapter Thirteen

Justin rose and crossed to the other side of the carriage and sat down next to Eleanor, his thigh pressed against the warmth of hers. He reached out and pulled the curtains across each of the windows, throwing the interior of the carriage into shadow, but not dark enough for them not to be able to see each other and know what he was doing, as he untied the ribbon on Eleanor's bonnet before removing it completely.

'We will reach Royston House shortly...' she protested breathlessly.

Justin reached up and tapped on the roof of the carriage.

'Your Grace?' his groom responded.

'Continue to drive until I instruct you otherwise, Bilsbury.' Justin raised his voice so that he might be heard above the noise of the horses' hooves on the cobbled street.

'Yes, your Grace.'

Eleanor seemed frozen in place, unable to move or look away as Justin deftly removed the pins from those fiery red-gold curls, before releasing them on to her shoulders and down the length of her spine, reaching almost to the slenderness of her waist.

Justin groaned low in his throat, closing his eyes briefly, as he imagined how sensuous those long curls would feel against the bareness of his own flesh, his shaft now hardening, thickening, just at imagining it. 'Dear Lord…!' He opened his eyes and raised his hands up to cup either side of her face before lowering his head to claim her parted lips with his own.

Desire, hot and strong, erupted between them, leaving no room for tentative exploration and seduction as Justin felt the instant and powerful surge of his own desire as his arousal curved up strong and pulsing against his stomach, his arms sliding about Eleanor's waist as he drew her firmly against him, breast to chest, the flatness of her abdomen pressing against the heat of his shaft.

She clung to him, her face raised as he deepened the kiss, sweeping his tongue over the softness of her lips before entering, then plundering the beckoning, enticing heat beneath.

For Ellie it was as if the last three agonising days of avoiding Justin had never happened, the instant heat of their desire making it seem as if this was a continuation of their previous lovemaking. Her love for him made it impossible to resist being crushed against him, his reaction to her telling her more surely than anything else that he was just as aroused as she was.

She became totally lost in the barrage of emotions as he continued to kiss her. Then he lifted her above him, the length of her gown rising up her legs as she straddled his muscular thighs, allowing him to pull her in tightly against him, her knees resting on the seat either side of him.

Her drawers had parted, allowing the fullness of his arousal to press up against the swollen heart of her, only the material of his pantaloons now separating them.

Ellie gave a breathless gasp as the rocking of the carriage rubbed his firm length against the sensitive nubbin between her own thighs, totally lost to sensation as Justin unfastened the buttons at the back of her gown. He broke the kiss to ease her slightly away from him to allow her gown to drop away, revealing her breasts covered only by the thin material of her chemise, his eyes becoming hot and glittering as he raised his hands to cup the twin orbs.

Ellie looked down, her cheeks flaming as she saw what Justin had done; her breasts were fuller, the nipples swollen and hard at their tips as they pouted up and forwards invitingly.

'You are so beautiful…!' he murmured huskily, gently pushing her chemise aside before his head lowered to draw one of those swollen berries into his mouth.

Ellie's whole body now felt suffused with heat as she thrust her fingers into his hair, every caress of that moist tongue a torture that coursed hot and molten through her veins.

She loved this man, needed—Lord help her, she needed—

She gave a low moan, throat arching, head thrown back, as Justin responded to that need, his fingers caressing unerringly that heat between her thighs, stroking in the same rhythm as his tongue now rasped against her other nipple, taking her higher, driving her insane with mindless desire.

'Unfasten my pantaloons, Eleanor…!' His breath was hot against her aching breast as he bit gently on her nipple. 'Let me feel your hands on me,' he pleaded gruffly.

Her cheeks burned as she sat back slightly, her fingers fumbling with the buttons of Justin's pantaloons in her haste to see and touch the hardness that had pressed against her so insistently, barely able to breathe as he leant back against the seat, lids half-closed, as she finally allowed that long, pulsing length to burst free, as if it had a will of its own.

Even as she gazed down in fascination a bead of liquid escaped the tip before sliding slowly downwards. Ellie looked at him uncertainly. 'May I…?'

'Please…' he encouraged hoarsely.

She quickly removed her gloves before touching that hardness tentatively, her fingers barely able to meet about its thickness. She was surprised, as she began to run her fingers slowly up and down it, at how silky the skin felt. She ran the soft pad of her thumb across the tip to capture a second bead of escaping moisture, looking up quickly as he gave a low groan. 'Am I hurting you?'

He gave a brief laugh. 'Only with kindness!'

Ellie gave a relieved smile, capturing her tongue between her teeth in concentration as she unbuttoned his waistcoat and pulled up his shirt to bare his chest before allowing her gaze to become fixed once again on the hard, silken length of his shaft. She continued to caress him instinctively, fingers tightening around his arousal, responding to his groans of pleasure as she began to lightly pump up and down. Justin's thighs began to thrust up into the circle of her fingers and she tightened her grip as she heard his loud gasp, the expression on his face now almost one of pain, despite his earlier assurances.

Ellie stilled. 'I am sure I must be hurting you—'

'No!' He lifted his hand, fingers curling about hers as he encouraged her to continue that rhythmic pumping. 'Do not stop, Eleanor, please do not stop…!' His head dropped back against the upholstered seat, lids completely closed, long golden lashes dark shadows against the harsh planes of his sculptured cheeks.

Ellie had never seen anything as beautiful, as intensely wildly beautiful, as the fierceness of his pleasure in her caresses. It was somehow empowering, so fiercely primal, to know that she could give such pleasure to the man she loved.

'Harder,' he encouraged achingly. 'Oh lord, faster…!'

Ellie's fingers tightened further about him as she followed his instructions, eyes widening as his shaft seemed to grow even longer, thicker, with each downward stroke, the head more swollen, and glistening with moisture.

Justin groaned harshly, the pleasure so intense, so all consuming as he thrust up into Eleanor's encircling fingers, every particle of him concentrated on that intense, mindless desire as he felt his release threatening to overtake his control.

It took tremendous effort of will not to give in to the need to spill himself, as he instead opened his eyes before capturing her wrist and putting a stop to her caresses. 'Together this time, Eleanor. We will come together.'

She blinked, her eyes a dark emerald in her own arousal.

'Like this,' Justin urged as he placed his hands on her waist to once again pull her thighs in tight either side of him, his breath leaving him in a pained hiss as he felt the burning heat of her against him, causing him to harden still further.

'Justin…?'

'Do not be afraid, Eleanor,' he soothed as he stroked gentle fingers down the length of one of her rosy cheeks. 'I swear I will not take your innocence. Or hurt you in any way. I only want to give you pleasure. To give us both pleasure. Do you trust me to do that?'

Did Ellie trust Justin? To give her pleasure? Oh, yes, she already knew how capable he was of sending her to the heights. But did she trust him not to break her heart?

Ellie feared it was already too late for that!

What other explanation could there be, she mused, other than that she had fallen in love with him, for the way in which she responded so willingly, so wantonly, to his every caress?

'Eleanor, *please?*' he begged at her continued silence.

It was unacceptable that this proud, powerful man should plead with her. That he should plead with anyone for anything!

Nor did she wish to continue to waste this precious time together lingering on her own emotions. 'Yes, I trust you, Justin,' she said, her hands clinging to the width of his shoulders as he sat up to edge forwards on the seat, his gaze once again holding hers captive as he began to move, the hardness of his shaft stroking against the swollen nubbin between her dampened thighs, the wetness there allowing his silken hardness to glide up and between her swollen folds rather than entering, breaching, the sheath beneath.

Ellie moaned in ecstasy as the nubbin between her thighs throbbed and pulsed in response to each stroke, her cheeks aflame with her arousal, her breathing ragged as she felt the pressure building inside her, taking her higher and ever higher, her breasts tingling almost painfully, as that heated pleasure between her thighs became almost too much to bear.

'Now, Eleanor!' Justin gasped between gritted teeth. 'I am going to—come for me now, Eleanor!'

His words meant nothing to Ellie, it was the tightening of his hands about her waist as he held her firmly in place, and the intensified throbbing and bucking of his shaft against her, that threw her totally over the edge and out into a maelstrom of almost unbearably erotic sensations.

Wave after wave of pleasure claimed her, as Justin's shaft continued to stroke to that same rhythm, before he also lost control, and a fiery liquid pulsed hotly on to her nubbin, sending her into a second, even more intense climax than the first.

Justin trembled and shook in the aftermath of the most intense release he had ever experienced, his ejaculation so fierce, so powerful, and lasting for so long he felt as if he had been ripped apart and was still in pieces, only the sound of their ragged breathing breaking the silence inside the carriage. Eleanor had fallen forwards weakly as her second climax faded, her head now resting on his shoulder as her body still shuddered and quivered with the aftershocks of that dual release.

It was incredible, beyond belief, that Justin should have responded so wildly, so intensely, to just the touch of her hands upon him and the heat of her between her thighs.

He enjoyed sex as much as the next man, had bedded more than his share of women the past ten years or so, but he could never remember experiencing such a depth of pleasure before, such a fierce release. It had seemed never ending, until he had felt as if it had started in his toes and been drawn up from his very boots.

His boots…

Damn it, not only were the two of them still fully dressed, but they were also sitting in his moving carriage—a carriage that now reeked of the smell of sex! What on earth had he been *thinking?*

Ellie was so weakened, so lost in wonder, that it took her several minutes to realise that Justin's shoulder had tensed beneath her brow. His chest was steadily rising and falling against her breasts, while his hands had fallen away from her waist.

She raised her head warily and looked at his harshly etched features; there was a frown between his eyes, his cheekbones appeared like blades beneath the tautness of his skin, and his jaw was tightly clenched.

So clearly not the face of an indulgent and satiated lover.

She moistened her lips with the tip of her tongue before speaking. 'Are you angry with me?'

'With myself,' he corrected harshly.

Her eyes widened. 'Why?'

'You can ask me that?' He gave a self-disgusted shake of his head as he placed his hands on her waist once again in order to lift her off him and sit her on the seat beside him. He briskly pulled up the bodice of her gown and refastened the buttons at the back before straightening his own clothing.

Ellie's legs felt decidedly shaky as she pressed her knees tightly together, gasping as she felt another wave of pleasure emanate from that still-swollen nubbin nestled in the auburn curls between her thighs. Her cheeks suddenly blazed again as she became aware that the uncomfortable dampness of her drawers was not entirely her own.

Could this be any more embarrassing? Not only had she once again lost complete control in Justin's arms, but the proof of his own uninhibited display was impossible to ignore. How could she have allowed this to happened again? It was utterly mortifying—

'This should not have happened again!' the

duke echoed at least some of her thoughts, his voice a growl in the silence. 'And it would not have done so if not for—' He broke off abruptly, eyes glittering darkly as he glared fiercely at nothing in particular.

'If not for what?' Ellie prompted.

'We have delayed long enough; I suggest you now tidy your hair and replace your bonnet,' he instructed as he pulled back the curtains and allowed in the sunshine before reaching up to once again tap on the roof of the carriage. 'Royston House, if you please, Bilsbury.'

Ellie continued to regard him for several seconds before turning away to look sightlessly out of the window, unwilling to allow him to see the tears which now stung her eyes as she did as he instructed and tidied herself.

The way Justin now spoke to her, and the harshness of his expression, could not have made it any more obvious that he deeply regretted what had just happened.

As she must now regret it, though for a completely different reason.

While technically she might still be an innocent, she was certain he had ruined her for any other man. She would only ever want him. Only ever love him. It was a total disaster.

Justin could not think of a single thing to say or do that would erase the expression of hurt bewilderment from Eleanor's face; that his behaviour had been reprehensible, totally beyond the pale, was beyond denial, as well as being a betrayal of his role as her guardian.

She still looked utterly dishevelled, delicate wisps of her hair having escaped her ministrations, her cheeks pale, her lips slightly swollen from the force of their kisses, her gown crushed and slightly soiled—and he winced just to think of the state of her underclothes.

Damn it, he had told himself after the first time that such a depth of intimacy must never happen between the two of them again. Nor did he believe it would have done so now, if he had not been so infuriated by her obvious enjoyment of Endicott's attentions, when recently she could barely spare him the time of day.

Which begged the question—why had Eleanor's obvious liking for Endicott so infuriated him, when the sooner she received a proposal of marriage from someone of Endicott's ilk, and accepted it, then the quicker Justin's own onerous responsibility as her guardian would come to an end? Just as her possible problematic connection to Litchfield would then become her husband's business rather than his own.

Which was exactly what Justin wanted, was it not? To be free of her so that he might return to his uncomplicated life before her come-out in society had caused him such inconvenience and irritation?

His uncomplicated life before Miss Eleanor Rosewood...

As Justin recalled, he had been lamenting the boredom of that life on the evening his grandmother had voiced her concerns regarding Eleanor's future, with the request that he provide her with a dowry and his protection. An emotion Justin could not recall experiencing even once since that evening.

True—except the very reason he had not found himself overcome with boredom this past week was because he had not had a minute to call his own in all that time!

His whole life had been tumbled into disarray since she entered it. He had not even found the time for his usual pursuits, such as his thrice-weekly visits to Jackson's Boxing Saloon. An oversight he intended to rectify at the earliest opportunity, if only in an attempt to prevent himself from once again falling victim to her physical charms.

That decision settled in his mind, Justin now turned his attention to the difficult task of diffusing the awkwardness that had been created by this latest lapse. 'There is never a teacup and saucer available when one so sorely needs one—'

'Do not try to make a joke out of this!' she turned on him fiercely.

He gave a pained wince. 'Once again I offer my apologies—Eleanor, are you crying?' He was appalled as he saw the silvery tracks of those tears falling down the paleness of her cheeks. 'Eleanor—'

'Or touch me again!' she warned even as she flinched away from the hands he had lifted with the intention of lightly grasping her arms. 'Or be mistaken into thinking these tears are caused by anything other than anger, and a recognition of my own stupidity, in having once again having allowed myself to fall prey to your experienced seduction!'

Justin's jaw tightened grimly at the insult

as he continued to look at her for several long seconds, aware of the challenge in her own gaze, before he drew in a deep breath and rose agilely to his feet to move and sit on the other side of the carriage. 'Better?'

Her chin rose as she replied just as tersely, 'Much.'

He let out a ragged sigh. 'Eleanor—'

'I really would prefer it if you did not speak to me again.' Her voice shook, whether with anger, or some other emotion, Justin was unsure. 'I have—I am in no fit state to talk about this now.' She gave a shake of her head, her gloved hands tightly clasped together in her lap.

Justin was surprised that either of them could speak at all after the intensity of their lovemaking! Indeed, his own body was currently filled with such lethargy, so physically satiated and drained, that he dearly longed for a hot bath in which he might ease away some of those aches and strains.

'Very well, Eleanor,' he acquiesced. 'But when you are feeling better—'

'I am not ill, your Grace,' she assured him with a humourless laugh. 'Merely full of self-disgust and recriminations,' she added honestly.

The fact that she was once again addressing him as 'your Grace' was enough to inform him of her state of mind, of her need to put as much distance between them, metaphorically, as she possibly could. 'Nevertheless,' he pointed out as gently as he could, 'we cannot just ignore what has happened in the same way that we did the last time.' Just the thought of a repeat of the three days that had just passed, when Eleanor had avoided his company as much as was possible, and spoke to him even less, was totally unacceptable. 'My grandmother, as you have already remarked, is a highly astute woman and a continuation of the recent tension between us is sure to alert her to the fact that there is something seriously amiss.'

Eleanor's eyes flashed a deep-emerald green and angry colour returned to her cheeks. 'Should you not have thought of that sooner, your Grace?'

Justin should have thought of a lot of things sooner! The fact that he had not was testament to his own state of mind. What little mind he seemed to have left about him whenever he was alone with her!

'Perhaps we will be lucky enough to have my grandmother attribute your obvious displeasure with me as the result of my earlier high-handedness in forbidding you from attending Lady Littleton's soirée this evening?' Justin suggested heavily.

'No doubt,' she agreed stiltedly.

Whatever his grandmother might choose to think or say was really unimportant, it was the antagonism Eleanor now showed towards him that concerned him the most…

Ellie heaved a sigh of relief as she saw they were approaching Royston House at last, barely waiting for the carriage to come to a halt and the groom—Bilsbury, no doubt!—to open the door, before stepping quickly outside, in desperate need to put some distance between herself and Justin.

She would need to bathe and change her clothing, too, before Edith St Just arrived home; as Justin had already remarked, his grandmother was indeed a very astute lady, and the dowager would only need to take one look at Ellie's dishevelled appearance to realise exactly what must have taken place between them in Justin's carriage on their drive back to Royston House!

It was to be hoped that the dowager had not arrived home ahead of them…

Ellie had no idea how much time had passed while she and Justin made love in his carriage, but it would not have taken the dowager so very long to take tea with Lady Cicely. It would be too humiliating if she had arrived home ahead of them—

'We will go inside together, Eleanor.' The duke put his hand lightly beneath her elbow to fall into step beside her as she hurried up the wide steps fronting the house.

Ellie shot Justin a fuming glance, especially as she saw that he looked just as fashionably elegant as he always did, with not a hair showing out of place beneath the tall hat he took off and handed to Stanhope once they had entered the grand entrance hall. 'I shall take my bonnet and gloves upstairs with me, thank you, Stanhope,' she refused with a strained smile as he offered to take them from her. 'If you could arrange for hot water for a bath to be brought up to me as soon as is possible?'

'I would like the same brought to my own rooms, if you please, Stanhope,' Justin requested.

'Certainly, your Grace, Miss Rosewood, I will see to it immediately.' The butler hesitated, his expression one of slight perturbation. 'I should inform you… A visitor arrived whilst you were out, your Grace.'

The duke raised his brows. 'And who might that be?'

Ellie was curious to know the answer to that question too; she had been acquainted with Stanhope for the past year, knew him to be unflappable, whatever the situation. And at the moment he was most certainly disconcerted, to say the least.

'Good afternoon, Justin.'

Ellie was aware of Justin drawing in a hissing breath beside her, even as she turned in search of the owner of that husky feminine voice. Her heart beat wildly in her chest as she found herself looking at an elegant and beautiful, blonde-haired woman, as she stood framed in the doorway of the Blue Salon.

A beautiful woman whom Justin undoubtedly recognised—but so obviously wished he did not!

Chapter Fourteen

It was a belief that was instantly born out by Justin's next accusing comment. 'What are *you* doing here?'

Ellie flinched at the angry displeasure she could hear in his voice, knowing she would shrivel and die a little inside if he should ever speak to her in so disparaging a tone.

But the elegantly lovely woman standing across the hallway did not so much as blink in response to that harshness as she turned to smile at the discreetly departing Stanhope before answering Justin chidingly, 'Really, darling, is that any way to address me when we have not seen each other for so many months?'

'And whose fault is that?'

She smiled sadly. 'On this particular occasion I believe it to be your own.'

Ellie felt as if this entire day had turned into a nightmare she could not wake up from. Firstly, the fierceness of their lovemaking in Justin's carriage, which had once again ended so disastrously. And now, it appeared, she was to meet a woman whom Justin had obviously once been—or perhaps was still?—involved with. A woman, moreover, who was so much more beautiful and sophisticated than Ellie could ever be.

Justin had not believed this day could get any worse, but the proof that it actually could was standing directly across the cavernous hallway. The last thing, the very last thing he had expected today was to find this particular woman waiting for him when he returned to Royston House.

'Are you not going to introduce us, Justin?' she now prompted as she looked pointedly at Eleanor. 'Or perhaps I can guess who you might be, without Justin's help,' she added ruefully when no introduction was forthcoming from him. 'You are no doubt Miss Eleanor Rosewood, the lovely young lady who was the stepdaughter of Frederick

St Just, and whom Edith has kindly taken under her wing?'

'I am Eleanor Rosewood, yes.' She sketched a curtsy, still looking confused.

A puzzlement Justin had absolutely no wish to satisfy, yet he knew he had no choice but to do so. 'Eleanor, may I present to you her Grace, Rachel St Just, the Duchess of Royston. My mother,' he added curtly as Eleanor continued to look at him blankly.

'Your *mother*...?' Eleanor gave a gasp, her expression one of wide-eyed disbelief as she stared at the woman who did not look old enough to be the mother of a boy of eight, let alone a grown man of eight and twenty.

She never had, Justin acknowledged begrudgingly, having always considered his mother to be one of the loveliest women he had ever set eyes upon. As a child he had thought her as beautiful as any angel. And she continued to be, despite now being in her late forties.

Her fashionably styled hair was as golden and abundant as it had ever been, her blue eyes as bright, her face and throat as creamily smooth, her figure still as resplendently curvaceous in the blue gown she wore—

The blue gown she wore...?

To Justin's knowledge his mother had not worn anything but black since the death of his father three years ago. And yet today, here and now, she was wearing a fashionable silk gown the same colour blue as her eyes, satin slippers of the same shade peeping out from beneath the hem of that gown.

Did this mean that his mother had finally—finally!—decided to end her years of solitary mourning for his father?

Ellie could only stare at the woman Justin had just introduced as his mother.

Was it any wonder she had assumed her to be something else entirely? This tall, beautiful woman definitely did not look old enough to be Justin's mother. Did not look old enough to be Ellie's own mother!

'I am sorry we did not meet when your mother and Frederick were alive, but so pleased that we are doing so now.' Rachel St Just smiled warmly as she seemed to glide across the hallway to where Ellie stood, the older woman hugging her briefly before then holding her at arm's length, her perfume light and floral—and hopefully masking the musky smell of Eleanor's own clothing!

'You are every bit as lovely as Edith wrote and told me that you were.'

'Grandmama wrote and told you about Eleanor?' Justin repeated slowly.

Ellie glanced at him, frowning slightly as she saw the incredulity in his expression, quickly followed by the narrowing of his eyes as he continued to look at his mother guardedly. Ellie noted that there was no attempt on the duchess's part to greet her son with the same physical warmth of the hug she had just received.

Perhaps the relationship between mother and son was so obviously strained that she knew Justin would reject such a gesture from her out of hand?

Ellie saw the sadness that appeared briefly on Rachel's lovely face in acceptance of that truth, before she smiled and asked, 'Is there some reason why Edith and I should not regularly correspond with each other?'

'None at all,' Justin replied tersely. 'I am merely surprised that one such missive, apparently about Eleanor, seems to have brought you back to town after all this time.'

'Oh, it was not just one letter, Justin,' his mother revealed. 'Edith has talked of nothing else but Eleanor for months now, until I decided I must come and meet this beautiful paragon for myself.'

Ellie now looked for any sign of the cynicism and mockery that were such a part of her son's nature, knowing herself to be neither 'beautiful' nor a 'paragon'—especially now, when her appearance was so bedraggled! But she could discern only kindness in the duchess's face as she continued to smile at her warmly.

Another glance at Justin showed that cynicism and mockery to be all too visible on *his* too handsome face! 'The dowager duchess is too kind,' Ellie answered his mother quietly.

'My mother-in-law is indeed kind,' Rachel agreed. 'But, I assure you, in this instance she was being truthful as well as kind.'

'Are you seriously telling me that you have decided to give up your years of solitary mourning in the country—' Justin eyed his mother derisively '—to come up to town out of a mere curiosity to meet Eleanor?'

The duchess raised golden brows. 'Why, what other reason can there have been?'

His jaw tightened. 'Grandmama did not write and tell you she has recently been… indisposed?'

Ellie saw now where Justin was going

with this conversation. He was concerned that Edith might have confided more fully as to the seriousness, or otherwise, of her illness with her daughter-in-law than she had him, and it was that very confidence which was now the reason for his mother's unexpected, and for Justin obviously surprising, return to town.

'I believe I will leave the two of you now and go to my room to bathe,' Ellie spoke softly into the tenseness of the silence that had now befallen them all.

Justin shot her a bleak glance, knowing their own conversation was far from over, but also accepting that the conversation he needed to have with his mother now took priority over any awkwardness that had once again arisen between Eleanor and himself. If, indeed, it had ever ceased!

Quite what he was going to do about Eleanor, and the habit he was rapidly falling into of making love with her at every available opportunity, was beyond his reasoning at this moment. The force of their lovemaking such a short time ago, and the unexpected appearance of his mother, had succeeded in completely destroying his ability for logic.

He also accepted that Eleanor, despite his mother's compliments, was looking less than her best—her hair so obviously in disarray beneath her bonnet, her gown appearing crushed, that she was no doubt feeling less than comfortable in the duchess's presence.

Justin gave an abrupt nod. 'We will talk again before dinner.'

Dark-green eyes looked away from his. 'I have a slight headache, your Grace, and believe I will take your advice after all and spend the evening at home in my bedchamber.'

His mouth twisted grimly at Eleanor's use of the word 'advice'—they both knew only too well that he had issued an order earlier rather than well-intentioned advice! 'Then I will call upon you in your room after dinner.'

That brought her gaze swiftly back to him, those green eyes flashing her displeasure. 'That will not be necessary, your Grace, when I have every intention of going to bed and then to sleep shortly afterwards.'

And she was no doubt hoping—perhaps even praying?—that when she awoke, this afternoon would turn out to be nothing but a nightmare!

Justin's own life was also becoming increasingly unbearable. Not only did he still have his grandmother's illness to worry about, and now his mother's unexpected arrival at Royston House to ponder over, but Dryden Litchfield, and his possible connection to Eleanor, still lurked threateningly in the background of these other, more immediate, concerns.

Boredom? Hah! Once again Justin acknowledged that he no longer had the time in which to suffer that emotion!

'Very well.' He thrust a hand through his hair. 'But if your headache worsens I wish for you to ring for Stanhope immediately, so that Dr Franklyn can be sent for.'

'I am not a child, Justin, to be told by you what I should or should not do!' Eleanor's cheeks instantly coloured a vivid red as she remembered they had an interested audience listening to their conversation. Her tone had been scathing to say the least, her use of his first name implying a familiarity between them which had certainly not been apparent until now. 'I apologise, your Grace,' she made that apology pointedly to his mother rather than Justin—obviously implying she did not feel she owed him an apology! 'I am afraid I am feeling less than well today myself.'

'You poor dear.' His mother's expression was wholly sympathetic. 'Would it be acceptable to you if I were to come up to your bedchamber and check on you later this evening?'

Justin turned back to Eleanor, derisive brows raised over challenging blue eyes.

Ellie had avoided looking at Justin following her irritated outburst, although she sensed his mocking gaze was now fixed upon her. Deservedly so; in her annoyance with him, she had forgotten all sense of propriety. In front of his mother, of all people.

'Perfectly acceptable,' she warmly accepted the duchess's suggestion.

'I will take care not to disturb you if you are sleeping.' Rachel continued to smile reassuringly, as if she had not noticed Ellie's familiarity towards her arrogant son.

'Your Grace.' Ellie bobbed a curtsy to the older woman. 'Your Grace.' Her voice had cooled noticeably as she gave Justin only the barest hint of a departing nod, not even waiting for his acknowledgement of that less-than-polite gesture before turning to hurry across the hallway, lifting the skirts of her gown to quickly ascend the wide staircase.

Even so, she could not help but overhear the duchess's next comment.

'Is there something relating to your young ward, which you feel the need to discuss with either Edith or myself, Justin?'

Justin continued to watch Eleanor for several more seconds as she hurriedly ascended the curved staircase, only turning his attention back to his mother once she had reached the top of those stairs and disappeared rapidly down the hallway he knew led to her bedchamber. 'Such as?' He eyed his mother coolly.

She sighed. 'I see that you are still angry with me.'

'Not at all.' His mouth twisted. 'Anger would imply a depth of emotion which simply does not exist between us.'

His mother gave a pained frown. 'That is simply not true! I have always loved you dearly, Justin—'

'Oh, please!'

'But—'

'I have no intention of continuing this conversation out here in the hallway, where anyone might overhear us.' He turned to stride in the direction of the Blue Salon, waiting until his mother, having hesitated briefly, now entered the room ahead of him, before following her and closing the door firmly behind her. 'Why are you really here, Mother?'

'I told you—'

'Some nonsense about meeting Eleanor.' Justin waved away his impatience with that explanation as he stood with his back towards one of the bay windows that looked out over the front of the house. 'To my knowledge, Eleanor has resided at Royston House with Grandmama for this past year, so why the sudden and urgent interest in her now?'

His mother sank down gracefully on to one of the sofas before answering him. 'Edith mentioned that, with your help, she intended bringing Eleanor out into society.'

Justin's hands were clasped tightly together behind his back. 'And have you come to offer your own assistance in that endeavour?'

She gave a sad shake of her head. 'I wish that you would not take that scathing tone when you address me.'

He drew in a deeply controlling breath, aware that he was being less than polite to the woman who had, after all, given birth to him.

'I apologise if I sounded rude.'

'That is at least something, I suppose—Justin, are you aware that your neckcloth is looking…less than its usual pristine self?' She eyed him with questioning calm.

Considering the depth, the wildness, of the desire which had seized him in his carriage just minutes ago, when Eleanor had unfastened his waistcoat and then pushed his shirt up his chest so that she might touch and caress him there, Justin was surprised only his neckcloth was askew as evidence of their passionate encounter!

'I believe we were discussing the suddenness of your decision to come up to town, not my neckcloth?' He refused to so much as raise a hand and attempt to straighten the disarray of that scrap of material, and to hell with what deductions his mother might care to make in that regard.

Eyes so like his own dropped from meeting his as his mother instead ran a fingernail along the piping at the edge of the cushion upon which she sat. 'It is not so sudden, Justin. I have known for some time that one of us must attempt to heal the breach which exists between us. And when you failed to visit me on my birthday this week, I realised it must be me.'

Justin had completely forgotten that it *was* his mother's birthday just four days ago. Indeed, he had been so preoccupied, with both his grandmother's illness, and this unaccountable passion he had developed for Eleanor Rosewood, that he was no longer sure what day of the week it was, let alone that he had missed altogether his mother's forty-ninth birthday!

He winced. 'Once again I apologise.'

She gave a teasing tilt of her head. 'Enough to give me the kiss you failed to give me earlier?'

'Of course.' Justin crossed the room to briefly press his lips against the smoothness of her cheek; it was a small price to pay, after all, for such negligence.

His mother nodded. 'And will you now sit here beside me and tell me all about Miss Rosewood?' She patted the sofa cushion beside her own.

A gesture Justin ignored as he instead walked over to one of the armchairs placed either side of the unlit fireplace. He folded his long length down into it in a deliberately relaxed pose, his elbows resting on the arms of the chair as he steepled his fingers together in front of him, all the time avoiding acknowledging the disappointed look he knew would be on his mother's face. 'Would Grandmother not be a more reliable source of information on Eleanor than I?'

'I do not believe so, no…'

His gaze sharpened as he looked across the room at his mother through those steepled fingers. 'Would you care to explain that remark?'

'Not really, no.'

Justin knew that he and Eleanor had both looked decidedly dishevelled when they entered the house together just now, but he was sincerely hoping his mother hadn't realised the cause. 'Then perhaps you would care to tell me your real reason for coming up to town?'

She looked pained. 'Could it not be that I wished to see my only son?'

His mouth thinned. 'Somehow I doubt that very much!'

'Oh, Justin.' His mother sighed heavily. 'Why do we always have to fight whenever we meet?'

He raised blond brows. 'Perhaps because we do not like each other?'

'Justin!' Tears filled his mother eyes as she sprang restlessly to her feet, her cheeks having blanched to a deathly white. 'That is just so—so cruel of you! I love you. I have always loved you!'

And Justin had always loved his mother, too. Even when he had been angry with her, hurt by her, resentful of her negligence, he had still loved her. He loved her still.

But those years, when he had very often not seen his mother or his father for months at a time, had created a gulf between them which he truly believed to be insurmountable.

'It is not my intention to be cruel to you, Mother. I just—why can you not just accept that there is too much between us, too many years spent apart, for us to be able to reach any common ground now?'

There was a strained look beside those tear-wet eyes and lines beside her unsmiling mouth. 'There are things—' she broke off, as if seeking the right words to say to him. 'You asked why I have come up to town. The truth is, when you forgot even to acknowledge my birthday, I decided—'

'Damn it, I have already apologised for my oversight!'

She shook her head. 'It is still a symptom of the way our relationship now stands. And there are things you should know, things I have not told you before now, which I think you have a right to know.'

Justin frowned. 'There is nothing you can say to me now that could ever take away all those years of neglect, when you chose to travel about the world with your husband—'

'My husband was your father, don't forget that! And we did not spend our lives simply enjoying ourselves, as you seem to be implying we were!' Her expression was anguished, her gloved hands clenched tightly together in her agitation. 'Nor was my decision to accompany him an easy one to make. But I made sure you were away at school before I decided to do so, and you had Edith and George if we had not managed to return for the holidays.'

'Yet my grandparents, dear as they both were and still are, were no substitute for my own parents!' This subject was too painful, too close to Justin's own heart, for him to remain his usual icily controlled self.

'Justin, I remained behind, stayed at home

with you, until you went away to school at the age of ten,' she reasoned anxiously. 'Do you not remember those years before then, Justin? The wonderful years we spent together in Hampshire, swimming or fishing together in the summer months, sledging and ice-skating on the pond in the winters? And the excitement we always felt when we knew your father was to return from—from his business abroad?'

His eyes narrowed to icy slits. 'I remember the years that followed far more clearly.'

Her shoulders drooped in defeated. 'You have become a hard and unforgiving man, Justin.'

He shrugged. 'I am what my life has made me.'

'Then I am sorry for it.' His mother gave a sad smile. 'You are an intelligent man. Can you not think of any reason why your father travelled abroad for almost the whole of your life, first to India, then to the Continent? Other than enjoying himself, of course,' she added with uncharacteristic tartness.

Justin glanced at her curiously, having absolutely no idea where this conversation was leading. 'I was always told that he went away on business…'

'And he was.'

'Then I do not see—'

'That business was not his own!'

'Then whose was it?' Justin made no attempt to hide his growing impatience with this conversation.

She looked rather irritated now. 'Can you really not guess, Justin?'

He stared at her, a critical gaze that his mother continued to meet unflinchingly, unwaveringly, as if willing him to find the answer for himself.

Justin tensed suddenly as an answer presented itself, sitting forwards in his chair suddenly. 'Can it be—?' He paused, shaking his head slightly in denial. 'All those years— did my father work secretly as an agent for the crown?'

He knew the answer he had found was the correct one, as a look of relief now flooded his mother's beautiful face, making it radiant.

Chapter Fifteen

'I know you are not asleep, Eleanor, so you might just as well give up all pretence that you are!'

Ellie was indeed awake, and she had heard the door to her bedchamber being slowly opened just seconds ago before closing again. But she had hoped, whoever her visitor might be, that they were now on the other side of that closed door.

She remained unmoving and silent now beneath the bedcovers, not wanting another confrontation with Justin. If she refused to answer him, surely he would simply go away?

Ellie's bath earlier had been very welcome and Rachel St Just, as promised, had visited

Ellie in her bedchamber before the family dined downstairs, that sweet lady arranging for Stanhope to bring Ellie some supper on a tray after she had confessed to still having a slight headache.

Shortly after that Ellie had heard one of the carriages being brought around to the front of the house, and then the departure of the St Justs to Lady Littleton's soirée. Several hours later, she still hadn't heard that carriage return.

She had assumed—wrongly, she now realised—that Justin, despite his reluctance to attend such social occasions, would have accompanied his newly arrived mother, and grandmother, to Lady Littleton's for the evening.

'Eleanor...?'

Her lids remained stubbornly closed, despite the fact that she could now discern the glow of candlelight through their delicate membranes. Justin had obviously moved closer to where she lay in bed.

'Damn it, are there not already enough women in this household who prefer to avoid my company this evening!' he muttered truculently.

It was that very truculence, a cross little-boy emotion, and so at odds with his usual arrogant self-confidence, that caused her lids to finally open, in spite of her previous decision to ignore him and hope that he would just go away.

'Ah ha!' Justin looked down at her triumphantly as he stood beside the bed, lit candle held aloft.

Ellie turned to lie on her back and rest up against the pillows, the sheet pulled up over her breasts as she looked up at Justin guardedly in the candlelight. She quickly realised he seemed to be leaning against the bed for support, his appearance also less than presentable; he had removed his jacket and neckcloth completely some time during the evening, several buttons of his shirt were unfastened at the throat and his waistcoat was also unbuttoned.

Another wary glance at his face also revealed that there was a brightness to his eyes and a slight flush to the hardness of his cheeks. 'Justin, are you inebriated?'

He blinked, before pausing to give the matter exaggerated thought. 'I believe I may have drunk a bottle of brandy, or possibly two, since dinner…'

This was just too delicious for Ellie not to

enjoy to the full. It was certainly impossible to ignore the fact that the haughty Duke of Royston, was so foxed he could barely stand! 'Perhaps you should sit down before you fall down—I did not mean there!' Ellie gave an indignant squeak as he immediately sat down on the side of her bed, causing her to scoot over to the other side if she did not wish to be crushed. 'Justin, you should not be in my bedchamber at all, let alone sitting on my bed!'

'Why not—?' He swayed slightly as he leaned forwards to place the candle and its holder on the bedside table. 'Uh oh…' He straightened again with effort, sitting still for several seconds before swinging his booted feet up on to the bed and lying back against the pillows beside her. 'Am I imagining things or is the ceiling spinning?'

'Justin!' Ellie sat up to frown down at him impatiently, her earlier amusement at his expense having completely disappeared as he lay back against the pillows with his eyes closed, golden lashes fanning across those flushed cheeks. 'Justin?'

His lids remained closed as he gave a wide smile of satisfaction. 'You have the hang of saying my name now, I see.'

'Justin!' she repeated with considerable exasperation as she took a grasp of his arm and shook it, with no apparent result as he simply settled more comfortably on to the pillows. 'You must get up now and leave immediately!'

'Why must I?'

'Your mother and grandmother will be returning soon—'

'They will not be back for hours yet.' He raised a hand to cover a yawn. 'And it was dashed lonely downstairs in the library on my own, whereas it is warm and cosy up here with you.'

Ellie stilled at this unexpected admission from a gentleman who gave the clear impression that he had never needed anyone's company but his own. 'Why is it that you think your mother and the dowager are avoiding your company?'

'Do they need a reason?' He gave a shrug.

To Ellie's mind, yes, they most certainly did; Rachel St Just had been so emotional earlier at seeing her son again, after what seemed to have been a lengthy separation, and the dowager was prepared to forgive her grandson anything since he had returned to live at Royston House. 'Why did you not accompany them to Lady Littleton's?'

He prised one lid open to look up at her. 'I may be in the mood for company, Eleanor, but I am not so desperate I would resort to that particular torture!'

She gave a rueful grimace at his obvious disgust. 'I was thinking of it more in terms of doing something which might please your mother and the dowager, and in doing so, perhaps regain favour with them?'

He gave a shudder as he closed that lid. 'I am not as anxious as that to regain their approval!'

'Obviously not.' Ellie sighed at this obvious display of his usual arrogance. 'Nevertheless, you really cannot remain here with me, Justin.'

'Why not, when your bedchamber is so much more comfortable than my own?'

Ellie did not see how that could possibly be true. The dowager had shown her about the main parts of the house when Ellie first came to live here a year ago and she seemed to remember the ducal suite as being opulent, to say the least, with its huge four-poster bed and deep-blue brocade curtains, Georgian furniture and luxurious blue-and-gold Aubusson carpets; her own bedchamber was nice enough, but only a quarter of that size, the bed barely big enough for the two of them to lie down upon together.

An observation which she should not even have been able to make! 'I cannot believe that. Nor do I think it wise for you to remain here any longer—Justin?' She eyed him uncertainly as he turned on the bed to face her, and in doing so making her self-consciously aware of the fact that she wore only her nightrail beneath the bedcovers, the bareness of her shoulders currently visible above the sheet, which was now trapped beneath his heavier weight.

'Did you know you have the most beautiful hair I ever beheld...?' Justin reached out to take a long red strand between his thumb and fingers. 'So soft and silky to the touch and like living flame to gaze upon.' He allowed the silkiness of her hair to fall through his fingers.

'I do not think this the time or the place for you to remark upon the beauty of my hair.'

'When else should I remark upon it when it is normally kept confined or hidden away beneath your bonnet?'

'Not always…' A blush brightened her cheeks.

No, not always…for had Justin not wound these silken tresses about his partially naked body just hours earlier?

He moved up on one elbow the better to observe how smooth and creamy her skin now appeared against that living flame. 'I could not see you properly in the carriage this afternoon.' He smoothed his hand across the bare expanse of her shoulder now clearly visible to him. 'You are very beautiful, Eleanor. Your skin is so soft…'

She held herself stiffly, but even so could not hide the quiver caused by the touch of his caressing fingers. 'Unless you have forgotten, Justin, I, too, am currently avoiding your company…'

He gave a wicked smile. 'I have forgotten none of what took place between us this afternoon, Eleanor.'

The colour deepened in her cheeks. 'Nor, unfortunately, have I. Which is why—'

'Unfortunately?' Justin's fingers curled about her shoulder to hold her in place. 'That is not particularly flattering, referring to our lovemaking like that, Eleanor.'

'Lovemaking which should never have

taken place!' She wrenched out of his grasp, quickly moving to the side of the bed and throwing back the covers to stand up, before retrieving her robe from the bedside chair and hastily pulling it on over her nightrail.

Justin lay back, taking unashamed advantage of being able to gaze upon the nakedness of the body he glimpsed briefly through the sheer material of that nightgown before Eleanor fastened her robe: firm, uptilting, berry-tipped breasts, slender waist, curvaceous hips and thighs above long and slender legs.

A pity, then, that the copious amount of brandy he had consumed earlier this evening appeared to have robbed him of all ability to do anything about it!

He gave a self-disgusted groan as he lay back on the pillows before lifting his arm to place it across his eyes. 'Does it seem over-bright to you in here?'

'You, sir, are seriously foxed!'

He gave a grunt of acknowledgement, having no need to look at Eleanor to know that she would be glaring down at him disapprovingly. 'Not at all a surprising state of affairs after the things I have learnt this evening. And not only that,' he added gruffly, 'but it seems I am to be bedevilled by desire for a young woman totally unsuited to the role of becoming my mistress!'

Could *she* be the young woman he meant?

If so, then he was perfectly correct; for she had no intention of ever becoming his mistress or any other man's, 'bedevilled by desire', or otherwise!

She drew in a sharp breath. 'You will leave my bedchamber right now, sir!'

'Can't,' he mumbled.

'What do you mean, you can't?' She continued to glower down at Justin as she stood beside the bed upon which he still lounged so elegantly, inwardly decrying the fact that he still managed to look so impossibly handsome, despite his less-than-pristine appearance. Or perhaps because of it…

Justin looked far more of a fallen angel in his current state of dishevelment, the gold of his overlong hair having fallen rakishly across his brow, with similar gold curls visible at the open throat of his shirt.

He cracked open that single eyelid once again as he answered her. 'I mean, dear Eleanor, that if my cock is incapable of rising to the occasion after I have gazed upon your delicious near-nakedness, then you may rest assured the rest of me is incapable of rising too!'

Ellie felt the embarrassed colour burning her cheeks. 'You are both behaving and talking outrageously! And likely you will seriously regret it come morning. Indeed, I believe you will wholeheartedly deserve the debilitating headache that will no doubt strike you down—Justin!' She gave a protesting hiss as he reached out to grasp her wrist before tugging determinedly, causing her to tumble back down on to the bed beside him. 'Stop this immediately.' She fought against the arm and leg he now threw across her breasts and thighs in order to keep her beside him.

He scowled at her impatiently. 'Damn it, woman, cease your struggling and try to be of some assistance to me for a change!'

She stilled as she realised he was not attempting to be intimate with her, but was merely using the restraint of his arm and leg as a means of stopping her from struggling any further. That she was not quite as immune as she'd like, to his close proximity and rakish good looks, was no one's fault but her own. 'In what way could I possibly be of assistance to you?'

He frowned. 'You are a woman, are you not?'

'I believe you are as aware of that as I.' She raised pointed brows.

'Exactly.' He nodded his satisfaction with that fact. 'And, as such, you understand the way a woman's mind works.'

'I understand how my own mind works, I am not so sure about other ladies.'

'In the light of there being no other lady available, with whom I might discuss this, you will have to do.' Justin blew out an irritated breath as he once again lay down beside her on the bed to stare up at the ceiling of her bedchamber. 'Explain to me, if you can, why it is a woman, who has lied to her only child for over half his lifetime, now expects that child to fall at her feet and ask *her* forgiveness for not understanding sooner, once she has finally—finally!—explained the reason for that lie.'

Ellie at him closely, seeing the evidence of his pain in the way his eyes had darkened and those grim lines had become etched beside his mouth. 'And would this woman, this mother, happen to be your own?'

He nodded. 'For years I have believed my mother and father to have been so engrossed in their love for each other, in their need to be exclusively with each other, that they had no room or love to spare in their lives for me, their only child,' he rasped. 'And now this evening my mother has told me—I can trust you not to discuss this with anyone else…?'

'Of course.' She bristled slightly at his need to ask.

He nodded distracted. 'This evening I have learnt what my mother and grandparents have always known, that my father was a hero and worked secretly for the crown for many years. That he risked his own life again and again. And latterly my mother chose to put herself in that same danger, when she insisted on travelling with him after I had gone away to boarding school. The two of them succeeded in collecting information which has saved many hundreds of lives over the years.'

And it was obvious, from the mixture of pain and pride Ellie now detected in Justin's voice, that he had not decided as yet how he felt about that…

Not surprising, really, when he had so obviously become the cynical man that he now was because for so many years he had held a quite different opinion about his parents.

It also confirmed Ellie's previous belief

that this might also be the reason Justin had repeatedly declared he had no intention of being in love with his own wife, when the time came for him to marry and provide an heir. For what man, who had believed himself to have been excluded from his parents' lives because of their all-consuming love for each other, would ever want to inflict that same neglect upon his own children?

Ellie moistened her lips with the tip of her tongue as she chose her next words carefully. 'I am sure that both your mother, and the dowager, understand your feelings enough to realise you will need time in which to completely absorb and adjust your thinking concerning the things you have been told this evening.'

Justin glanced at her. 'How would you feel if you were to learn that your own father had not been who you thought all these years?'

Ellie shrugged. 'I hope that I would eventually find a way to come to terms with that truth.'

Justin's eyes glittered. 'That would surely depend upon who your father is!'

'Was,' she corrected softly.

'Well…yes,' he conceded awkwardly.

'It appears your own father was something

of a hero.' Ellie said, sensing that they were now talking slightly at odds with each other, as if Justin's conversation was about something entirely different to her own. 'And I have every reason to believe, despite never having met him, that my father was an honourable man, at least.'

'Yes.'

'Unless…' she eyed him warily '…you have heard otherwise?'

Too late Justin realised that he had allowed his mother's revelations, and an over-indulgence of brandy after not eating enough at dinner, to loosen his tongue in a way he would not otherwise have done and had now appeared to have cast doubts in Ellie's mind about her own father.

How much worse would those doubts be if she were ever to discover that both Justin and the Earl of Richmond, suspected Dryden Litchfield of being her real father, as a result of his having raped her mother!

Damn it, here he was, wallowing in self-pity—probably exacerbated by that over-indulgence of brandy, the effects of which seemed to have dissipated entirely during the course of this current conversation—when the truth was his own father had been a hero of major proportions, his mother, too, when they had both decided to travel to places that were often highly dangerous.

What an idiot he had been. How utterly bloody selfish. Instead of getting blind drunk, what he should have done earlier this evening was get down on his knees and thank his mother for all that she and his father had sacrificed for their king and country.

His mother had been right, of course, in that he *had* forgotten those years before he went away to boarding school. Happy and contented years when Justin had his mother's almost undivided attention, interspersed with weeks or months when his father would return to them and the three of them would then do those things together.

Eleanor, on the other hand, had no memories whatsoever of any father, either in her childhood, or now. Frederick would have been less than useless, he thought acerbically. And the one Justin might give her, if Litchfield should indeed prove to be her father, was nothing short of a nightmare.

'I have not heard anything detrimental about Henry Rosewood, no,' he answered carefully.

'You seemed to imply otherwise a moment ago...?'

'If that is so, then I apologise. I assure you, they are nothing more than the ramblings of an inebriated man.' He swung his booted feet to the floor before sitting up on the side of the bed. 'I apologise for having disturbed your rest, Eleanor. I believe I shall now go to my own bedchamber and endeavour to sleep off the effects of my over-indulgence.'

There was no denying that he had been inebriated when he'd first entered Ellie's bedchamber, but she did not believe that to be the case now. Nor did she care for the way in which the conversation had turned to the subject of her own father just a few minutes ago, then just as quickly been deflected by Justin. As if he were privy to some information which he did not intend to share with her...

His next comment in no way alleviated that suspicion. 'Good lord, look at the time!' He glanced down at the watch he had taken from the pocket of his waistcoat. 'You are right, my mother and grandmother will be returning at any moment and they must not find me here in your bedchamber when they do.' He replaced his pocket watch before straightening in preparation for departing.

Ellie now sat up against the headboard of the bed, her legs curled up beneath her. 'Justin, you would…share the information with me, if you were to learn anything of my father which might damage the dowager duchess in society?'

He turned to look at her sharply. 'And what of your own reputation?'

She shrugged. 'I came from obscurity and will quite happily return there, but I could not bear to think that I had caused the dowager, or indeed yourself or your mother, any social embarrassment before I did so.'

Justin's expression softened. 'And would you not regret or miss anyone or any part of that society on your own account?'

Having been reluctant at first, Ellie knew she would now miss many things. The warmth and kindness of Edith St Just, and now her daughter-in-law, for one. The friendship of Magdelena Matthews, which, never having had a close female friend before now, had become so very dear to Ellie these past few days. And lastly, she would miss Justin himself.

She had not spent all of her time earlier

this evening in bathing and eating a light supper, but had found more than enough time in which to dwell on what she truly felt for Justin. To come to the realisation, that much as she might wish it otherwise, she was indeed in love with him to the extent that, if she ever *were* to be rejected from society, from *his* society, that she might, out of a need to be with the man she loved, even go so far as to accept his offer, if he were ever to make it, of becoming his mistress.

'I should miss the St Just family,' she now answered him honestly. 'You have all been extremely kind to me—'

'I have not been in the least kind to you, Eleanor!' he contradicted harshly.

'But of course you have.' Her expression softened as she looked across at him. 'Your...methods of doing so may have been slightly unorthodox,' she allowed ruefully. 'But, nevertheless, you have done much to make it possible for me to be accepted into society.'

That might be so, Justin acknowledged with inner frustration, but he also held the knowledge that would allow that same society to completely shun her!

Damn it, something would have to be done about this situation with Litchfield, and sooner rather than later.

Chapter Sixteen

'Something must be done about Litchfield, Richmond!' Justin voiced that same sentiment the following afternoon, scowling across the distance that separated the two men as they sparred together at Jackson's Boxing Saloon.

'I agree—if only so that you no longer feel the need to try to beat me into the canvas!' Lord Bryan Anderson drawled ruefully after Justin had landed a particularly vicious jab to his jaw. Both men were stripped to the waist, the perspiration from their efforts obvious upon their sweat-slicked bodies.

Justin drew back. 'Damn it! I apologise, Richmond.' He straightened before bowing to the other man, as an indication that he considered their bout to be a draw and now over.

The Earl of Richmond eyed him curiously as they strolled across to where they had left their clothes earlier, his muscled physique appearing that of a much younger man, the hair on his chest reddish-gold rather than the premature white upon his head. 'Your concern for your young ward is…admirable.'

Justin paused in towelling himself in order to give the earl a sideways glance. 'Your implication being…?'

Richmond chuckled softly. 'She is a beautiful young lady.'

'And possibly in possession of a father who is considered as being anything but a gentleman!'

The older man appeared thoughtful as he sat down to towel off the worst of the evidence of his own physical excess. 'And does that fact affect your own regard for her?'

'Do not be stupid, man!' He scowled.

'Some men might feel—'

'Then some men do not know how to appreciate a diamond when it is placed in front of them.' Justin's scowl darkened as his face emerged from pulling his shirt over his head.

'But you do?'

His mouth twisted. 'So much so that I am

giving serious thought to—' He halted, realising he was being indiscreet.

'Yes?'

Justin changed his tack. 'Eleanor cannot be held responsible for who her sire may be.'

'Even if it should indeed turn out to be Litchfield?'

'Even then,' he said grimly, having realised the previous evening, after he had chosen to go to Eleanor's bedchamber to confide in her, that his 'regard' for her was of a more serious nature than he had previously allowed for.

His mother's revelations about his father seemed to have somehow stripped away all of his defences, to such a degree that he could no longer hide the truth, even from himself.

He had been so determined to maintain his lack of emotional involvement where women were concerned, that he had not fully understood until after he had returned to his own bedchamber the previous night, completely sober but unable to sleep, the difference she had already made in his life.

The main change had been that he had moved back into Royston House, after years of refusing to do so. He might have excused that move to Eleanor as the need for him to be close at hand if his grandmother should become ill again, but inwardly he had always acknowledged that it was really Eleanor, and the need he felt to protect *her,* most especially from men such as Litchfield, that had been his primary reason for returning home.

A need to protect her which had just resulted in a deeper, even more startling, realisation…

'It is curious, is it not,' Richmond continued slowly, 'considering Litchfield's licentiousness, and obvious disregard for whether a woman consents or not, that there are not more of his bastards roaming the English countryside.'

Justin shrugged. 'We do not know that there are not.'

'Then perhaps we should make every effort to prove that?'

'For what purpose?' Justin asked curiously.

Richmond avoided meeting his gaze as he buttoned his waistcoat. 'I have my reasons.'

'Which are…?'

'I would prefer not to discuss them at this point in time.'

'Damn it, Richmond!' Justin exploded.

'If you have any knowledge whatsoever that might indicate Litchfield is not Eleanor's father, after all, then for God's sake have a little pity and share it with me!'

'Why is it so important to you?' the earl asked.

Justin glanced away. 'My grandmother is very fond of Eleanor—'

'And you are not?' Richmond derided.

Justin's jaw tightened. 'Mind your own damned business!'

'I trust you will forgive me for saying so, but my impression is that you have become more than a little "fond" of Miss Rosewood yourself.'

Justin's eyes narrowed to steely slits. 'You go too far, Richmond!'

'It is to be hoped, as Miss Rosewood is a young lady unprotected in the world by any but your own family, that you have not gone too far with her yourself,' the older man warned.

Justin drew himself up to his full, impressive height. 'I have appreciated your assistance this past week, Richmond, and have always regarded you as more than just an acquaintance, but that does not give you licence to question me about my relationship with Eleanor.' Especially when Justin was unsure himself, as yet, as to exactly how to proceed with her!

The two men's gazes clashed in a silent battle of wills, Richmond the one to finally back down as he sighed. 'I apologise if I have given offence, Royston.' He gave a stiff bow.

'Your apology is accepted.' Justin smiled. 'In fact, if it is not too short notice, then why not join us for dinner this evening at Royston House, and then you may see for yourself how ill-treated Eleanor is!' he teased.

'I would never accuse you, or any member of your family, of ill treatment towards anyone,' Richmond protested.

'I trust you will allow me to make Litchfield the exception, if it becomes necessary?' Justin drawled, cracking his knuckles meaningfully.

'Let us hope that it does not.' Richmond grimaced. 'I have heard tell that your mother has recently returned to town.'

'All the more reason for you to rescue me from yet another evening of dining in an allfemale household!'

The earl gave a rueful smile. 'In that case,

I believe I should very much enjoy dining with you and your family this evening, thank you.'

'It is settled then.' Justin, now fully dressed and ready to depart, nodded his satisfaction with the arrangement. 'As it happens, I am expecting another report on Litchfield to be delivered later today, which we might discuss once the ladies have left us to our brandy and cigars.' But, considering the pounding in his head when he had finally woken up at lunchtime today, and which had still not completely gone away, Justin very much doubted he himself would be imbibing!

'I had no idea that you were so well acquainted with Richmond!' The dowager duchess eyed her grandson curiously as the family gathered in the Blue Salon that evening to await the arrival of their dinner guest.

It was the first time that Ellie had seen Justin since he had left her bedchamber so late the previous evening. She had left the house that morning before he had appeared, hopefully suffering with that severe headache she had predicted the night before when he did!

Although he did not appear to be suffering too badly this evening…

Just to look at him in his black evening clothes and snowy white linen, the last of the sun's rays shining in through the windows giving his hair the appearance of molten gold, the severity of his features thrown into light and shadow, those piercing blue eyes sharp with intelligence, was enough to make Ellie's heart beat faster, much to her own annoyance.

She had been unable to fall sleep the previous night once he had left, as she thought over all he had told her, and realised how those things must have affected his views about marriage.

It was easy to see how, as a child, Justin would have made the assumptions he had concerning his parents long and frequent absences, and what he had believed to be their almost obsessive love for each other that they would abandon their only child in order to be together.

Just as she now believed it was the reason he had decided that such a love in his own marriage was not for him.

Unfortunately, that understanding made absolutely no difference to how she felt about him.

It was no longer the girlish infatuation she had felt for his rakish good looks and arrogant self-confidence just a few short weeks ago, but a deep and abiding love that would surely cause her heart to break when she had to leave him. As she surely must. Loving him as passionately as she did, marriage to another man had become an impossibility for her. But she also had to accept that one day Justin had to marry, if only to provide his heir—and she could not remain at Royston House as witness to such a cold and calculated alliance.

Except he was not married as yet, or even betrothed.

'Can you possibly be referring to Lord Bryan Anderson?'

Justin had been surreptitiously watching Eleanor until that moment, as he admired the creamy swell of her breasts visible above the low neckline of the deep-emerald silk gown she wore, a perfect match in colour for her eyes and lending a deep richness to the red of her hair as she sat demurely in the armchair beside the unlit fireplace.

It took some effort on his part to turn his gaze away from her beauty in order to concentrate on answering his mother's query. 'He is recently returned to society himself following the death of his wife last year.'

'I had no idea the countess had died!' A frown now marred his mother's brow.

'Possibly that is because you have hidden yourself away in the country these past three years?' the dowager reminded her.

'Yes.' Rachel nodded distractedly.

Justin was at a loss as to what significance the death of Richmond's poor wife—surely a blessing to all concerned, after so many years of suffering?—could possibly have to any of them personally.

'Justin looks quite bemused, Rachel!' His grandmother gave a chuckle.

Humour at his expense, obviously, although he failed to see the reason why. 'Mother?' he queried cautiously as he saw the becoming blush that now coloured her cheeks.

'My dear boy, it has been such a time of revelations for you!' His grandmother looked amused as she continued, 'My dear, if Rachel and Robert had not met and instantly fallen in love with each other, then

Richmond might now be your father in his stead...' she explained gently.

Although not a part of this conversation, Ellie had nevertheless been following it with great interest. An interest which now turned to concern for Justin as he looked suitably stunned by the dowager's comment.

Ellie reacted purely on instinct as she rose quickly to her feet to move to Justin's side—surely this latest disclosure would prove too much, even for him, on top of all he had been told about his father the previous day? Indeed, the hand he placed briefly in front of his eyes, as he shook his head, would seem to indicate as much.

Until he lowered that hand to reveal a teasing grin. 'Perhaps it is not too late, Mama? After all, you are now both widowed.'

'Justin!' his mother gasped, the blush deepening in her cheeks.

His grin widened. 'You could do far worse than Richmond, Mama. Did you meet him at the Royston Ball, Eleanor? And if so, what is your opinion of the man?' He turned to her, that mischief gleaming in the warm blue depths of his eyes.

Ellie returned Justin's smile as she gratefully responded to the warmth in his eyes. 'I danced a quadrille with him, I believe, and found him to be a very charming and handsome gentleman.'

Justin quirked a mocking brow. 'Not too charming or handsome, it is to be hoped?'

Now it was Ellie's turn to blush. 'In a fatherly sort of way,' she finished quickly.

Justin continued to study her admiringly for several long seconds. They had not had the chance to talk alone together as yet today and he had felt slightly wary about trying to do so, uncertain of his welcome after his reprehensible behaviour the night before in such an inebriated state. But he had felt slightly reassured a few moments ago when she had come to stand beside him as he learnt of the friendship that had once existed between his mother and Richmond. Almost as if Eleanor felt a need to protect him...

An irony in itself, when Justin knew that he was the one who needed to protect her, even from himself on occasion!

'There you have it then, Mama.' He turned back to his mother. 'You have both Eleanor's and my own blessing if you should decide to—'

'Really, Justin, this is not at all a suitable

conversation, let alone an amusing one, when the earl is due to arrive here at any moment.' His mother gave him an admonishing glance.

He smiled unapologetically. 'I was merely assuring you that you have my wholehearted approval if you should decide to…renew your acquaintance with Richmond.'

His mother looked more flustered than ever. 'And I am telling you that I have no need of such approval, when I have no intention of being anything more to the Earl of Richmond than the middle-aged mother of his friend!'

'You are still a very beautiful woman, Rachel,' the dowager put in.

Her daughter-in-law threw up her hands in exasperation. 'You are all gone mad!'

'Ah, but what a wonderful madness it is, Mama.' Justin was no longer able to resist the desire he felt to touch Eleanor in some way, so he placed his hand lightly beneath her elbow.

She looked uncertain. 'I believe that must be the earl I hear arriving now,' she murmured.

Justin was not so sure as he heard the sound of a raised voice outside in the hallway, followed by Stanhope's quieter, more reasoning tone, and then another shout.

'Justin, can you see what that is all about?' The dowager looked concerned.

He nodded, releasing Eleanor's elbow. 'Stay here,' he advised the women before crossing the room in long determined strides. He had barely reached the door before it was flung open to reveal an obviously furious Dryden Litchfield standing on the other side of it and an uncharacteristically ruffled Stanhope just behind him.

Litchfield's face was mottled with temper as he glared at Justin contemptuously. 'Just who the hell do you think you are, Royston?' he snarled.

'There are ladies present, Litchfield,' Justin reminded with cold menace.

'I don't give a damn if there is royalty present!' The other man's voice rose angrily. 'You have a bloody nerve, poking and prying about in my private affairs—'

'I remind you once again that there are ladies present!' Justin held on to his own temper with difficulty, inwardly wishing to do nothing more than to punch Litchfield on his pugnacious jaw, an action as unacceptable, in front of the ladies, as was the other man's swearing.

Litchfield snorted. 'I am sure they are all well aware of what an interfering bastard you are—'

'You, sir, will remove yourself, and your foul tongue, from my hallway immediately!' The dowager duchess, obviously having heard more than enough, now stood up to glare imperiously at their uninvited visitor.

Litchfield gave her a sneer. 'You all think yourselves so damned superior—'

'Perhaps that is because they are superior?' Eleanor interjected. 'Certainly to you. In every way.'

Justin turned slowly to look at her, his chest swelling with pride as she stared at Litchfield down the length of her tiny freckle-covered nose.

Her chin was tilted at a determined angle as she stepped forwards. 'It is entirely unacceptable for you to burst in here, uninvited, and then insult the dowager and her family.'

'Don't get hoity-toity with me, missy, when I know your own mother to have been no better than a who—'

'That is quite enough, Litchfield!' a third male voice thundered across the entrance hall.

Ellie's startled glance moved past Lord Litchfield to see the Earl of Richmond moving swiftly across the hallway, his evening cloak billowing out behind him, his handsome face dark with anger.

'You will excuse my interruption, ladies.' He gave them an abrupt bow before turning his attention back to Dryden Litchfield. 'We will take this conversation elsewhere,' he ground out.

'And why would I do that?' the other man challenged insolently.

The earl narrowed hazel-coloured eyes. 'Because if you do not do as I suggest, then I will have no choice but to have you arrested forthwith.'

'Arrested?' Litchfield scorned. 'For what, pray?'

'I believe there are any number of charges which might be brought against you.'

'By whom? You?' he sneered.

'If necessary, yes,' the earl bit out grimly.

Litchfield gave a contemptuous shake of his head. 'I believe all your years of being married to a madwoman must have addled your own brain, Richmond—' His words came to an abrupt halt as the earl's fist landed squarely on his jaw, his eyes rolling back in his head even as he toppled backwards.

Stanhope, in a position to catch him as he fell, instead stepped aside and allowed the other man to drop to the marble floor of the grand entrance hall, his top lip turned back contemptuously. 'Shall I have one of the footmen assist me in ridding us of this… person, your Grace?' He looked enquiringly at a grim-faced Justin.

'Yes—'

'No,' Richmond put in firmly before turning to bow to all the St Just family. 'I apologise for my impertinence.' He looked at the duke, his expression stern. 'But information has come into my keeping this evening which I believe dictates we must settle this matter with Litchfield once and for all right now, Royston.'

Ellie was still bewildered by Lord Litchfield's insulting remark about her mother. Shocked that this obnoxious man should have even known the sweet and gentle Muriel! Nor did she completely understand his comment concerning the Earl of Richmond's deceased countess, although there was no mistaking his intended insult—and the earl's swift retribution for it!

The duke scowled at the unconscious man. 'Have him carried to the library, Stanhope.'

'Justin, would it not be better if we were to all hear what the earl has to say?' the dowager asked, quite pointedly, it seemed to Ellie.

The duke met his grandmother's gaze, a silent message seeming to pass between the two of them before he turned back to the earl. 'Richmond?' he said finally. 'My grandmother, at least, is already conversant with…some of the events of the past.'

The earl winced. 'The truth of that is… not as we thought it might be, Royston.' He glanced uncomfortably at Ellie as he spoke.

Which only served to further increase her alarm, following so quickly on the heels of Lord Litchfield's earlier remark about her mother. 'Justin, what's going on?'

Justin could tell Eleanor was deeply disturbed by recent events.

He was also troubled by Richmond's implication that Litchfield was not Eleanor's father, after all.

For if not Litchfield, then who…?

Surely not someone Muriel Rosewood had met after returning from India; the timing of Eleanor's birth was all wrong for that to be the case.

Then perhaps some other gentleman Muriel had been close to in India?

Chapter Seventeen

'You will ask chef to delay dinner for half an hour,' Rachel St Just instructed Stanhope once the butler and a footman had deposited Litchfield on the rug in front of the unlit fireplace, the dowager having refused to allow him to soil any of the Georgian furniture with his less-than-clean appearance. 'After which, you may come back and remove him from our presence,' she added with a disdainful curl of her top lip.

Justin had never admired his mother more than he did at that moment, the truths she had told him yesterday at last allowing him to see her for the redoubtable woman that she was, rather than the mother he had believed to have abandoned him for so many years.

Richmond, he noted abstractly, was also regarding her with similar admiration.

'Justin…?'

He drew his breath in sharply, knowing he had been avoiding looking at Eleanor for the past few minutes as he saw to the removal of Litchfield, knowing he could delay no longer. A lump formed in his throat as he turned to see that she looked more lost and vulnerable than ever.

He stepped forwards with the intention of taking her in his arms.

'Lord Anderson,' the dowager made what was undoubtedly a timely interruption at the same time as she shot Justin a warning glance, 'would you care to tell us what you meant when you threatened to have this obnoxious creature arrested?'

'I fear the reasons for that are not for the delicate ears of ladies.' The earl's voice contained an edge of restrained anger. 'Suffice it to say, the man is completely beyond redemption.'

'What did he mean by his remark about my mother?' Eleanor asked.

'Royston!' the dowager protested as Justin moved determinedly to Eleanor's side.

He chose to ignore that second warning

and instead placed an arm protectively about her waist. 'I believe it would be beneficial if you were to sit down,' he suggested kindly.

Ellie was stunned by the compassion and gentleness of his expression as he guided her to an armchair, both of them emotions she was unaccustomed to seeing on the face of the man she loved. There had been concern for his grandmother's health, yes. Also that inborn arrogance that was so much a part of him. Passion and desire, most certainly. But she had never seen the endearing combination of more tender emotions in him before now.

'You are keeping something from me,' she spoke with certainty as she refused to sit down.

He straightened tensely, a shutter falling over those deep-blue eyes. 'Eleanor—'

'Royston is not the one responsible for keeping something from you,' the Earl of Richmond interrupted firmly.

'Then who is?' she wanted to know.

'I am.' The earl looked uncharacteristically nervous as he crossed the room to take one of Ellie's hands in his both of his. 'And it is my sincerest wish—'

'What the hell are you doing, Richmond?'

Justin exploded, immediately filled with a possessive fury that the handsome man was touching her so familiarly. He still wasn't sure Richmond didn't have a *tendre* for her.

'Justin, please…!' His mother sounded distraught at his aggression.

His glittering blue gaze remained fixed on Bryan Anderson, his jaw clenched. 'Take your hands off her!'

Ellie blanched. 'I do not believe Lord Anderson means to give offence, Justin,' she murmured.

'He is offending me by touching you!' Justin continued to glower at the older man. 'I told you to let her go!'

'Really, Justin, do try to remember the earl is a guest in our home,' his mother reproved. 'Your own invited guest, in fact.'

Lord Anderson gave Ellie's fingers a reassuring squeeze before releasing her to turn and bow to the two St Just ladies. 'Do not be alarmed, ladies. As Eleanor's guardian, Royston's objection to what he thinks is my familiarity with Miss Rosewood is perfectly in order.'

'I don't just think anything—you *were* damned familiar!' the duke bit out tautly.

Ellie reached out to place a hand lightly

on his tense forearm, unsure why he was reacting so strongly. 'Please allow Lord Anderson to continue.'

Justin drew in a deep controlling breath, before nodding in reluctant acquiescence. 'Just keep your hands to yourself,' he warned the earl.

At any other time it would have been thrilling for Ellie to imagine that Justin's behaviour might mean that he truly cared for her, that he actually disliked seeing another man's hands upon her. Except she already knew that he did not, that he had stated quite clearly, on several occasions, that he would never fall in love with any woman. His protectiveness towards her now was, as Lord Anderson had already stated, merely part of his role as her guardian. 'Lord Anderson?' she asked.

'It is my sincere wish that you will try to understand and forgive what I am about to tell you, El—Miss Rosewood,' he swiftly amended as Justin gave a low, warning growl. 'To believe me when I say that if I had known at the time, I would have behaved otherwise—' He broke off, obviously finding this difficult. 'There is no easy way to say this. No way that I can soften the blow for you—'

'Then why say it at all?' Justin said darkly. 'Surely there is no need, when you have already stated that Litchfield was not the one responsible?'

'He is not.' Richmond's face appeared very pale against his white shock of hair and black evening clothes. His gaze returned to Eleanor. 'May I first say how like your mother you are, my dear.'

She blinked. 'You knew my mother?'

He nodded. 'Many years ago, in India.'

Her throat moved as she swallowed before speaking. 'Then you must have known my father, too?'

'I was Henry Rosewood's commanding officer.' Richmond told her. 'He was a well-liked and heroic officer.'

A tinge of pleased colour warmed Eleanor's cheeks. 'I never knew him, and—my mother talked of him so rarely.'

'Perhaps because it was too painful for her to do so,' the earl suggested gruffly.

'Perhaps.' Eleanor smiled sadly.

'The likeness between you and your mother is—startling. I had no difficulty in instantly recognising you as Muriel's daughter when I first saw you the evening of the Royston Ball,' Richmond continued emotionally. 'A fact I noted to the duke shortly afterwards.'

'He did not mention you had done so.' Eleanor gave Justin a brief puzzled glance.

'Perhaps because I did not see it as being of particular importance at the time.' He shrugged.

'But it is now?'

Justin had admired Eleanor for her intelligence more than once, but at this moment he might have wished her a trifle less perceptive.

'Justin, is it possible this business has something to do with that private matter I requested you look into?' his grandmother asked sharply.

God save him, he was surrounded by intelligent women! 'Yes,' he sighed.

The dowager looked down in horror at the man still prostrate upon her Aubusson rug. 'Surely not…?'

'Richmond seems to think not, no,' Justin confirmed drily.

'That is something, at least!' His grandmother raised a relieved hand to her ample bosom.

Justin agreed wholeheartedly with that sentiment. Although he could not help questioning Richmond's certainty on the matter.

Ellie looked dazed, having no idea what the dowager was referring to. But then, most of this past few minutes' conversation was a complete mystery to her. 'I still fail to see why Lord Litchfield forced his way in here uninvited this evening. What on earth was the matter?'

Justin's mouth twisted contemptuously. 'He obviously took severe exception to learning I had employed someone to investigate into his private affairs.'

She blinked. 'Why would you do such a thing?'

The dowager stood up. 'I am afraid I am partly to blame for this, Ellie.' She ignored her grandson's glower at her use of the shortened name. 'I asked Justin to…to look into a certain matter for me and it would seem that this is the unfortunate result.'

Ellie was none the wiser for this explanation. 'But surely this can have nothing to do with me?'

'I am afraid it has everything to do with you, my dear.' The dowager raised her hands in apology. 'But I had no idea, when I made my request to Justin, that the matter would become so complicated.'

Again, Ellie was no nearer to understanding this conversation than she had been a few minutes ago. 'And what request did you make of Just—the duke?'

'I merely—I had realised—' The dowager appeared uncharacteristically flustered as she quickly crossed the room to take both Ellie's hands in her own. 'There is no easy way to say this, my dear, so I shall simply state that Henry Rosewood was killed in battle exactly a year before you were born.'

Ellie literally felt all the colour drain from her cheeks as she absorbed the full import of this statement. Henry Rosewood could not have been her father.

She stumbled slightly as she pulled her hands free of the dowager's to drop down into the armchair she had earlier refused. Tears blurred her vision as she looked up at Justin accusingly. 'You knew about this.' It was a statement, not a question.

A nerve pulsed in his tightly clenched jaw. 'Yes.'

'How long have you known?'

'A week, no more. Eleanor—'

'No! Don't!' She lifted a restraining hand

as Justin would have moved to her side, grateful when he halted in his tracks. She needed to—had to somehow try to assimilate exactly what this all meant to her.

Obviously she was Muriel's daughter. But not Henry's. And if not Henry's daughter, then whose—?

Her horrified gaze moved to Litchfield, who still lay unconscious upon the rug in front of the fire. No! She could not bear to be the daughter of such a dreadful man! It would be worse, even, than learning that she was illegitimate—

'I am your father, Eleanor.'

Ellie was barely aware of the combined gasps of all the St Just family as she raised her stunned gaze to look at Lord Bryan Anderson, the Earl of Richmond.

'I am your father, Eleanor,' he repeated as he came down on his haunches beside her, his hazel gaze unwavering upon her face as he took the limpness of her chilled hands in his. 'I swear to you I did not know it until a few hours ago, but I know now, beyond a shadow of a doubt, that I am your father. And you can have no idea how very much it pleases me that I have a daughter,' he added emotionally, tears glistening in his eyes.

Ellie continued to stare at him for several long breathless seconds, looking for—hoping to see—some likeness to herself in his face. His eyes were a mixture of blue, green and brown, his features both strong and handsome, his hair that premature shock of white, his form both fit and muscled for a man his age.

But she saw nothing, no likeness to herself, to confirm that he was, indeed, her real father.

'My hair was once as auburn as your own,' the earl supplied, as if he knew her thoughts. 'I received a severe shock in my mid-twenties, which turned my hair completely white. You see, my wife of only a few months was involved in a hunting accident, from which she never fully recovered, physically or mentally. We never had a true marriage again.'

'So you were married when you and my mother—when the two of you—'

'I was,' he confirmed grimly.

Darkness started to blur the edges of her vision as the shock of it all suddenly hit her with the force of a blow, that darkness growing bigger, becoming deeper, as she felt herself begin to slip away.

'Out of my way, Richmond!' she heard Justin shout, before strong arms encircled her just as the darkness completely engulfed her and she collapsed into unconsciousness.

'For goodness' sake, stop your infernal pacing, Justin, and go up to the girl if that is what you wish to do!'

Justin made no effort to cease his 'infernal pacing' as he shot his grandmother a narrow-eyed glare. 'I am the last person Eleanor wishes to see just now.'

'Nonsense!' the dowager dismissed briskly. 'Once she is over the shock she will be gratified to know she is the daughter of an earl—'

'The illegitimate daughter of an earl!'

'I am sure Richmond will wish to acknowledge her as his own.'

'Whether he does or he does not, I very much doubt that Eleanor will thank any of us for our part in this,' Justin muttered dully. 'In just a few short minutes she has gone from believing her father to be Henry Rosewood, to that reprobate Dryden Litchfield, only to finally learn that her father is actually the Earl of Richmond.'

Doctor Franklyn had been called to attend to Eleanor, first giving a minute of his time to declare that Litchfield was only suffering from a badly bruised jaw from Richmond's blow. After which Justin and Richmond had both very much enjoyed telling that obnoxious gentleman exactly why it was he would not be talking of this evening's events, or those of the past, to anyone. The information they had both gathered, on Litchfield's behaviour this past twenty years or more, was more than enough to put him behind bars if charges were levelled against him, several other reputable ladies having also suffered at his brutal treatment. Knowledge they would prefer did not become known to the public, but which they would quite happily testify to in private, if necessary.

As for Eleanor, this last few minutes was too much for any young woman to accept with equanimity. Damn it, he was having trouble coming to terms with Richmond as her father, so how could she possibly be expected to do so!

Nor, knowing her as he did, would she easily forgive his own part in keeping such knowledge from her.

Justin had carried Eleanor upstairs after she had fainted, and she was upstairs in her bedchamber even now, being attended to by

Dr Franklyn and watched over like a protective hawk with its newly hatched chick by Bryan Anderson.

By her real father…who had a lot more authority to be there than Justin did.

The earl had spared only enough time, as they waited in Eleanor's bedchamber for the doctor to arrive, to tell them all briefly how it had come about.

Richmond's own enquiries into the events in India twenty years ago had resulted in more than just the damning information he had gathered on Dryden Litchfield. He had received a letter earlier this evening, from the wife of a fellow officer who had also been a particular friend of Muriel Rosewood, in which she had stated that Muriel had given birth to a baby girl exactly nine months after leaving India. Exactly nine months after Bryan Anderson had spent a single night with Muriel before she sailed back to England.

'Do not judge him too harshly, Justin,' his mother now advised as she placed her hand gently on his arm. 'He had already lived five years of hell with his deranged wife when this occurred. It is all too easy, during wars and hardship, for such things as this to occur.

And let us not forget that Lord Anderson offered Muriel refuge in his own home following Litchfield's attack upon her.'

'Before then bedding her himself!'

'Eventually, yes,' she allowed. 'But you know him well enough to realise it would not have been without her consent. And, as a woman, I can tell you exactly why Muriel would have welcomed the attentions of a gentleman such as Bryan Anderson. She needed his physical reassurance, that pleasanter memory, to take home with her to England after suffering Litchfield's brutality.'

'It would seem that she took far more than a pleasant memory back to England with her!' Justin's hands were clenched into fists at his sides.

His mother nodded. 'And decided, quite admirably, that it was not fair to tell Richmond of the child she was expecting. Think, Justin, of the dilemma it would have placed him in if he had known, how he would then be torn between loyalty to his deranged wife and the woman who was now the mother of his daughter. I am sorry I did not know Muriel better when she was married to Frederick, as she is to be commended for her unselfish actions twenty years ago. She and

Richmond were not in love, after all, had merely been thrown together in adverse circumstances, which then led to the birth of a daughter.'

Justin sighed. 'I am not the one who will need convincing of the rightness or otherwise of that, Mama.' Eleanor was his only concern in this matter. A tenderness of feeling he knew was not returned—indeed, he had every reason to think that she now wished him to Hades for his part in keeping the truth of the past from her!

Certainly he had not been the first person she had asked for once she had recovered from her faint. No, Richmond had that honour.

'As this seems to be an evening of confessions...'

Justin's lids narrowed as he glanced sharply at his grandmother. 'What other deep dark secrets are we to be made privy to now?'

The dowager pursed her lips. 'I am afraid I was not completely truthful with you last week regarding my own health, my boy.'

He rolled his eyes. 'It was all a ruse, was it not, Grandmama? Another effort on your part to persuade me into residing at Royston

House once more? To eventually get used to the idea of matrimony?'

The dowager's eyes widened. 'You knew all the time?'

'I was certain that was the case, yes,' he allowed with a wry smile. 'You hadn't allowed anyone else to be present in the room, even Eleanor, during Dr Franklyn's visits. Nor am I so lacking in intelligence that I did not see the vast improvement in your health within hours of my having moved back here. Tell me, Grandmama, how did you achieve the effect of the whitened cheeks that night you sent for me?'

The dowager gave a sniff of satisfaction. 'A little extra face powder was most convincing, I thought.'

'Oh, most,' Justin conceded drily. 'No doubt your letters to my mother these past months, informing her of Eleanor's introduction into society, and my own presence back at Royston House, were also part of your machinations?'

'You are being impolite, Justin!' The dowager looked suitably affronted.

'But truthful?'

'Perhaps,' she allowed airily.

He grinned. 'Well I am sorry to disappoint

you, Grandmama, but my own reasons for moving back to Royston House had absolutely nothing to do with your pretence of ill health.'

'I am well aware of it.' She gave an imperious nod of her head.

He raised his brows. 'You are?'

'Oh, yes.' She smiled smugly.

'Grandmama—' He broke off as Dr Franklyn appeared in the doorway of the Blue Salon where they all waited for news of Eleanor. 'Well, man, do not just stand there, tell us how she is!' Justin barked.

'Miss Rosewood is quite recovered now,' the doctor assured. 'And she shows no signs of suffering any lasting effects from her faint.'

'And?' Justin scowled darkly.

'And what, your Grace?' the doctor replied.

'Did she not ask for—for anyone?' he pressed urgently.

The doctor's brow cleared. 'Ah, yes, I believe she did ask if she might speak with—' Justin had already left the room, taking the stairs two steps at a time, before the doctor had finished his statement '—the dowager.'

Chapter Eighteen

E llie was quite unprepared for the way Justin burst into her bedchamber, only seconds after the doctor had departed.

'What do you mean by entering Ellie's bedchamber uninvited, Royston?' Richmond frowned his disapproval of the younger man's actions.

To say this past hour had been…life-changing for her would be to severely understate the matter. To learn that Henry Rosewood, a man she had never known, was not her father after all and that Lord Bryan Anderson, the Earl of Richmond, was, had come as a complete shock to her.

But once she had got used to the idea, it was actually a pleasant one.

She should perhaps continue to be shocked, distraught, and take weeks, if not months, to acclimatise herself to the things she had learnt this evening, to all that Lord Anderson had gently explained had befallen her poor mother in India twenty years ago.

Except Ellie found she could not summon any of those emotions…

It had always been difficult for her to feel anything more than respect and affection for the man who had died before she was even born, and Frederick St Just had never been more to her than her mother's second husband, a man with whom Muriel was so obviously not happy. For Ellie to now learn that she had a father, after all, and such a well-liked and respected man as the Earl of Richmond, was, she now realised, more wonderful than she could have imagined.

It had also given her hope that perhaps her changed circumstances, despite her illegitimacy, meant that she and Justin were not so socially far apart as she had always believed them to be. The earl had already told her he was going to publicly acknowledge her as his daughter and he was influential enough to carry off the scandal with aplomb.

Although the fact that Justin had just

walked into her bedchamber, as if he had a perfect right to do so, obviously did not sit well with her brand-new father!

Justin ignored the older man's disapproval, having eyes only for Eleanor as she sat on the stool in front of the dressing-table; her face was still very pale, her eyes dark-green smudges and the freckles on her nose very noticeable against that pallor. 'Should you not be in bed?' he demanded as he quickly crossed the room to stand in front of her.

'I only fainted—'

'You have received a severe shock.'

'But a pleasant one.' She turned to reach up and clasp her father's hand, the earl returning the shyness of her smile with one of warm affection. 'Justin, may I present my father, Lord Bryan Anderson, the Earl of Richmond. Father, Justin St Just, the Duke of Royston.'

Justin's admiration for this young woman grew to chest-bursting proportions at the gracious elegance and ease with which she made the introductions. Most females in Eleanor's present situation would be having fits of hysterical vapours by now, crying and carrying on to an unpleasant degree. But she was made of much sterner stuff than that, had so obviously absorbed, and then swiftly accepted her change in circumstances.

'Richmond.' He nodded stiffly to the older man.

'Royston.' The earl's nod was just as terse.

Eleanor gave a puzzled smile. 'I thought the two of you were friends?'

'We were,' the two men said together.

She looked taken aback. 'What has happened to change that?'

Richmond gave a humourless smile. 'Will you tell her, Royston, or shall I?'

Justin's frustration was evident as he glared at the earl; this was not the way he had wanted to approach this. 'I am afraid, Eleanor, that your father seems to be aware of the closeness that exists between us and he is feeling protective and disapproving, to say the least.'

'Oh,' she gasped, her cheeks flushing a becoming rose.

'It would be impossible not to know,' Richmond rasped, 'when the very air seems to quiver and shift whenever the two of you are in the same room together!'

'Oh,' Eleanor breathed again.

'The question is, what are you going to do about it, Royston?' Richmond said bullishly.

'Oh, but—'

'I,' Justin cut in firmly over Eleanor's protest, 'am going to do what any gentleman should in these circumstances, and ask for the honour of your daughter's hand in marriage.'

Ellie stared up at Justin, sure that he had gone mad; her circumstances might have changed, but her heartfelt desire, her determination to marry a man who loved her as deeply as she loved him, had not changed in the slightest!

In truth, she loved Justin, more than anything else in the world, just as she was certain she would continue to do so for the rest of her life. Nor could she deny that she had felt a brief thrill just now—a very brief thrill—at the thought of becoming his wife. Until good sense had prevailed and Ellie accepted that Justin had made the offer only because honour dictated he do so and not because he loved her, too.

She stood up. 'I would like to answer that request for myself, your Grace,' she said stiffly, her chin raised proudly high. 'And my answer in no. Thank you. Nor is there any reason why you need make such an offer.' She looked at her father. 'There may be a detectable *frisson* in the air whenever we are together, Father, but I assure you, nothing has happened that the duke should ever feel he must propose marriage for.'

'If you would allow us a few minutes alone, Richmond?' Justin quirked a questioning brow at her father.

'My answer will not change—'

'Richmond?' Justin spoke ruthlessly over Ellie's objection.

'I believe, Eleanor, that it is in your own best interest to listen to what Royston wishes to say to you,' the earl encouraged, satisfied that Justin wanted to do the honourable thing by his daughter.

Her lips pressed stubbornly together. 'My answer will not change, no matter what he has to say. And Justi—his Grace is well aware of the reasons why it will not.'

'It is always a bad sign when she resorts to calling me that,' Justin confided, smiling ruefully.

Richmond did not return the smile. 'You understand that I will fully accept whatever decision Eleanor makes?'

He sobered. 'I do.'

'Very well,' the earl said briskly. 'I will rejoin the two ladies downstairs. I am sure I must still have some explaining to do in that quarter.' He grimaced.

Eleanor looked distraught. 'There is no need for you to leave—'

'There is every need, damn it!' Justin's temper was not as even as he wished and he made a visible effort to suppress it.

'I will not leave the house until I have spoken to you again,' Richmond reassured Eleanor gruffly as he bent to kiss her lightly on the cheek. He gave Justin a warning frown before crossing over to the door and closing it quietly behind him as he left.

Leaving a tense and awkward silence behind him.

A silence Justin knew, as Eleanor glared at him so mutinously, that it was his responsibility to fill. 'Will you at least agree to hear what I have to say?'

Her eyes flashed deeply green. 'I do not see the point in it, when you are already aware that I refuse to marry any man whom I do not love and who does not love me.'

Justin continued to meet that stormy gaze as he answered her huskily. 'Yes, I am.'

She grimaced. 'There is your answer then.'

'What if I were to say I am already in

love with you, and was willing to wait, in the hope that you would eventually fall in love with me too?'

Her face paled as she shook her head. 'You do not love me.'

Justin had spent years hiding his emotions behind a barrier of arrogance and cynicism, out of a desire, he now knew, not to be hurt and rejected again. There was no place between them for that barrier now.

Nor did he attempt to prevent that barrier from falling away from his emotions, as he moved down on one knee in front of her. 'I love you more than life itself, Eleanor Rosewood-Anderson,' he stated clearly. 'More than anything or anyone. If you feel anything for me at all, desire or even only liking, then would you please marry me and allow me the opportunity to show you my love, prove it to you, and perhaps one day persuade you into loving me in return?'

Ellie felt numb as she stared down at him, sure that this usually proud man could not just have declared on bended knee that he was in love with her and that he wished to make her his duchess.

'There will never be anyone else for me, Eleanor,' he continued fervently at her continued silence. 'Much as I did not want to ever fall in love with any woman, I know that I love you beyond life itself. I think I've been in love with you since the night of my grandmother's illness when you summoned me here—which was not a true illness, by the way, but a wilful machination on her part to persuade me into moving back here—and then you brought me to task for my tardiness.'

'The dowager was not really ill?' Ellie found it safer to focus on that part of his statement rather than those other wonderful—unbelievable!—things he was saying to her.

'Not in the least,' Justin said with a twinkle. 'Nor was it my true reason for moving back to Royston House.'

'What was your true reason?' Ellie's heart was now beating so loudly in her chest she felt sure he must be able to hear it. Justin had said that he loved her. More than anyone and anything. Beyond life itself!

'To protect you,' he revealed grimly. 'From Litchfield and other men like him.' He sighed deeply before admitting, 'Also I know now that I was beside myself with jealously of the attentions being shown to you by so many younger men. It was my intention to thwart those attentions as often as possible.'

Justin had been jealous? The proud, the haughty, the arrogant, the self-assured Duke of Royston, the man who gave the impression of needing no one, had been *jealous* of the attentions shown to her by dandified young boys like Lord Charles Endicott? Did Justin not know—could he not *see* that no other man existed for her but him? That they never had, and never would?

'Oh, Justin…!' Eleanor sank gracefully to her knees in front of him before raising her hands to cup either side of his dearly beloved face. 'I have *loved* you for months now. Have fallen even more deeply *in love* with you this past week or more. I will always love you, Justin. I could not have responded to you as I do, have made love with you in the way we have, if I was not already in love with you!'

Such an expression of joy lit up his face at her declaration, a glow in the deep blue of his eyes, his cheeks flushing, the wideness of his smile making him appear almost boyish. 'How much I love you, Eleanor!' He swept her into his arms, cradling her against him as if she were the most precious being upon the earth. 'Please marry me and be my duchess,' he pleaded as he moved back slightly to look at her with all of that love shining in his eyes. 'I promise you will never ever have cause to regret it.'

'Yes! Oh, yes, Justin, I will marry you!' Eleanor's expression was as joyous as his as she launched herself into his arms and the two of them became lost in the wonder of their love for each other.

One floor below them, in the Blue Salon, Edith St Just smiled with a quiet inner satisfaction at the knowledge that, on the morrow, she would be able to show her two closest friends the name of the young lady, written on a piece of paper to be held in safekeeping by Lady Jocelyn's butler, in which she had predicted who would become Royston's duchess.

That name was Miss Eleanor Rosewood…

* * * * *

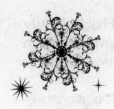

Merry Christmas
& A Happy New Year!

Thank you for a wonderful
2013...

A sneaky peek at next month…

HISTORICAL

IGNITE YOUR IMAGINATION, STEP INTO THE PAST…

My wish list for next month's titles…

In stores from 3rd January 2014:

- ❏ From Ruin to Riches – Louise Allen
- ❏ Protected by the Major – Anne Herries
- ❏ Secrets of a Gentleman Escort – Bronwyn Scott
- ❏ Unveiling Lady Clare – Carol Townend
- ❏ A Marriage of Notoriety – Diane Gaston
- ❏ Rancher Wants a Wife – Kate Bridges

Available at WHSmith, Tesco, Asda, Eason, Amazon and Apple

Just can't wait?

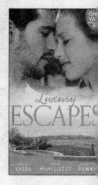

Join the Mills & Boon Book Club

Want to read more **Historical** books?
We're offering you **2 more** absolutely **FREE!**

We'll also treat you to these fabulous extras:

- 🌹 Exclusive offers and
  much more!

- 🌹 FREE home delivery

- 🌹 FREE books and gifts with our
  special rewards scheme

Get your free books now!

visit www.millsandboon.co.uk/bookclub
or call Customer Relations on 020 8288 288